A TWIST IN THE RIVER

Stig Abell believes that discovering a crime fiction series to enjoy is one of the great pleasures in life. His first novel, *Death Under A Little Sky*, introduced Jake Jackson and his attempt to get away from his former life, in the beautiful area around Little Sky. This book is the fourth in the series, and Stig is absolutely delighted that there are more on the way.

Away from books, he co-presents the breakfast show on Times Radio, a station he helped to launch in 2020. Before that he was a regular presenter on Radio 4's *Front Row* and was the editor and publisher of the *Times Literary Supplement*.

He lives in London with his wife, three children and two independent-minded cats called Boo and Ninja (his children named them, obviously).

 @StigAbell
 @TheStigAbell

Also by Stig Abell

Death Under a Little Sky
Death in a Lonely Place
The Burial Place

A TWIST IN THE RIVER

STIG ABELL

A JAKE JACKSON MYSTERY

HEMLOCK PRESS

Hemlock Press
an imprint of HarperCollins*Publishers* Ltd
1 London Bridge Street
London SE1 9GF

www.harpercollins.co.uk

HarperCollins*Publishers*
Macken House, 39/40 Mayor Street Upper
Dublin 1, D01 C9W8, Ireland

First published by HarperCollins*Publishers* Ltd 2026
1

Copyright © Stig Abell 2026
Map by Liane Payne © 2026

Epigraph from 'The Dry Salvages', part of *Four Quartets* by
T. S. Eliot, used with permission

Stig Abell asserts the moral right to be identified as the author of this work.

A catalogue record for this book is available from the British Library.

ISBN: 978-0-00-864371-3 (HB)
ISBN: 978-0-00-864372-0 (TPB)

This novel is entirely a work of fiction. The names, characters and incidents portrayed in it are the work of the author's imagination. Any resemblance to actual persons, living or dead, events or localities is entirely coincidental.

This book is set in Sabon LT Pro at HarperCollins*Publishers* India

Printed and bound in the UK using 100%
Renewable Electricity at CPI Group (UK) Ltd

All rights reserved. No part of this publication may be reproduced, stored in a retrieval system, or transmitted, in any form or by any means, electronic, mechanical, photocopying, recording or otherwise, without the prior written permission of the publishers.

Without limiting the author's and publisher's exclusive rights, any unauthorised use of this publication to train generative artificial intelligence (AI) technologies is expressly prohibited. HarperCollins also exercise their rights under Article 4(3) of the Digital Single Market Directive 2019/790 and expressly reserve this publication from the text and data mining exception.

This book contains FSC™ certified paper and other controlled sources to ensure responsible forest management.

For more information visit: www.harpercollins.co.uk/green

For Nadine and her bathtime reading

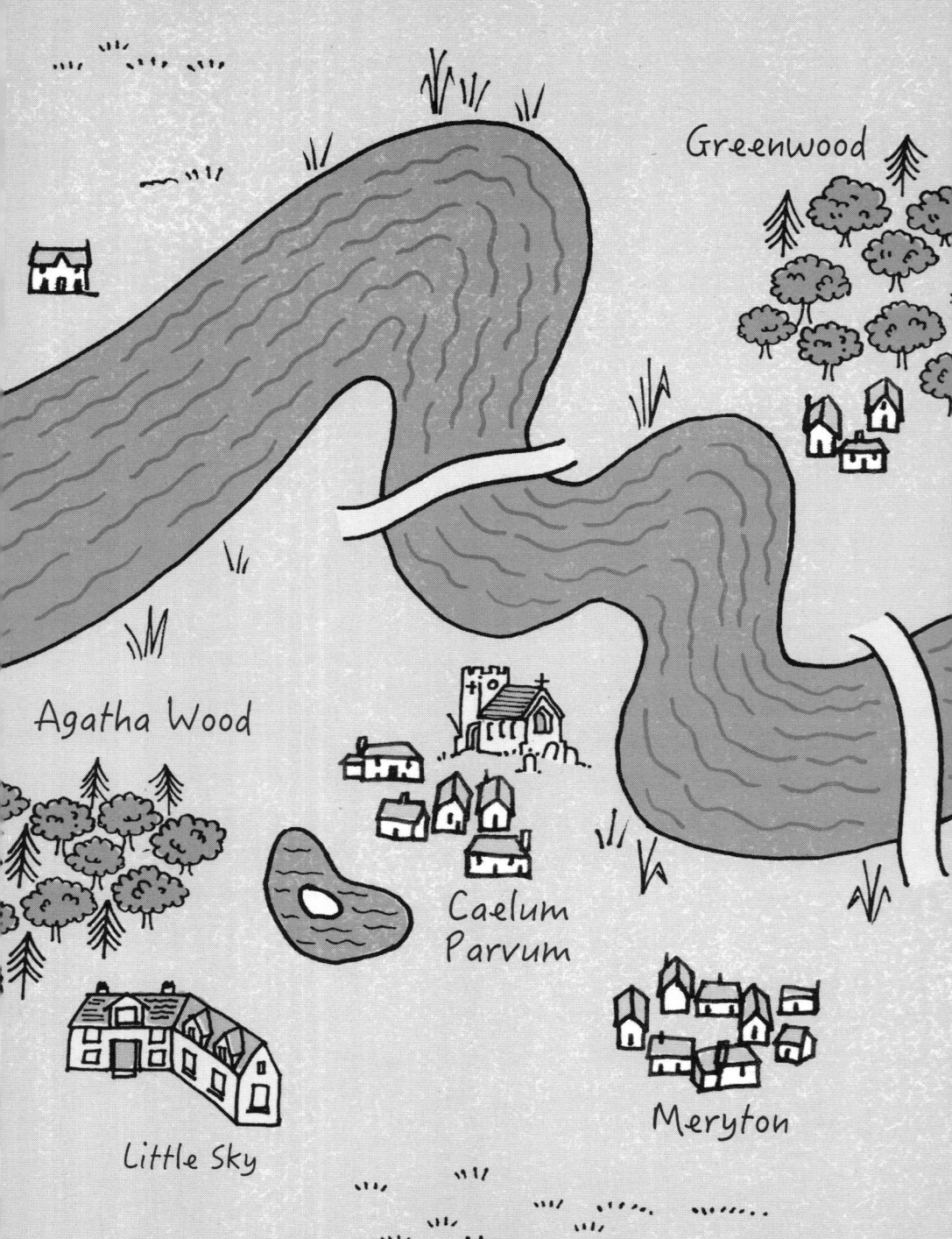

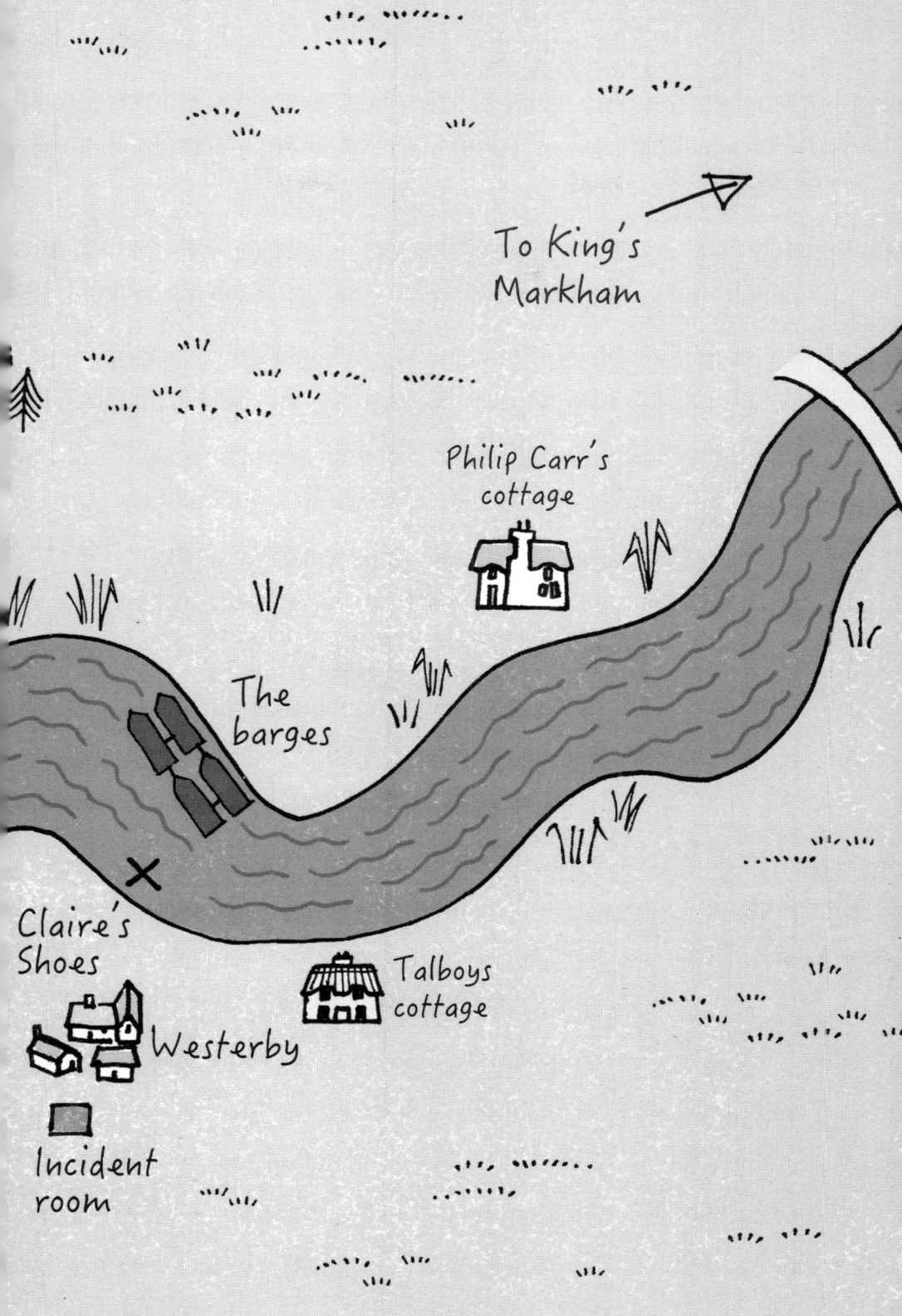

I do not know much about gods; but I think that the river
Is a strong brown god – sullen, untamed and intractable,
Patient to some degree, at first recognised as a frontier;
Useful, untrustworthy, as a conveyor of commerce;
Then only a problem confronting the builder of bridges.
The problem once solved, the brown god is almost forgotten
By the dwellers in cities – ever, however, implacable.
Keeping his seasons and rages, destroyer, reminder
Of what men choose to forget. Unhonoured, unpropitiated
By worshippers of the machine, but waiting, watching and
waiting.

T. S. Eliot, 'The Dry Salvages'

Prologue

There has always been the river. Sometimes it comes at a canter, sometimes in a torrent, depending on weather and whim. This early evening, it is placid and smooth, a blue-grey snake that lies more or less still, ready to strike.

A woman, hot from her run, takes off her shoes and socks and cools her aching feet in the satin chill of the water. The air is thick, the river is inviting. Around her is the peace that comes just before dusk in the countryside, the day all but over, the swelter gone, the breeze rising to greet the beginnings of night.

Elsewhere a man, also warm from his constant movement, backpack cutting into his shoulders in familiar – and welcome – thrum of pain. He moves down the river path, up again, never still. At night he sleeps nearby, watches the insects settle and swarm above the surface, little motes of life. Above him bats flit, soundless, twisting and swerving into the living clouds. If you only eat midges, he thinks, you must need to keep hunting the long night through, just to fill your tiny bat belly. Larger creatures appear too, especially if he doesn't move much: big fish rise up gulping to the surface, mouths puckered; voles and shrews, ratty and swift, dart in and out of the water, slick and slippery as if they have been oiled. Once he saw an otter, incongruous as if from a picture book, resting on the bank, paws across its chest.

People are drawn to water, day and night. To eat and drink, to gather and stare. They ignore him, mostly. If he is walking, head down, they let him go by, a figure lost in his own private world. Sometimes they jog past him, huffing at the temerity of his existence, daring to slow them down for a micro-second. As dusk comes, and he finds his spot for the night, he becomes completely unseen, ignored. A part of the landscape, the unconsidered backdrop. He witnesses romantic assignations, kisses and cuddles, hungry hands clawing atop scanty summer clothes. Skinny-dips in the river: shrieks of joy and cold, bright flares of flesh in the gloom.

Not just joy, of course. There is never just joy in the world. He sees fights, hears shouts and curses, wounding words that can never be taken back. There is danger here. The river, which loops and bends, bracketed by thick lines of trees and vegetation, is always both public and private. You can do all sorts, especially in those moments of half-light early and late.

And whatever else happens, the river keeps going, ever onward. Unlike life, which can be suddenly stopped when you least expect it.

Book One: Watershed

Then in a wailful choir the small gnats mourn
Among the river sallows, borne aloft
Or sinking as the light wind lives or dies.
                        John Keats, 'To Autumn'

Chapter One

Jake Jackson, happy, is standing in a second-hand bookshop, lost in thought. His fingers trace the spines of books that all bear the scars of reading. Softly battered, marked by time and use. Shabby, like him. Outside, through the bay window, the afternoon looks mild and warm and sleepy, a final soft exhalation of summer. No cars move down this cobbled street. Not that many people either.

He is in Meryton, the largest town near Little Sky, the farmhouse where he lives. Three streets of shops, a school, two churches, three pubs, and mostly small, snug cottages, built for local labourers over the past few centuries. Jake doesn't come here often, but he loves books, especially detective books, and can't be without access to a bookshop. He enjoys the randomness, the serendipity of visiting a place where he can't predict what exactly might tempt him, stocked as it is by the whims and subjective tastes of those unknown folk who live close by. He likes objects that have been given up, spurned even, something he can reclaim. In any case, he has no choice. Little Sky is not on a postal route, and so he cannot receive deliveries by men in shorts representing faceless companies. His house has no internet access either, so the world of online shopping is removed entirely.

Every couple of weeks, he gets a lift the ten miles or so along meandering lanes to Meryton, buys a few books, and runs them home, following the route of the river that lies across the landscape like a solid line scribbled on a page. It has become a pleasant ritual in a life where such minor moments of routine are plotted and treasured.

Jake hears a gentle cough and peers over his shoulder, pushing his long, sun-streaked hair clear to meet the eyes of the man standing behind the cash register. The bookseller is entering late middle age, thick-rimmed black glasses contrasting with a pale and freckled face, his hair grey, his cropped stubble white as chalk. Behind him is a sign with the name of his establishment in ornate lettering: BOOKS DO FURNISH A ROOM. Some sort of literary joke.

Sam Fryer ('I should've opened a chippy,' he once told Jake) has been running the shop for decades, having fled his former life in the city as a teacher. He had a radical background there: was a marcher, a heckler, a self-righteous protester on behalf of social justice, but had eventually grown worn down by his failure to change the world, and worn out by the demands of teaching unwilling children. His shop was his passion, his escape.

Sam had not given up his history in one conversation, but in several, over many months of Jake's regular attendance. His voice soft and searching, his eyes calm, pale grey as pebbles. Jake had told him – in similarly protracted fashion – some of his own past: his life as a policeman, a detective in fact, a loyal member of an institution Sam had once so lustily reviled. Now both older, both removed from that urban world, they could be wry and understanding of one another's former lives.

'Jake, will you make your mind up and buy something? I'd like to close up in a second.'

There is a clock on the wall to the side of them, ticking thoughtfully. 'It's barely even five o'clock, Sam. I've no idea how you make this place pay.'

Sam is clearing his desk, stacking papers and books. 'I overcharge the likes of you. It's a seller's market. If you didn't have me, where would you go?'

Jake carries his book choices to the desk, well-thumbed paperbacks as ever, selected with no great theme in mind, with names that have grown familiar to him over time: Fred Vargas, Ellis Peters, Lucy Foley, Ian Rankin.

He hands over a twenty-pound note, and waves away the change. If you have money, he thinks, you should always share it generously with people who provide something you value. And Jake is, by any standards, wealthy. He inherited a farmhouse called Little Sky from his uncle Arthur, along with his love of books, a library of thrillers, and enough money to live comfortably forever. Arthur's death had defined Jake's life, enabled him to leave the force and the city, embrace the rolling quietude of the deep countryside, seek peace.

Sam ushers him out of the door, where he nearly bumps into a solid figure walking swiftly past. He carries a heavy backpack, like a soldier's, three or four times the size of Jake's, and he is marching like a soldier, head down and fast, yomping along as if part of an invisible cohort somewhere on the moors. Jake's impact moves him a fraction sideways, but scarcely checks his momentum. He does not look back, waves off Jake's apology, and heads relentlessly on. His body is thick and trim, his T-shirt blackened with sweat, his hair shorn almost to the skin, like a penitent.

Jake shouts another apology, to no avail, and turns back to Sam, who looks rueful.

'You'll not get much out of him.'

'I've seen him around the place, along the river. Always marching up and down.'

Sam is leaning against the doorway, rolling a cigarette. 'That's Martin. He buys the occasional book here, but I wouldn't say I've got to know him. He always looks like he's running away from something, and in a sense he is.' Sam lowers his voice, rests a hand on Jake's shoulder. 'I hate to gossip, as you know.' Jake grins at the manifest untruth. 'But he left his name when he was waiting for a book, and I googled him. Martin George. There was a man of that name a few years ago, lost his wife and daughter. The youngster was killed, the wife assaulted, you know, raped, in their house while he was out.'

'Jesus. Poor guy.'

'It's worse even than that. He was on early shift, left for work in the middle of the night, accidentally left the door open. Just forgot to check it properly, left it swinging, an invitation to the wrong person. Someone went in, opportunistic, I suppose. Wife never forgave him, moved away. It broke him, as it would, wouldn't it? He gave everything up, lives more or less on the river now, spends his days walking about the place, sort of restless. He's, I don't know, empty when you speak to him, emptied out.'

Sam has lit his cigarette and taken several deep puffs, and now stubs it on the wall, red sparks careening to the ground. 'Anyhow, I've not got time to chat. That's the whole reason I kicked you out in the first place.' He pats Jake once more, a gesture of kindly solidarity, and heads inside.

Jake slides his purchases into his own backpack, and shrugs it tight onto his shoulders. It is a lovely late afternoon for a run, warm but not hot, the air a balm against his skin. He is wearing old cloth shorts, once blue but now grey with over-washing, and a dark green vest. His arms are well-muscled, a pale blue vein snaking across each bicep, his calves knotted beneath hairs that have been coppered by the summer sun. He walks in the direction Martin has gone, then takes two turns which bring him to the river's edge.

He could hear the water before, but now he sees it, navy blue flecked with foamy white as it courses, heedless, past him. The low sun coats its surface like bronze polish. It is wide at this point, a hundred yards across or more, and in the distance to his left he can see the structure of a bridge, once stone now concrete, casting long shadows into the water. He sets his feet on the small pathway that borders the river. The ground in front of him is already a patterned carpet of discarded leaves, those freshly bleached greens and yellows mixed with umber and ochre, life's rot, muddied and soft and scuffable.

Jake begins to jog, keeping the water to his right as he goes, a constant companion for the next ten miles. His stride is long and easy, his daily regime of running around the vast perimeter of his property making his legs feel hardy, his lungs full and wide. He sees almost nobody. A cottage, from which smoke snakes into the silvery blue of the early evening, the only sign of hidden life.

There is hardly any traffic on the river either. A man in an ancient rowboat, in the shade of a willow, thick-jumpered and still, a fishing rod leaning out precariously into the water. A single barge, grubby and water-beaten, huffing and puffing past, scarcely faster than his running pace. Quiet once more. The path follows the bends of the river, long and sinuous, like a casually outstretched arm. The light begins to fade with the afternoon, the water darkens, now chestnut-coloured, glossy as paint.

He can feel the pull in his muscles, the mild strain that makes getting to the end of exercise worthwhile in the first place. A larger boat passes him, a sailboat, broad and impressive, large-bellied and billowing with the insistent breeze.

That belly of the sail reminds him of pregnancy, makes him think of Livia. He had met her three years before, the local vet, and they had fallen in love. He had never had children, not in his first marriage, which ended in a welter of miscarriages and regret. He thought he might never have them, but this last summer – amid an investigation into murder on an archaeological dig – Livia had shyly, magnificently confirmed she was having his baby. That fact is now the centre of his existence, something that he weighs continually, clutches in his mind, a blessing and a burden of responsibility. He is desperate for nothing to go amiss, for disaster not to strike. He feels always a second away from bad news, knows he has an endless foreshadowing of a flinch. It annoys Livia, he can tell, that he has this edginess, this fear that seems as solid and growing as the child inside her.

Jake shakes his head to clear negative thoughts. He is nearly home, the shape of his surroundings now recognizable: a hawthorn tree, trunk wizened and wrenched forward like an old man leaning on a stick, its berries already weighing down the branches, pinpricks of blood against the lush green of the leaf; the bank of cornflowers on a hummock rich with wild grass, a needless tuft in the landscape, shaggy and speckled with blue. He strikes off on a path that takes him past Livia's house. He slows to let his breathing settle, the throb of his pulse loud in his ears.

Inside the garden, Livia is sitting on a chair by the door, her mind elsewhere, green eyes wide open, as she frets a piece of material in her hands. She stands as she sees him, her expression a little absent, preoccupied, her legs long and brown, still glinting in the incoming dusk.

'Lovey, I was going to leave a message for you. That woman by the river, they've found her phone, her shoes, but no other sign of her. Do you think she's lying somewhere? Do you think she's dead?'

Chapter Two

The missing woman is called Claire Davidson, small, short-dark hair, early thirties, a nurse with a husband and two children. She had been gone a couple of days and already there was a hue and cry about her. Livia had followed the story from the outset, it had preyed on her mind, and she now spent too much time monitoring its progress, hungry for news of Claire's fate.

Claire had been on a walk or run by the river, some form of exercise. She'd been wearing lycra, mainly pinks and purples, and had headed off on a route that should have taken her – according to her regular habits – no more than an hour or two. Then nothing. Disappeared from the land completely.

Jake knows most of this only from Livia herself. He tries to divorce himself from the news, in any form. At Little Sky, it is easy. Once he had lived an urban life as a detective, over-filled with incident, with events of cruelty and chaos. He had spent time trying to explain it all, to piece together what had led to disappearances and assaults and deaths, to make sense of what appeared so often senseless. Now, where he can help it, he no longer seeks information about what is going on in the world.

He leans forward into Livia's hug, inhaling the cherry perfume of her hair, feeling that hard knot in her stomach nestling against him. 'Liv, is this the hormones talking, d'you think? You seem very invested in that woman.'

She jabs him archly. 'Well forgive me for caring about another human being.' She sighs, as the jab becomes a stroke, her fingertips pushing down the fibrous hairs on his arm. 'You're probably right. But only a bit. I feel sorry for her, that's all. In the photos, she has this kind, this searching, this – I don't know – hapless face. And I hate the thought of something happening to her. What do you think's gone on?'

'It's an odd thing, but people really do disappear, especially in places a little out in the wilds. She could've been attacked, sure, but she could've decided to go for a swim, people do, and just not been ready for the water.'

'You swim all the time, it must be safe in summer, mustn't it? I'm always walking past half-naked folk diving in the river.' She sniffs at him. 'And, by the way, you could do with some sort of plunge right about now.'

He pulls up a chair, mock-frowning, feeling the damp droop of his vest, smelling the animal tang of drying sweat. 'That's what comes from grabbing me as soon as I walk in.' Livia has poured him a cold glass of home-made lemonade from a jug half-filled with ice and mint. It is sharp and herby. He swallows a large mouthful. 'No, the water's pretty cold even at this time of year. Definitely still dangerous.'

'Hard to believe an impromptu swim could be deadly, though. And where's her body?'

Jake stands up and stretches. 'You'd be surprised. Water's never really safe. And you're always telling me not to see conspiracies everywhere.'

The garden is small, and overlooks fields that stretch into the distance, pale greens, stubbly browns, and one shock of yellow, a wide patch of rapeseed that has not yet been harvested. In the apple tree above them, a solitary cuckoo offers a modest serenade, two paired notes floating gently down, simple as a flute. Behind them, in the kitchen, he can hear Diana, Livia's daughter, singing less tunefully to herself as she does her homework. She was a welcome product of an unwelcome liaison with a father she has never met, and is now eight, a big fan of Jake, somewhat changeable on the subject of a new sibling on the way.

Her head pops out from the open door for a second, an animal from its burrow, hair wild with dark curls, her eyes green like her mum's but paler and softer, a washed-out watercolour.

'You look like a right sweaty mess, Jake.'

'Afternoon to you, little one.'

Her lips twist in weary scorn. 'I'm not little any more. Anyway, bye.' She retreats and resumes her song.

For a second, as the light begins to fail, Jake feels protective of Livia and Diana, the beginnings of his family. An irrational impulse. He reaches over and strokes Livia's hand. 'You're sleeping here tonight, aren't you? Why don't I come tomorrow morning and we'll go and join the search. I'm sure you'll be able to find out where it's happening.'

Livia clasps hold of his wrist gently, running her own fingers – which are brown and delicate, faintly creased with age – over his calloused palms, writing small circles on each patch of roughened skin. 'I'd like to do that, I reckon.

Good thinking, lovey. Are you not staying over? I've got a house call in a few minutes, then I'm dropping off Di at her riding club.'

'I think I'll get home, clean myself up and sort the house out. You guys can then stay the weekend in the sort of luxury you're accustomed to.'

They kiss goodbye, Jake feels the customary clench of affection in his stomach. His legs have stiffened and he is slow in his walk out of Parvum, and towards home. His journey takes him one final time near to the river, a slinking, steady presence, almost black in the soft dusk, moving with solemn languor. It looks peaceful, sombre and safe. And yet he knows that it can be a killer.

Chapter Three

Water is still on his mind when he gets home. The sky has paled to ballet-shoe pink. There is still welcome warmth in the air and the ground. Jake drops his backpack by the door, kicks off his clothes and walks to the pier that stretches into Chandler Lake. The name is a deliberate nod to crime fiction, as it is with the other landmarks of his vast, undulating, isolated property: Agatha Wood, Poirot Point, fields called Bosch, Morse and Wimsey.

 He had always been suspicious of wild swimming, and the online trumpeting and tribalism that seemed to accompany it. But the shock of chill water to the body has become an experience he craves, pitched somewhere between therapy, trial, and sensory jolt. It's like a proof of living, as he now leaps in and feels his breath torn from his body, the enveloping velvet of coolness, the dark depths beneath the soft-hued sky. There is danger here, but also release. He wonders how Claire had felt about the same sensation, if indeed she had.

*

The next morning, Livia is waiting for him and together they drive in her battered Volvo to a hamlet called Westerby, a scattering of houses in one of the bends of the river. It was here that Claire Davidson had last been seen, and where her belongings had been found. There is another search planned for this morning, and they can see when they arrive a gathering of volunteers, many clad as if for a summer picnic: bare legs and sunhats, bottles of water and dark glasses. Some are brandishing their phones, complaining about a lack of signal.

Jake recognizes some of the locals. Families from Parvum, a dad he half-knows from Diana's school. Sarah from the village shop, the Jolly Nook, is closest to the river, slightly aloof, arms folded and apprehensive, kicking the turf as she waits and listens to a suet-faced, lumbering figure who is probably a farmer. Rose and Lily are there too: brother and sister, he a harmless scoundrel, she an archaeology student, both sitting on the damp ground, faces raised in anticipation of the heat of the day. Livia greets them with hugs and flops down beside them. Jake's progress is checked by a hand to his arm. He spins round and sees another familiar face, Jo, one of his closest friends in the area. She is a journalist, reluctantly running the news operation of a local newspaper that has mostly become a vapid and garish website, a cantankerous, charming, loyal figure, who had long been close to Livia and has warmed to Jake since his arrival.

Her face is closed, disgruntled. She has a cigarette in one hand, and expels smoke as she talks. It feels fitting, she is fairly smouldering with annoyance.

'Jakey, I thought you and Liv would come along to this. There's a pretty good turnout of the local citizenry, mostly good sorts. But there's a few strangers too, look yonder.'

A group of people standing on the wall by the bridge. Young, at least younger than Jake, the men in T-shirts with the arms rolled up to their shoulders, hair fluffed up at the front in poodleish fashion, the women in tiny shorts and long shirts. They are filming each other and themselves on their phones, a general hubbub of singsong narration audible even at this distance.

Jo snorts with derision. 'This whole story is getting too big already. It's partially my lot's fault, I know. We've all been pitching the tale of the bouncy white nurse and her mysterious disappearance, real heartstring stuff. The nationals have got excited, there's a broadcast truck somewhere blocking the road into the village. Hairy-arsed engineers sipping their tea in the street. I can handle that; I'm used to it, I'm part of it, if I'm honest. But this shower over there really boil my piss. Influencers. They've come here to solve a mystery for their fucking TikTok following.'

Jake is quiet, as Jo runs slightly out of steam.

'Jake, do you even know what TikTok is?'

'No more than I need to.' He shakes his head. 'But are they any worse than journalists, really? You're ghoulish, and your readers are ghoulish, everyone loves a pretty tragedy even if they pretend not to.'

Jo laughs. Her bobbed hair, with tinges of grey she has stopped trying to conceal, flutters in front of her face and she huffs it away. 'They're so fucking . . . guileless about it all, though. We dress things up and talk about the public interest and important ideas like scrutiny and transparency. They just want to look good, get likes and be close to the action. They should at least pretend to care, shouldn't they?'

One of those to whom she is gesturing, a woman with red

sunglasses and a sort of blond beehive hairdo, is sprawled on her side as close to the flowing water as she can, filming herself issuing dire warnings about the dangers of the river behind her.

'I see your point, Jo. But they'll get bored of this in the end.'

'Let's hope they get bored because we find her.'

Jake points to another cluster, just young men this time. They are in shorts and vests, standing with their arms taut, their triceps bulging. 'Some more charming strangers?'

Jo stubs her cigarette out carefully. 'Nah, they're locals, lads from Meryton. If I were to be uncharitable for a moment – and I know you'd not expect that of me – I'd say they want to be in the background of whatever videos are being made, and appear on the telly. They've been flexing their muscles like that for the last half hour, while trying to pretend they're not. It must be exhausting.'

One of them, prison-built with thick arms and small legs, a ghost of a moustache, hair shaved at the sides and allowed to grow long at the back, is staring fiercely at the river, letting his hands clench and unclench. Jake watches as he is brought back into the group with a push, rejoining their desultory conversation with his hands still bunched at his sides.

He turns back to Jo. 'Who's in charge here, then? Is there a plan?'

'Your pal McAllister's running the show really, but he's delegated this morning's search to those coppers there.' She gestures to a man and a woman in black trousers and white shirts. 'They'll give you a map, and an area to cover, and then off you go.' Chief Inspector McAllister was a recent arrival to their community, and a welcome one. He had worked closely with Jake when they looked into the murders at the archaeological dig.

As the police officers begin dividing the crowd into groups, Livia stands. Jake watches as she walks over and waits to collect a map, rubbing her belly with one hand, her back with the other, unconsciously framing the life within. It's a habit she has adopted early on, a sort of pose of pregnancy. Jake likes to see it, and wonders if anyone else can read its meaning. She is wearing light grey cotton trousers and a yellow vest, her skin darkened by the summer months, the brown base of her stomach, hard as an upturned bowl, only briefly visible when she shifts position. It is not quite big enough to excite attention, not quite small enough to ignore if you look for it.

Jo has grabbed a notebook from somewhere. 'You get going with that gorgeous lady of yours. I'll stick around here and bother the police. Not that they talk to journalists any more. In their scheme of things, we exist somewhere between petty thieves and arsonists. Scum, really.'

'Is that what they think of you, or you think of them?'

She winks, then leans across and pecks him on the cheek. Scents of coffee and smoke. She moves off to hug Livia, before heading on towards the two officers.

'I said we'd cross the river and go one or two miles up.' Livia is serious, but there remains a breezy energy about her. 'Rose and Lil are going to stick on this side, and then we could meet up.' She points to the map. 'At the Old Souls Bridge here.'

'Are you all right going that far?'

She pushes a finger to his mouth. 'No pregnancy fussing. I'm not ill, I'm not an invalid. I'm a healthy animal with another one waiting its time inside me.'

'Silly me.'

They cross the bridge briskly and head up the pathway. Most of the other groups have stayed on the other side of the river, some going upstream, some down, some heading off across the fields – softly rolling and green in parts, otherwise more hardscrabble, with brown, post-harvest soil turned over and baked hard and crumbly in the sun.

Soon Jake and Livia are alone. They hold hands for a few strides, arms swinging, before they both realize they should not be approaching the journey as just a gentle walk in the sun. It is hard not to relax into the morning, though, the sky now blue with gently scudding clouds, the reassuring burble of the water. They pass a pair of birds bobbing near the reeds, long pale necks, with heads of mottled orange at the back, black feathers sticking up on top. Avian punks, croaking like bad singers.

'I love bad-haircut birds.' Jake is oddly pleased by the sighting.

'We in the veterinary community prefer to call them great crested grebes, you know.'

'They look a bit like those gym lads. Posers.'

'It's how lots of animals pick their mates – who's the best poser?'

'That's certainly how I picked you out. I remember that hot day, you were in small shorts, tiny vest, sexily chasing sheep in a field.' He taps her on the bottom gently. 'Posing and sweating.'

She digs him in the ribs. 'Working, as you well know. I never sweat.'

A companionable silence falls. They start to concentrate their attention more on the riverbank, a thin strip of mud three feet beneath them, massed thickets of plants, some rotting wood. There has been rain this summer, more than usual, so the water is high and fast, especially for the season. It is clear enough, bottle-green in this light, but so deep that the silty depths are invisible. At each clump of vegetation they crouch, looking into the morass, checking if anything is trapped.

'Would we really be able to find anything in the water at this point?'

Jake creakily stands. 'It's possible, but I've been on jobs where a body stays hidden for ages even with divers in the water. Once everything gets so wet, it merges into the surrounding wetness.'

'I heard some expert on the radio saying that he'd find Claire in a morning's work.'

'I've never trusted people who are one hundred per cent confident about anything. Especially experts showing off on the radio.' He inhales. There is the faint smell of dirt and decay, sickly, in the air. 'Doubt always seems to be a healthier approach in life generally.'

They move on. Two boats pass, small motor launches, their inhabitants waving cordially. Thicket to thicket they go. Livia has found a long stick, almost head-height, which she uses to prod into each murky dampness. They look up the river, the surface shimmers and slides, a soft haze hovers. Right before the course twists westwards, it widens and, in the cleft of the bend, they see a mooring area, a stationing of barges tied together.

'What's that right the way up there?' Livia is curious.

'I've walked near it before. It's like a barge community. Maybe four or five of them, more or less permanently docked, if that's the word you use. I've never met anyone who actually lives there, though.'

'Maybe someone might have seen Claire.'

'I'm sure they'll have been asked.'

'Do you want to check?'

Jake stretches. He's not exactly pushed for time. 'Why not?'

They increase their pace with a destination now in mind. Jake feels the sweat trickle down his back, pooling at his waistband. Livia looks as cool as normal. The sun never seems to overheat her body, her skin welcomes the rays as a healthful gift, darkening further each day, leaving just the few contrasting, creamy, private patches shaped by tan-lines. Jake tries to put those areas out of his mind for the moment.

They are within hailing distances of the barges. The first appears deserted, gently rocking with the current, some bright red geraniums a splash of living colour against the prevailing browns and greens. On the second – its name *Offshore* painted in baroque, looping letters – sits a woman, hair as white as wool, incongruously dressed in a rain jacket. Her occupation is summery enough: she is shelling peas into a metal bowl, which glints in the sun like the surrounding water.

Livia hails her as they come alongside the barge. Her face, at rest rather forbidding, breaks into a smile and she beckons them aboard. They sit down beside her on the bench, which is sanded smooth and faintly warm.

'Those look good. Where d'you get fresh vegetables on a boat like this?' Livia is friendly and solicitous as ever.

She beams, teeth broken and greyed. 'Ah, not that I should be boasting about it, but we've got what you might call an informal garden beyond those trees there.' She gestures with her head, her hands busy squeezing, peas popping into the bowl with a satisfying ping. 'I'm sure we should've asked permission, but we've been here for so long, nobody's ever worried too much about it. My name's Maud, by the way.'

Jake and Livia introduce themselves.

'And how long before the little baby comes?'

Livia gulps, a little taken aback. She had only told Jake about it a few weeks ago, and they have told nobody else. 'I'm only a few months, and still think most people can't spot it.'

'Don't worry, my dear. I've got an eye for that sort of thing. Always had. Pregnancy suits you too.' Maud beams. 'You'll make a lovely-looking family, I've no doubt. Big feller like your man, lovely exotic beauty like yours.'

Jake winces a little at 'exotic'. Livia takes no offence. 'I don't know what to say to that, Maud.'

Maud offers a hand, strong and meaty, the product of a lifetime's outdoor work. 'I'm too old to mind my tongue too much.' She smiles, beatific. 'Now you came to me, can I help with anything?'

Jake explains their search for Claire. Maud nods sagely. 'I'd heard something on the wireless. I'm out on deck most days, all day in the summer, weather permitting, and I'm sure as can be I've seen nothing floating past. We get plenty of joggers on the riverside, though, and I generally pay them no mind. They look so unhappy, I reckon, especially the women. So joyless. When I was young, I didn't need to charge around the place, all sweaty and sad-looking. I ate properly and walked everywhere, and looked like a woman should look. Curves, here and there. Some of this lot wear so little, I see more of their unmentionable bits than my old man did when we were courting.'

She nudges Jake suggestively. 'I might not be much to look at now, but I was a real head-turner when I were a lass, let me tell you. I do say, though, that when you get to a certain age, you might as well be comfortable. My old man was the same too.'

'Is he about?'

'He passed on a while back, God rest him. A real waterman, you know. We spent years up and down the rivers, and then came here a long while ago to settle. Never regretted it, and I like the company now. I'm the local old biddy, and that suits me.'

Jake looks across at the row of moored barges, shackled loosely together, never still. 'It's a little community, I guess.'

Maud nods approvingly. 'There's a family at the end, David and Rajni, she's another dark beauty like you, my love. Their kids are teenagers now, though I can scarce believe it. Next to them are Alex and Julia, sorry Yulia. From the Ukraine, don't you know, got out before the war. Hard-working pair, them; not around too much. And then there's Vaughan Mitchell, nearly as old a bugger as me. Used to work in the city, spent a small fortune doing up his barge, changed its name, which I told him you should never do. Terrible luck. Now it's called *The Playboy*, would you believe. He's not as bad as all that, though.'

Jake realizes that Maud could keep a conversation like this going indefinitely. He tries to bring things back to Claire, but it becomes obvious that Maud has seen nothing to help them.

'We lost a woman to drowning, you know, must have been near ten year ago. She had one of the barges. Lovely woman, a teacher. Jill something. Taught reading books. One night went in, was pulled out three days later, drowned as a cat. As I say, I've been up and down the rivers all my life. You never lose respect for the water.'

Jake and Livia get to their feet, start making noises of farewell. Maud grips Livia's arm. 'You'll come back and let me know what happens to her, if you find her, won't you? And maybe I'll see you with a little one someday. I was never blessed with children, though we dearly wanted them. It's a treasure, you know. Priceless.'

Jake looks her in the eye. 'We think so too.'

'Yes, I'd say you do. Bless you then, and take care.'

They walk on for a few minutes more, Livia starting to flag a little. Overhead, a peregrine falcon hovers, its wings dipping in the invisible thermals, its yellow feet stark and ungainly. As they reach a small stream flowing into the main river, it suddenly stoops, dropping to the ground, lost to sight.

The stream, running back through a copse of trees, oaks and elders, is crossed by a piece of stonework, Old Souls Bridge, which Jake has read dates back to the medieval period. It is pleasantly hefty, its huge building blocks cool and reassuring, flecks of mica set into the denseness of the granite. Rose and Lily are not there, and so they decide to rest a while. Livia lies flat on the broad wall, hands on her stomach, shoes cast aside, stretching her feet experimentally in different directions. They are compact, slender, packages of tiny bones. Jake perches nearby, grabs one and squeezes: the knuckly ankle, the sole cool and slightly leathery.

'Go on then.' Livia sighs expansively. 'I might be gross and hot, but I'll accept a foot massage if you're offering.'

They spend half an hour luxuriating in the bosky quiet, paddling in the shallows, letting the icy water soothe them further, but there's still no sign of Rose and Lily, so they decide to make their way back. The sun is at its peak, the sky bereft of cloud, dreamlessly blue. They don't drop their guard as they go, eyes focused downwards, though the sun glares white on the river's surface.

It is Livia who spots it, her stick trailing in the water, snagging against unseen flotsam as she goes. It pulls her up, a mass of damp cloth snagged on a root. With effort, she drags it out, sodden and dripping.

'What was Claire supposed to be wearing?'

Jake checks the information on the map. 'Pink shorts and a purple and black Nike running top.'

'Like this one, do you think?'

They lean forward and see the white swoosh in the top corner. Shoes and phone left on the bank upstream, her top in the water down here. No other sign of her anywhere. The thought sobers them. Livia sends a short text message on her phone to the number on the top of the map. They mark the spot of their find by shifting a piece of rock across the path, weighing the garment down, before moving off in silence to talk to the police in person. Livia's hand, as she clings tightly to Jake, stays as cold as the water itself.

Chapter Four

Night-time, Livia's homely cottage, the air surprisingly chill. Autumn seems to sneak in further with each descent of night. The heat dissipates, the dark swells, there is a dampness you can feel in your lungs when you breathe it in. Livia has a fire going and lies on a sheepskin rug with her feet before it. She was too tired to walk up to Little Sky when they returned from the search, too dispirited about the prospects of Claire's survival.

A record plays in the corner, fittingly enough: 'Come, sweet death' by Bach, all lugubrious cello. Jake is using the laptop to talk to Martha, for what Livia has dubbed 'The Irascible Loners' Book Club', where the two of them discuss detective fiction, usually with little agreement. Martha is a crime author herself, though that is not her defining feature: she spent years as a member of the secret services before being invalided out after close-up gunshots took her legs off below the knees, and still moonlights as an investigator between novels. While she is caustic and bloody-minded, her published stories are actually gentle, comic capers, tales of unlikely heists by a middle-class gang of art thieves.

Jake has been telling her about the books he had bought the day before, trying to get her to try Fred Vargas, whom she has hitherto dismissed as 'too weird and French'. They are now on stronger common ground, sharing their enjoyment of P. D. James, the later novels especially.

'Do you think she was in love with Dalgleish?' Jake is ruminative.

'A typically male question, as I'd expect from you.' Martha is smoking cannabis using a pipe, from habit, and to combat the pain from her injuries. Whatever her narcotic consumption, Jake has found she remains sharp and brilliant, one of the best case investigators he has ever come across.

'In fact, have you noticed something?' Martha warms to her point. 'Every time a female novelist writes a strong male lead, the first thing men say is: do you think she fell in love with her own character? They said it about Sayers and Ngaio Marsh, they say it about James. Nobody ever accused Colin Dexter about being all gay for Morse, did they? Though, now you mention it, don't male authors just tend to live vicariously through their heroes instead? They're always suspiciously hunky. Have you noticed how much Morse gets the women going, despite being old, gouty and stinking of fags? The least sexy sex symbol in fiction, and yet all these surprisingly big-boobed young things fall for him.'

Livia chuckles sleepily. Jake raises his arms in mock-surrender. 'All right, all right, it was a boring point to make. I'm tired, we walked a long way today, you know.'

'How insensitive. The one thing I'd love to do if I could, and you're moaning about it.'

There's a pause. Then her face breaks into a grin. 'God, I love doing that. Gets you every single time, you soft bastard.' She makes her voice shrill. '"Oh no, I've offended the disabled lady, I'm such a terrible, illiberal person."'

Another chuckle from the area near the fire. Jake throws a cushion in Livia's direction.

'We were only out there in the first place, because Liv here feels she needs to do something to find that poor nurse.'

'What a fucking cow Livia is. I hate kind people too.'

'That's it, I can't win, I'll shut up. Unless you've got some info about the nurse you want to share, make Liv feel better . . .'

Martha inhales thoughtfully. 'Even I'm amazed there's so much play on it in all the various bits of media. I looked it up, you know. More than 170,000 folk go missing every year, and the country weirdly fixates on just a handful, mostly kids or safe-looking white women of child-bearing age. I'd draw some pretty searing social conclusions, but I can't quite be bothered. No, Claire seems to be in the river. Who knows how she got there and why?'

Jake runs his finger along a groove in the table. 'And why was she not wearing a top? If she'd been hot to begin with, she could've left it with her shoes.'

'Maybe she went for a paddle first. I agree, it's odd.'

Livia speaks up from her corner. Flickers of fiery light lick against her skin. 'I just can't believe there's no footage, or evidence, to tell us either way.'

'You deliberately live, Liv, right out there in the wilds. No CCTV, no handy satellites above, or at least none that the government wants to admit to.' Martha snorts softly to herself. 'It's salutary, when you think about it. The world is bigger than we pretend, and that's on balance a good thing. Why do you care so much about this one, out of interest?'

Livia raises herself up on her elbows. Jake can see a vein softly pulsing in her neck. 'Ordinary boring reasons. I just think of her children, I guess, her husband.'

'Unless he did it, of course. Jake here will tell you how often and how quickly police look at the old feller. And I bet in houses throughout the country, people have clucked at each other when they've talked about it, and blamed him.'

Jake waves in agreement, and then offers his thoughts. 'Shoes off, and phone left on the riverbank: they both suggest she went in of her own accord. Three days ago was warm, maybe she was running, fancied a paddle, and slipped. Took off her top and had a bit of a dip. Or had a seizure, banged her head. Or had a moment of despair and threw herself in. The water's faster than it should be at this time of year, there's a strong current. Do you buy that, M?'

'Occam's Razor. Simplest explanation's usually the right one. And Jake is definitely the person I turn to for rank simplicity.'

'If Jake's right' – this is Livia, frowning – 'there's no version of her going in where's she still alive now, is there?'

'There's not many other versions that are possible at this stage, whatever we think happened. Either she's done a runner, without shoes or a phone, and is hiding out somewhere. Unlikely. Or someone has grabbed her for unknown reasons, left obvious evidence of her disappearance, and has decided to keep her hidden. That's not a very nice thought either.'

Livia slowly eases herself recumbent once more. 'Fine. Don't offer sops to reassure me. Can you please go back to debating books? I can handle this sort of thing in fiction, not in real life.'

They take her at her word, speak lightly for a few moments more. After he has said goodbye (Martha is always curt and peremptory, always the first to blip off when the conversation winds down), Jake sits and listens to Livia's heavy breathing. She has fallen asleep, curled up, feline, as the fire starts to ebb, the few glowing coals gradually blanketed by a thick tissue of ash. He carries her to bed, no burden, for all that he realizes he now has two people in the crook of his arms.

The next morning, Diana packed off in a lift to school, the mess of the house highlighted by a piercing sun, Jake and Livia are drinking coffee when a loud knock sounds at the door. Jake levers himself up, and goes to answer. Standing outside is a man, shortish, haggard and sleep-deprived, thinning brown hair, jeans and an old T-shirt that look like they have been worn for more than a day. Jake smells the desperation, rising like sweat from him.

He makes a grab for Jake's arms. 'You're Jake Jackson, aren't you? Please. Please. I need your help.'

Chapter Five

The man lets go, then bustles past him into the living room. Jake turns to follow.

'How d'you know who I am?'

'You're the famous ex-copper who solves crimes round here. Most people know that. I asked around and thought I'd try your girlfriend's place before that massive hike up to where you're supposed to live.'

'And, if you don't mind me asking, who the hell are you?' Livia is standing, arms folded, scepticism written across her face.

'My name is Steve. Steve Davidson. Claire's husband.'

A hush. No sound other than the distant squawk of a gull. Livia's expression softens as she draws him to a chair by the old dining table. 'We were out looking for her yesterday. Would you like a coffee?'

He winces out a smile. 'That's kind. Yes, please. I've not slept or eaten much for the last few days. I'm living on coffee, more or less.'

She brings him a steaming mug, and, unasked, a piece of

fruit cake, as they all three sit around the table. Steve looks like the very picture of a bereft and bereaved husband. Jake speaks to him like he is coaxing a spooked horse.

'I'm not sure why you'd be looking for me. I'm not sure I can help much at all.'

Steve's hands shake as he brings the mug to his lips. He has ignored the cake. 'They told me you'd found her top yesterday afternoon, and I was thinking of you anyway. You solve cases other people miss, don't you? Claire even mentioned you a couple of times over the last few years, when she read about that dig, or some other thing. I can't remember now.' His voice cracks.

Livia reaches out a hand and pats his. 'Jake is good at solving crimes, Steve. But he can't just find missing people any better than anyone else. We'll help look, of course we will. I'd give anything to think of something that can bring her back to you. But . . .' She falters.

'But, what? She's probably at the bottom of the river? I can't bear that.' The pitch of his voice rises, becoming a wail that swells until it sticks in his throat. 'I can't bear that.' He grabs Jake's arm, spilling his coffee, ignoring the spread of dark liquid across the old, rough surface of the table. 'What if someone's grabbed her, what if she's alive somewhere, waiting for a miracle, some piece of clever detective work? What if you're the chap that can save her?'

Jake remains carefully calm. He almost never raises his voice, in any situation. And getting excited would certainly not help here. 'Why would anyone want to grab her?'

Livia begins quietly mopping up the coffee with a cloth. Steve's fists grip his thighs, clutching at the taut material. 'I don't know. She meets all sorts as a nurse, doesn't she? Crazy folk, druggies. Why does anyone attack anyone? Will you help me find out?'

Jake lets this pause linger, as he thinks. 'Steve, I'm happy to speak to the chief in charge of the investigation, who's a good man. I can look over whatever he's got. And Livia and I will do all we can to help the search. But I can't promise more than that, and I have to tell you I believe the police will already be doing all they can.'

Steve rises, pathetically grateful, shakes Jake's hand. 'OK. I've got what I came for, at least. I've a feeling you might be the difference.'

Jake holds on to his hand, brings his own head close to Steve's, looks him in his troubled, bleary eyes. 'You've got to keep strong. For yourself. For the kids. Stay hopeful, but stay realistic. I'm no superhero. I'll go this morning to see the police. You hold on tight to things, you hear.'

Steve's eyes fall to the ground. A sob wells up from the base of his stomach, guttural. He swallows it, nods to them both and leaves, shutting the door carefully behind him.

Livia comes to stand near to Jake, traces a finger across his arm. 'God, I never want to hear a noise as despairing as that again.' She picks up the mug and plate, the cake untouched, and takes them back to the kitchen, giving her own sigh as she goes.

Chapter Six

There's an incident room in an old village hall, a mile or so from Westerby. Jake walks there straight from Livia's house, tracing the route alongside the river. A cool pallor has descended upon the morning, the sun obscured beneath a flat expanse of pewter cloud.

Jake sees the circus from a few hundred yards away. A large broadcast truck, five or six cars parked on verges, journalists vaping or standing slightly apart from the crowd, making calls. The hall itself is old and ivy-clad, a large stone lintel above the door that looks medieval.

It smells, like all such places, of the past, of community congregation, of disinfectant and boy scouts and bureaucracy. Fusty as cabbage. Jake walks past the idlers outside, some of whom probably have an idea who he is: the crime correspondents, and some of the locals.

Inside, the main hall – the floor brown and scuffed, piano in one corner, flags and pennants adorning the walls – a series of tables have been set up, some with computer equipment on top. There are chairs laid out. An urn of hot water is on a ledge in the corner surrounded by tea-making detritus, the surface mapped with patches of stickiness. People shift and whisper, but there is little energy in the room, no suggestion of impending news.

Jake waves at DCI McAllister, who is sitting, arms folded, head back, staring at the beams in the ceiling. He pulls up a chair beside him, pats him equably on the thigh.

McAllister smiles. 'Why did I have a feeling you might show up?'

Jake raises his hands. 'I'm not trying to interfere.'

'Ah, I'm just joshing.' He sips a cup of jaundiced-looking tea. McAllister is a dark, saturnine Scotsman, with wiry hair, and a permanent shadow across his chin. He regards Jake as a sort of consultant, the man who had helped when McAllister was first transferred here from Glasgow. Jake has tried to be an ally, and a sounding board, ever since.

Now he tells him about the husband's visit, and they compare notes about what is known about Claire and her final moments. McAllister does not have much more information than Jake, which is a concern to both of them. He looks harassed by this particular case, his normal facade of placating irony worn a little thin. Claire's inexplicable disappearance, all the media attention. They speak softly so as not to attract the interest of anyone else in the room.

'It still sounds most like a swimming accident to me.' Jake is tentative.

'Aye, I think so. I'm not that sold on ideas of suicide. From what we can tell, there was no great secret tragedy in Claire's life. She had all the problems lots of folk do, right enough: stressful job, kids with issues, marriage occasionally under strain, a bit of ill health, but nothing out of the ordinary.' He reflects for a second. 'We're none of us ever in perfect shape, are we? She could've taken her shoes off and jumped in, but it's no way to kill yourself really. I think accident most likely. Foul play not impossible. But that doesn't seem to satisfy the hordes outside.'

'Are they becoming a problem?'

McAllister works a knuckle, hidden beneath a feathery tuft of hair. It reminds Jake involuntarily of the grebe he saw on the river. 'No more than usual. Actually, a bit more than usual. For some reason, people care about her, want answers more urgently, more urgently than I can give them.' He pauses. 'That shouldn't be a bad thing.'

'Livia's more invested in this than she's been in other stories, so something's going on. Maybe it's the end of summer, maybe Claire's pretty and mumsy and so we can't imagine her dead, maybe we're all tired of women getting hurt and she's being made to stand for something bigger than she is.'

'Maybe. But I'm not sure that helps us. Any bright ideas?'

'You know what you're doing. I'll take a look at the case file quietly before I go, but I've got nothing special on my mind.'

'Do it in the office back there, will you? I can live without reports of you as the hairy saviour of the hapless local police.'

An hour or so later, Jake leaves the hall through a side door. A light drizzle is falling, which he barely notices. He had learned nothing unexpected from what he had read. A great deal of resources had been expended over the previous few days, and McAllister had handled matters in his usual thorough, methodical way. There were pages of witness statements, from people on the river, co-workers from the hospital, local searchers. As far as could be determined,

Claire had left after an early shift, driven home and headed out in her exercise clothes, never to be seen again. She had been working in A&E, ten hours, and it had been a busy day but not unusually so: more than one high fever, a bicycle accident. One other case had attracted her especial attention, and thus Jake's: a woman who had attended with marks on her face and body, sullen and afraid, the looming presence of a partner beside her. Claire had apparently marked her file as a possible victim of domestic abuse, but no action had yet been taken on it. Jake had written down the details on a card, which he pocketed as he left, but he wasn't convinced there was much of a connection to explore there.

As he stands in the mithering damp, the not unpleasant sensation of rain on his face, he notices someone taking shelter beneath a tree, ten yards away, staring at him. He recognizes her from the search yesterday, the girl with the beehive hair who had been filming herself. She waves, then turns to speak into the camera on her phone, which is striped yellow and black. Seconds later, she hastens towards him, long, rustling raincoat slipping from her shoulders. Beneath it, she is wearing denim shorts and a pink T-shirt.

She reaches out a hand. 'Jake, isn't it? The local superhero detective?' Her eyes, friendly but intense, bore into him.

'Hardly. Just Jake is fine.'

'I'm investigating Claire's disappearance. Are you?'

'I'm helping, I suppose, but just as a concerned citizen. You know: part of the search volunteers.'

'Can I talk to you on camera? You're a character made for the internet, as you may or may not realize. Mysterious, good back story, someone unwilling to conform to the traditional professional stereotypes.' She traces a sharp fingernail lightly against his cheek. 'Not unhandsome in the right light.'

Jake smiles. 'Gosh, how flattering. No, I've got nothing useful to say, and I don't want to get in the way of the cops. You should take care too. This isn't a game, you don't want to be part of making things more difficult.'

'I don't treat any story like a game, Jake. My followers would see straight through that, and my rep is all I've got, you know, to trade. How about just a selfie then? I really am pleased to meet you. I'm Dani Jones, by the way. Detective Dani on YouTube and elsewhere. And I know, you're not on social at all, you big caveman.'

She manoeuvres herself next to him, her face close to his, holding her phone up high. Her expression immediately sets in a practised pout, like a waxen image, eyebrows raised theatrically, lips puffed, tongue poking from the corner of her mouth. He probably looks baffled and dishevelled, but smiles anyway, for pride's sake, mouth tightly closed over his teeth.

Dani lets him move off, and walks companionably alongside him. 'Have you got any theories, Jake?'

He shakes his head. 'I promise you, Dani, I'm not working this at all. Nice to meet you, though. I'm wandering off home now.'

'I'm working on a theory she was killed by a man who met her at the hospital. Any comment on that?'

Jake thinks of the card in his pocket and shakes his head. 'I just hope we find her.'

Dani frowns, speaks to his retreating back. 'I think "hope" might be a bit too passive an approach for my tastes.' She watches him head through a small gap in the drystone wall – craggy and grey, lined with moss – and towards the river. 'I'll see you around, Jake. I'm not going anywhere, I promise.'

When he looks back, he sees she is striding into the hall, through the door he had just exited.

The address in his pocket – of the potentially abused woman at the hospital – is from a village between Westerby and home, and he decides to take the detour, whether stung by Dani's remarks about passivity or not, he cannot quite tell. The rain has stopped and all the green around him is now accentuated. Small puddles nestle in dips and crevices, little jewels of light, the fallen leaves beneath his feet sodden and smooth.

The village is actually called Greenwood, no doubt a misnomer in the depths of winter, but now immediately apt. There is a single road through it, of dark and damp asphalt. Jake finds the right house, a cottage with a short drive linking it to the road, and ponders his next move. He has no grounds to intervene, no prompt other than curiosity.

He has the names of the couple – Louise and Paul Sansom – and he supposes he could get McAllister, or more likely Martha, to look at any relevant violent history the husband might have. His other resource is a woman called Aletheia, with whom he worked as a detective in the past, and who has helped him with the various cases he has become entangled in since his retirement. She is an expert Searcher, in the parlance of his old force: a peerless investigator into the backgrounds of suspects, who works for both the police and the secret services. She'd help, of course, if he asked for it, but Jake is conscious he's spent the past three days insisting that there's likely a sad, simple explanation rather than something more sinister.

The cottage is quiet, curtains shut, the whole building

seeming to squat, flinching from the hot, hostile sky and the towering trees. Jake stands for a while, contemplative, and then heads towards the village centre, where he sees a pub, its doors open to the sun and passing trade.

Inside, it is gloomy, except for the stencil of light through the doorway itself, a patch that illuminates a scuffed and scarred wooden floor. There are two men at the bar, both tall and thick set, heavily stubbled, wearing dark jeans and tight T-shirts. Their arms look strong, muscles taut beneath the flesh, but their stomachs are bowling-ball round. They have half-empty pints in front of them, glazed eyes.

Jake goes to the bar and orders a beer. He realizes he looks a little incongruous, even though he had dressed up to see the police: soft cotton trousers and a dark vest. He looks across to the men, nods affably. 'I'm looking for a guy named Paul Sansom, you know where he might be? His place looks empty.'

Jake's glance is returned with evident rancour. The taller of the pair speaks first.

'Who wants to know?'

Jake is not intimidated. He sips his beer. 'Obviously, I do. I'm just checking up on him. His wife was put in hospital recently.'

They both move closer, standing to frame Jake. The same man continues to speak. 'How's that your business? You don't look like police. Don't look like one of those reporters.'

Jake does not break eye contact. 'Let's just say I'm someone interested. Are you friends of his?'

'Paul's a mate, yes. And he wouldn't like us talking about him. He wouldn't like you much either. He does his talking with his fists mostly.'

'Including on his wife?'

'Now, I didn't say that.'

Jake turns to the man on his right. 'Do you speak at all, or just hang out with this lad because of his handsome looks?'

A landlord has appeared, solicitous, behind the bar. Right-hand man pokes a stubby finger, the nail torn, into Jake's chest. 'I ain't got nothing to say to you.'

'And neither of you know where Sansom is?'

The landlord, with a lined, kindly face, breaks the tension. 'Paul Sansom works on a crew that puts road signs up. They went off on a job Tuesday up North. They'll be back tomorrow. I know that because he headed off straight after he took his missus to hospital, came in here for a quick pint then. That's all we can tell you.'

Jake thinks it over. If it's true, it might well put him away from the area at the crucial time, or it might be a convenient alibi. No reason to back down right away. He keeps his chest wide, finishes his beer quickly. 'If it comes up, you might tell him he should keep his fists to himself. I better not hear of his wife in hospital in the future.'

A smirk, and a beery belch near his face. 'What you going to do about it, hippy?'

Jake locks eyes once more. 'He really won't want to find out. Big blokes who hit women are scum. They're weak, just don't want people to know it. I'm sure deep down you realize that too.' He keeps his voice calm, pushes past them and heads back into the light. It is satisfyingly bright outside, the atmosphere clear and fresh. As he emerges, he catches sight, on the other side of the road, of a woman taking hurried leave on a scooter. No helmet, blond beehive hair bobbing. He watches as she disappears from view.

Chapter Seven

'So did you really achieve anything with all that?' This is Livia, after night has fallen, ensconced in the library at Little Sky. Diana is asleep, the house is quiet, the windows open to the breeze.

'Almost certainly not, no. I probably should've left well alone. I even felt that as I was doing it. Problem is, this guy Paul could be relevant, and is worth checking up on.' He exhales. 'But I also know I got a little wound up back there. I've never liked big fellers who throw their weight around, and I've not always had the confidence to stand up to them. Now I can't resist.'

'Are you going to leave it?'

He weighs it up in his mind. 'I might – if you don't mind, lovey – go and see the wife. The evidence for the beating looked pretty solid. I could see if she needs help at least. While asking one or two questions.'

'Of course I don't mind. I'll come with you. I want to help too.' He looks at her in the pallid twilight, her face in repose, sleepy sea-green eyes. She rolls towards him, a frown of concentration.

'Why was that Dani girl there outside the pub?'

Jake shrugs. 'She seems to be taking the whole case very seriously. I wonder if she'd chased down the same lead out of the hospital. Who knows? I doubt she's onto something, but she strikes me as someone not easily put off. I guess she might need to let it go too, like us. In the end, I think Claire got hot and bothered, went for a swim in the river, and had a terrible accident. It's not thrilling, it's not good for social media, but it's probably true.'

Livia places her head against his chest. She is wearing loose pyjama leggings and a vest. He can feel the warmth emanating from her body, her skin soft and faintly tacky, like clay that has been fresh-fired by the heat of the sun. 'Look at you with your online expertise. You'll be on TikTok before you know it.'

He laughs. 'I'm off to the sauna for twenty, then I promise to stay offline and take you to bed.'

'You'll be lucky if I'm awake when you get back. I'm sleeping for two, you know.'

Jake had built the sauna in his first summer at Little Sky, and he and Livia had a developed a ritual of long, languorous sessions followed by shriek-filled dips in the lake. She had decided to give them up during her pregnancy, which Jake thinks is the right decision, but he is not quite willing to share the privation himself.

He strips off his clothes, the tops of his legs pale in the half-light, and wanders through to the kitchen. He puts his things in the basket by the stove. A room of shiny surfaces lit by moon-glimmer, silent apart from the ticking of a clock. Sprawled on the floor is Cyprian, Livia's ginger cat, who has made the permanent move to Little Sky before her. She has settled in well, stalking the fields in idle pursuit of the small birds that flit near the hedges, archly observing the chickens who live in raised houses in one of the fields, regularly dismembering and presenting fieldmice with a cat's conscienceless precision.

Livia still needs her own cottage, as it is closer for work and connected to the technology an on-call vet requires. They have discussed what will happen when the baby comes, how Little Sky will become shared, not just Jake's private domain. He is happy about that, but wonders how it will all work when Livia does go back to her job. He puts the problem from his mind as he wraps a towel around his waist.

Inside: the air so hot it sears his lungs, a soothing orange light to read his book under, the hissing of the coals mitigating the oppressive silence. He lies naked, soon covered in sweat, his hair plastered, holding his book above his head, before he puts it down, watching its pages curl in the heat.

He holds out against the swelter until his skin reddens, his heart begins to thump, and he can feel the pulse in his neck throbbing beneath the skin. He staggers outside, moonlight bleaching him white. Naked lunatic. The lake is cool and refreshing, and he swims out towards Reacher Island, now just a blot of dark shapes against the blue-black sky. Stars are scattered above him, pearly pinpricks, as he floats on his back, watching his chest rise and fall, his breathing slowing, every inch of him alive in the moment.

Inside, Livia is making mint tea in the kitchen, and he takes her in his arms, still damp from the water, his towel discarded on the floor. She eases Cyprian out into the night with one foot, before coming back into the centre of the room, slipping out of her flimsy clothing. Jake gasps at her carnal reality, as he always does, a throb of desire at the familiar sight of skin, and curves, the now-rounded stomach atop the bold thatch of hair, the sheen of perspiration in the warm night.

'Some couples don't have sex during a pregnancy, you know.'

'Some couples don't know what they're missing.'

She pushes him down on to the overstuffed chair by the stove. Out of the corner of his eye, Jake watches the cat stalk away, tail aloft and aloof. Then all thought of anything else is forgotten.

The next morning, lateish, they drive to Greenwood, Livia at the wheel of her old Volvo. He points out the Sansom house, and they walk down the drive, Livia in the lead. They had decided that, as a woman, she should do the talking; she would be up front with Louise, and assess the level of danger, if any.

There is no reply to her knock. They wait, listen to the heave of the trees. She knocks again. Jake catches a movement at the window.

'I think if we stick around, she'll realize she has to speak to us.'

Livia nods, counts a minute and knocks once more. The door opens an unwelcome fraction. They can see a pale face, her features still smothered by shadow.

'Louise?'

A faint movement of her head.

'Louise, my friend works with the police, and he and I

just want to check you're OK. You went to hospital with quite serious injuries, and we want to make sure you know there's people who care about that.' As she is speaking, Jake recognizes anew the scant authority for them being there.

'I'm OK.' Louise's voice is scarcely louder than the wind.

'Would you mind if we came in for a chat? We won't stop long.'

Livia gives the door a slight push with her hand as she speaks, and it opens with no resistance. Louise is wearing grey tracksuit bottoms and an old hooded top, her dirty blond hair piled up on her head. Her eyes are watery and suspicious, her face on one side is livid with bruising, blacks and purples and reds. When she turns, she moves like an old woman, though he knows she is not yet thirty.

'You can come in, but you'd best be on your way, soon enough. I don't want to have my husband come back to find you.'

She leads them to a sitting room which is sparse and tidy, dominated by a huge TV screen on the wall. The news is playing silently, tales of violence and sorrow from around the world. Livia gestures to it. 'Did you see the story about Claire Davidson, the missing nurse?'

A nod.

'Do you remember her?'

'I thought it was her on the telly. Paul said it wasn't, but he spent most of the time at the hospital looking at his phone. Did she go missing that day? How awful.'

Livia and Jake sit close together on the cracked leather sofa, after Louise eventually motions them to do so. She perches on an armchair, hand near her mouth, nibbling her fingernails. In the light of the room, her skin looks washed-out, leached of life, the bruises even blacker, starker.

Livia leans forward, trying to keep pity from her voice. 'Claire left a note saying she thought you might've been abused by your partner. Did she say anything like that to you?'

Louise is staring at Jake, he can feel the hostility emanating from her like a fever. He makes as if to stand, and she flinches.

'I can wait outside if you'd like. I don't want to make you uncomfortable.'

Her flinch becomes almost a sob, a sagging of her body, as though it is broken. 'Oh, why does it matter who knows what? This Claire woman was kind, took me into a room and looked at me. Said she knew what'd happened and wanted to help. Told me I could be brought in to hospital and she'd pretend there were more tests I needed, to give me the chance to talk, private like.'

'What did you say?' Livia is soothing.

'I did what I always do. Tried to wish my problems away, I guess.' Louise tugs at her hair. 'I don't know.' The pause fills the room, a sense of futility pasted across her features. 'I don't know what to say to people like you, people like that Claire woman. My life is my life, I've made my decisions, and I know what I'm in for.'

Livia persists, even if doubtful of getting through. 'That doesn't mean you have to put up with anything at all. You've always got choices.'

A bitter grin animates Louise's face for a second. 'That's what posh women always say, and it just makes me think they don't get it, don't get real life. Paul's the main thing in my world, and I can handle him most of the time. I've had my moments when I've gone for him as well, you know. Most of the time he's sweetness, less he loses his temper. If

I moaned about that, kicked up too much of a fuss, what'd we have to come back to?'

'Sounds like a real sweetheart.' Jake can't help himself.

Louise's face distorts with contempt. 'As if you've never had one too many and taken a swing. All men are like that in the end.'

Livia reaches out her hand; Louise does not flinch this time. 'Let me promise you something. Not all men are like that. And no woman should put up with it. Did Paul know Claire had talked to you about this?'

Louise shook her head. 'I kept it quiet. Even took a number to call if anything bad happened again. Why do you ask?'

Livia considers her response, opts for honesty. 'We're helping look for Claire. We just want to make sure nothing's happened to her.'

'So you're not here to help me at all. You don't care about me, you care about her.' She stands, stiff as a marionette. 'I think you should leave.' Her top rides up a little. The underlying skin is pale, but there is more bruising here, more blacks and blues bleeding into one another.

Louise snatches Livia's hand away, pulls down her top. 'I said I think you should leave.'

Livia takes a piece of card from her pocket, writes her number down. 'You can call this any time. We do care about you. We wouldn't have come otherwise. We'd like to help Claire, but we want to help you too. I want you to believe that.' She holds Louise's stare, her face open and credible. Louise is starting to speak, when the crunch of a key in the front door interrupts them. She steps back, aghast. Before anyone can say anything a man fills the door into the living room, squat and broad, a billiard ball for a head.

His voice is pregnant with portent. 'Lou, I didn't know you had folk over today. You didn't tell me.'

Livia becomes brisk. 'We're involved in the search for the missing nurse, and are checking on people who'd spoken to her, like your wife.'

He doesn't move from the door. 'You'd think the police could do that themselves.' He turns his attention for the first time to Jake. 'Hang about, are you the hairy bastard that was asking questions about me in the boozer? They told me you was some sort of hippy. I was coming looking for you. You've saved me the fucking bother.' He steps forward. His face is ruddy with anger, maybe drink, his expression one of entitled rage; his arms are half-outstretched, stranglers' hands to the fore. 'So what do you want to know about me, and what do you want with my missus?'

Chapter Eight

Jake can see the beads of sweat trickle down Paul's head, smell the beer on his breath, feel the aggression pulsing from him, seeping from his pores.

'We're looking into that nurse going missing, Claire Davidson. You two were some of the last people to speak to her.'

'I don't know nothing about a nurse. Lou went to hospital, got fixed up, I went out on a job. That's all that happened.'

'Did you talk to her?'

Paul takes a step back so he can fix his eyes more easily on Jake. 'To who?'

'Claire, the nurse.'

'Lou did, I was just waiting around.'

Louise edges forward, places her hand on Paul's arm. She addresses her words to Livia, who is standing, wary, her expression otherwise unreadable. 'Claire was kind and all, but we weren't with her for long enough to have much to do with her.' She turns and looks at Jake meaningfully.

Jake thinks about leaving it at that, but can't entirely

suppress the angry feeling, something deep in his gut, when he sees the smouldering figure in front of him, recalls the battered softness of his wife's skin. 'So how come Louise was in the hospital in the first place?'

Paul looks across at her. 'What did she tell you?'

'Nothing, which is why I'm asking you, champ. See, I used to be a copper, and I worry about healthy women going to hospital looking smashed-up like that, you know?'

'I never agreed to have a copper in the house. Why don't you get out. Both of you. She never should've let you in.'

Livia moves to leave. Jake sighs. 'We'll go. We didn't come here to cause a scene in your house. We came to help out a woman.' He didn't specify Claire or Louise, indeed is not sure how much he has managed to help either much. 'But you need to watch yourself.'

He moves to shift past Paul, whose torso is rigid, stiff with bravado. Jake pushes against him. He can feel the man's muscles twitching beneath his tight T-shirt. Paul pushes back.

'You need to mind your own fucking business.'

Another push from Paul. Jake staggers slightly, steps forward to right himself, and collides once more against Paul's body. It's an accident that is taken as a provocation. The mask finally slips and Paul grunts, tries a big swing at Jake's face, which he ducks easily. All Paul's control has gone now, all that tension pouring from him.

Jake recognizes instantly that Paul knows his way around a fight. But so does Jake. Instead of backing away, he holds his hands up, an old trick he'd learned in combat training. It's a distraction, a sub-conscious message of surrender that makes the attacker feel secure. It also gets his hands high, and ready. Paul blinks, and Jake corkscrews a punch with his left, turning it into an upper-cut at the last minute beneath Paul's jaw, snapping his teeth together like a closing box. It's not a hard punch, but a cruel one, painful and startling. Paul reels backward. Jake steps to one side, and delivers two more strikes, as quick as he can, into Paul's kidney and stomach. More concise cruelty. The air explodes from him, he gasps and gets nothing, drops down to one knee.

It has all taken less than five seconds. Jake pushes him roughly to the ground. Paul has bitten through his lip, so a small piece of pink flesh is loose and dripping blood. There are tears in his eyes. Jake's voice is as quiet as ever.

'You might be good at fighting people smaller and weaker than you, but you're out of shape and slow. Only you know what a coward you really are, but I can see it.' Jake looks up briefly at Louise, who has not moved.

'So here's all I'm going to say. If I hear you've taken out your rage on Louise, I'll come back and you won't be getting up. If I hear you had anything to do with that nurse's disappearance, I'm coming back too. Do you understand me?'

Paul spits out a gobbet of bloody phlegm on the linoleum floor. He half raises himself on all fours. His voice is strained.

'I hear you. But you need to watch your back as well, hippy. You came to my house, remember that.'

They leave him behind, breathing heavily, and walk to the door. Louise shuffles after them. The pupils of her blue eyes are dilated wide. 'You had no business being here. All you've done is made him mad. I'm gonna suffer somehow, I know it.'

Chapter Nine

With that, the door closes behind them. Livia strokes Jake's arm. 'Come on, let's get back to the car before he comes after us.'

Jake grins ruefully. 'I'm not sure I handled that brilliantly. But he's done for the day anyway.'

They get in the car. No movement in the house behind them. Livia's voice is steady. 'He was ready to really hurt you, though, until you put him down. And I like that you don't go looking for trouble like that, but you sure know how to handle it.'

'Let's just hope I've not made the whole thing worse. He's going to feel unmanned by all that. Damn it. It's almost never a good thing to get involved like this, unless you offer a proper route out.'

'I'd agree, but there's Claire to think of too. We were right to ask questions. She could've given us a line to her.'

'Could've but didn't. I better ask McAllister to send someone round to let him know they have an eye on him, too.'

'He won't file a complaint against you?'

'No chance. Admit a hippy like me took him down in his own house? He couldn't handle it.'

The sun peers out from behind one of those flighty clouds, bathes the car in mellow light. Jake's heart rate is back to normal, the stinging pulse in his knuckles the only physical sign of the altercation. They park at Livia's house and walk up to the Jolly Nook, the shop-cum-pub at the heart of Parvum. Sarah is in her usual position, standing atop an old pile of newspapers, surveying the lines of shelves that are filled with local produce, meat and vegetables and preserves, along with biscuits and cakes from her own oven.

'Hello, my ducks, nice to see you. And looking blooming as ever, especially you, Livia. Jake here always looks more bedraggled than blooming, but I love him anyway. Someone's got to.'

Livia gives her a hug. 'I do my best to as well. How are things?'

'Mustn't complain, mustn't complain. Well I do, but none of you listen much. Can I get you a cuppa? Jake, you look hungry – finish this scone for me.'

He demurs, to no avail. She pushes a plate into his hands, and goes back into her kitchen. She brings three more scones and puts them on the counter. Jake is, without reluctance, eating. Sarah has the gift of kitchen alchemy, bringing happiness through pastry.

'I'm having a cider with my lunch. Would you like some?'

She brings out two more glasses, and a long bottle half-filled with pale gold liquid. 'This is very light, good for the daytime, more like apple juice.'

Livia places her hand over her glass. 'Not for me. I've got work later.'

Sarah pauses for a fraction, and raises a knowing eyebrow, but makes no comment. 'Jake, you can keep an old lady company.'

He isn't sure he wants to have cider, however light, but feels obliged to camouflage Livia's non-drinking. Sarah is right. The cider is delicate, no fizz or kick, the flavour more of elderflower than apple. The three of them stand companionably.

'There was a man the other day looking for you, Jake. Youngish, mean-looking. I said you were away.'

Jake wonders whether it was Claire's husband or Paul Sansom, even though neither is particularly young. He is just about to find out more, when the tinkle of the doorbell disturbs them. McAllister walks in, his set and serious face warming into a smile when he sees Sarah. She beams, heads back into the kitchen, returns with more scones.

'Chief Inspector, you'll be wanting something to keep you going. You look gaunt with all your work.'

McAllister pats his stomach, and grabs a scone. He is trim enough in his dark suit trousers and white shirt, a uniform that never varies. 'Sarah, you always think I need feeding. My wife wonders why I come home and don't want dinner. She thinks I'm having an affair.'

'For someone who's worried about eating too much,' Jake cuts in, 'you've certainly inhaled that scone.'

McAllister looks as flustered as he ever does, which is not much, and casts an eye upon Sarah's other pastries. 'Well, don't want to be rude. I was here on business, to leave a message for you actually.'

'And you thought lunchtime might be a good time to drop in.'

Jake and McAllister find their way to a picnic table outside, leaving Livia and Sarah to talk.

The afternoon is gorgeous in its aspect, the perfect mixture of breeze and sun, a warmth to wallow in. Jake fills McAllister in on what happened with the Sansoms. He agrees to send a constable around. 'I was going to do it anyway, given the report from the hospital. Though', he cautions, 'if anyone asks I'll be very clear I don't condone ex-coppers slapping folk around, whatever we think they've done. You should keep away from him from now on – I'd hate to have to arrest you.' Jake nods, before McAllister continues. 'Do you like him as a kidnapper or killer?'

Jake shakes his head, watches something flutter in a nearby tree. Small shock of red and yellow. A second later he hears the high-pitch trill, insistent and voluble. A goldfinch, a beautiful bird. Amazing, he thinks, that he recognizes its call now. One of the virtues of quiet living, away from the obscuring hubbub and clamour of the city: you start to hear things afresh, attune your brain to the incidental noises of common existence.

He turns his mind back to the conversation. 'I don't. He's a bully and a beater, but I think anyone he went after, you'd see the body quickly. He's not . . .' He searches for the word. 'Furtive or clever. And not a kidnapper.'

McAllister nods and pulls a further scone from his pocket. 'Say nothing,' he mumbles between mouthfuls. 'The scanning boys have been up and down the river. They've found an anomaly – what you or I might call a dark blob – that could be something, and we're going after it first thing tomorrow. You're welcome to come along.'

'Are you sure you want me there? I thought my support might be a pain if it became too open.'

'Ach, it might be too late for that.' He reaches for his phone, spends a few seconds stabbing at the screen inexpertly, then shows it to Jake. It's a video of Dani, 'Detective Dani', headlined: 'The hairy hero detective joins the search.' Jake watches for a moment, footage of him taken at a distance, intercut with Dani narrating her own account of the investigation into Claire's disappearance. The final shot is a screen with the words: 'Did a killer come from the hospital?'

'Are you bothered?'

McAllister exhales. 'Not really about your involvement, at least not for now. It's a big public search after all, and you've got something of a local reputation. I wouldn't be thrilled if this Dani talked to Paul Sansom, but they don't strike me as easy soulmates. No, come along tomorrow morning; I'd be pleased to get your thoughts. My boys think it's almost certainly a body, and it's been in the water a while.'

Chapter Ten

Very early morning, the sun no more than a hint beneath the horizon, stars paling as the black becomes blue. It's cold as Jake slides out of bed and brews some coffee. He feels it warm in his stomach as he walks, feet clad in leather boots, soon sopping from the early dew. The dive site is an hour or so along the river, still and dense-looking, chocolate-coloured in the half-light, shiny as icing on a cake. Nobody in the world seems awake but him.

Then he sees lights ahead, movement, hears the murmur of human activity. The river turns back on itself a little here, creating a bulge of land about the size of a cricket pitch, carpeted with boggy grass that once may have been half-submerged in marsh. Two searchlights have been set up, small but fierce, directed at the water. There is a police van a few hundred yards away, still on the path, providing the power.

McAllister is standing, muffled in his black coat, directing operations. He waves at Jake to stand next to him. In the river, beneath the light, he can see two divers, one crouching in the shallows, hands feeling beneath him like he has lost his keys, the other standing, then plunging into the central course of running water, gleaming like an otter.

Jake surveys the whole landscape. An impenetrable wood behind them, open fields running towards the skyline on the other side of the river. Further along the path is a solitary cottage, its chimney leaking grey smoke, smudged line against the sky. Jake nods towards it. 'Do the folk there know what you're doing?'

'We had to get them to open the gate to let the van in. Two women, some sort of pottery makers, I think. Nice enough.'

'They're watching through binoculars in the top window. I can see the glint.'

'That's no crime. They might get lucky and see something.'

'Do you think *we'll* be lucky?'

McAllister stamps his feet. 'I fear so, Jake. We'll see.'

Jake pours himself a cup of tea from an urn sitting in the back of the open van. He finds an old stump a few yards downstream and sips the steaming drink, watching the day coalesce around him, brightness – pale orange at first – filling the gaps between the trees.

He starts when the cry of 'boss!' pierces the quiet. One of the divers is waving vigorously. Jake hangs behind while McAllister goes to the water's edge. A further moment and he steps back, to allow something heavy to be lifted from the water, limp and ungainly. They place it carefully on a stretcher that has been brought up especially. McAllister waves Jake over. The lights have been turned back from the water, down on to the ground, harsh and unforgiving.

McCallister swears softly. 'A body, just where they said it'd be.'

Jake crouches down. It is naked, the skin mottled and stretched, water-bloated. Jake feels his heart race.

'Chief.' Jake's voice is a little hoarse. McAllister is looking behind them, talking to one of his staff.

Plans are being struck to move the body, bring in other experts. Jake speaks again, but to no avail.

'Chief, for fuck's sake.' His voice is, finally, louder than normal. McAllister turns. 'What is it?'

'Claire Davidson is a middle-aged woman, short with a bob of dark hair. Look.'

They both stare at the body, lifeless like a fish gaffed from its watery home. But still a recognizable shape, still a person there to recreate in your mind. It looks very much like a young woman, slightly taller than average, hair that is blond at the tips and reaches all the way down to her waist. Skin overwhelmingly pale, as if bleached. The only patch of colour the pink of her toenails.

'Chief, you've found a body. But this isn't the one you were looking for.'

Book Two: Tributary

Fame is like a river that beareth up things light and swollen, and drowns things weighty and solid.
                                    Francis Bacon, *Essays*

Chapter Eleven

Three days pass. Still no sign of Claire. The media, new and old, spasming at the latest development: two women gone, one unrecovered, what did it all mean? The new body is identified as Jade Fortescue, mid-twenties, a trainee solicitor, single and on a week's holiday from work. That explained why she had not been noticed missing sooner. The autopsy was hurried through, and death was estimated sometime after Claire's disappearance, maybe by as much as seventy-two hours, though the state of the corpse in the water made precision difficult.

Cause of death was also similarly hard to determine. Some water in her lungs, suggestive of the fact that she was alive when she entered the river. There was bruising on her body, but that was also consistent with rough treatment by the river itself, which had been made fat and fast by the unseasonal rain, and would have borne her helpless, hither and thither, dragging her against reeds and rocks. Her nakedness was notable. Had she lost her clothes somehow in the process of becoming such flotsam, or had she entered the water naked, and if so, why? A frenzy of speculation had built with no obvious resolution. At some point, Jade's heart had stopped, the heart of a fit and healthy woman teeming with future, and beyond that nobody was able to venture with confidence.

Jake had avoided the circus as far as possible. At this stage, he could do little to help, and so had let the machinery of justice move into its practised gear, collecting physical evidence, establishing the days and weeks that led up to her sudden quietus. Livia had been shocked by the discovery, her anxiety about Claire made yet worse, more vivid and real. It subdued her, troubled her. Jake could tell, and wanted to help, but also realized that she would need to work through this herself. He couldn't make the world a better place, a world with no sodden women dredged ungainly from the water, and it would be arrogant to pretend otherwise.

This morning, he is mulling things over as he digs in his garden. Death and injustice feel momentarily distant. A perfect day to be outside. It is warm, but the heat now feels ever more transient; it pleasantly caresses rather than swelters, like it had done in the summer; it feels finite, and all the better for it. At dawn at this time of the year, the dew is always heavy, the air nipping at the extremities, little autumnal pinches to remind you what is coming; dark comes quicker in the evening, the breeze rising from the lake, the trees throwing off ever leaner silhouettes.

He is turning over the soil in one of his vegetable patches. It is black and rich, smells of both life and decay. The other patch is still teeming with produce, too much for one family, he thinks, and most of it will have to be given away: pendulous peppers, reddening on the vine; French and runner beans; courgettes and onions. The stalks sag with plenty, look over-burdened, blowsy with too much; the leaves are turning sepia-coloured, eaten by unseen caterpillars and other crawling creatures.

He is content enough when he lets his mind drift, becoming preoccupied with the manual task at hand. His old friend Peter – one of the first people he had met at Little Sky, dead these three years – had encouraged him to plant and grow. What was that phrase he used to tell him, wagging his dirt-lined hand with pleasure? 'We must cultivate our garden, Jake – the greatest line in all philosophy.' Jake was no philosopher but it seemed right enough to him.

The door to the kitchen is open, and he has his record player on loud, piano pieces by Karol Szymanowski, something he'd picked up as part of a bulk purchase at a record store and become fond of. He has his shirt off, welcomes the soft sting of the sun on his skin. He sits down, pours the remainder of the coffee from the pot, feels the cool grass against his legs. The lake is afire with reflected sun-glare, but something beyond it also glimmers, winking insistently. He puts his mug down, tries to see what is catching the light, without success. No matter. He has finished his digging, and would be happy for the walk down the valley.

He takes his time, touring the property as much as striving for one spot. Wolfe Orchard is at its most fecund now, a carnival of fruit, apples and pears, the cider scent of sweetness and plenty. His chickens strut and preen, the sun making their feathers shine like oil on water. When he gets past the lake, he sees it is Dani sitting beneath one of his elder trees, phone on the floor beside her, an expensive-looking camera around her neck. She is dressed for the warm day in not very much, small shorts, crop top, her skin still pale as a wraith. She is not slender, but not overweight, generously built; she makes Jake think somehow of things natural and abundant, like milk or cream. Her blond hair is piled high on her head like before.

She looks him up and down appraisingly. 'Easy on the eye. The land around here, I mean. Pretty to look at.'

'Were you taking pictures of me?'

'Would you like to see them?' She smiles distantly.

'Not really. Don't you need my permission to take them?'

'You're the policeman. You can arrest me if you like.' She is flirting, but abstractly, as if performing a role.

'What do you want?'

'What I always want, Jake. Stuff to excite and intrigue. This is a fascinating case, shocking really, murder in quiet paradise, the targeting of innocent women. And you're an eccentric cast member to spice things up: good back story, a bit of a wild card.' She sighs. 'And, as I've said before, not entirely unhandsome.' She reaches out and traces a finger down Jake's stomach. Again there is something arch and self-mocking as she does so.

She looks over Jake's shoulder, back towards the river and away from his house. She then steps forward, closer than he would like. 'So what's your theory now, Mr Wildcard?'

He takes a step back. She takes one forward. Ironic giggle. Another step back. 'I don't have one, but one woman missing and one dead is no small thing. It's more than just content.'

'Disapproval noted. But, you're wrong. Everything is content. Anyhow, I want to hear more of what you actually think.' She makes a sudden, jerky move back, as if stung. Looks again over his shoulder, speaks past him.

'Oh gosh, I didn't see you there. You must be Livia, the girlfriend. I'm afraid you've caught us.'

Livia walks up, breathing heavily. A flutter of worry for Jake, at the combination of heat and pregnancy. 'Caught you doing what?'

'I don't know. Talking out of school.' Dani stays arch. 'Jake, you and I must continue this some other time. Nice to meet you, Livia.' She pats his hand, lets it linger, and walks back towards Morse Field. After a hundred yards, she stops and starts talking into her phone, presumably filming herself, screen held at a distance with practised ease.

Livia is standing beside Jake, hands on her waist, as if easing a pain in her back. 'What was that all about?'

'God knows. I saw the glint of her camera and came to see what it was.'

'I saw that. You were making a very close investigation of that young thing, in her tiny shorts, all that floury skin on show.'

'She was getting close to me, I think you'll find.'

'And you looked devastated about it.'

'Liv, come on.'

'Don't patronize me on this. I'm pregnant and hot. I feel fat and loathsome, not at all helped by seeing you half-naked being felt up by that pasty Kardashian. She's trouble. You know it, and I know it.'

He puts his arms around her. She tries to shrug him off, but he clings on. 'Objection noted. I promise to only speak to people over the age of thirty-five from now on. I'll ask for ID first. And I'll wear big thick leggings and a rugby shirt at all times outside the house.'

Livia's face is puckered, lines across her forehead of consternation, which then reluctantly relax into an amused pout. She is natural, Jake thinks, in every way Dani seemed studied. She leans upward and pecks his cheek. 'Come on, I've got the afternoon off. You can come swimming with your whale of a girlfriend in this big cool lake of ours, and then treat me like a queen, seeing as I seem to be bossing you around like one.'

They wander back to the house. Peace regained for the moment.

Chapter Twelve

Jake likes to hold in his visual memory the sights and sensations of Livia like this, Edenic, floating in the water, her copper skin strewn with rivulets of trickling liquid, her nakedness splendid as a piece of art.

She had brought news from Martha, who said she was following the case despite herself and wanted to speak that afternoon. Livia has been trying to shift her own attention from the subject of the lost women, but keeps returning to it, helpless. She thinks about it when she is making her rounds as a vet, she thinks about it even more when she is away from work.

They get dressed and picnic beneath the beech by the house, salad pulled fresh from the garden with mustard and cider vinegar, bread and butter studded with rock salt. Jake finds some soothing music, starting with a song called *Spiegel im Spiegel*, delicate cello, turns it down and lets it float over them. After they've eaten, Livia snuggles into a cushion and falls asleep, the leaves above separating to allow striations of swaying sunlight upon her, scattering of gold. Jake brings his book, and sits nearby, occasionally watching her shift and murmur.

Mid-afternoon, when she wakes, Jake is staring past her, thinking. He leans over and kisses her mouth, lips slightly dry, the musty smell of sleep upon her.

She shoves him off gently. 'Jake, you don't kiss a woman who's just woken up and hasn't brushed her teeth after lunch.'

'Do you think we should get married?'

'I was just talking about bad breath, Jake, let's not overreact.'

He slides across to her, takes her hand, feels the cool of a fingernail beneath his thumb. 'I'm serious. We're going to have a baby together, should we get married first?'

'Is that a proposal? Because it's not the most romantic thing I've ever heard. Peter Wimsey asked Harriet to marry him IN LATIN next to an old bridge in Oxford.'

'You're so disgustingly literary these days.'

'It's all this living with a bookish boyfriend.'

'So what you're saying is that, if you've brushed your teeth, and if I'm romantic enough, you might say yes. And maybe in Latin.'

She wrinkles her eyes, charmingly, does deign to kiss him back. 'You're going to have to risk it and find out, lovey, aren't you?'

A little later, he strolls back to Livia's house in Parvum, in order to use her computer to call Martha.

She answers promptly, clearly already at her desk. No sign of recreational intoxicants for once. She is even wearing glasses, big dark rims; her blond hair is now purplish at the tips.

'Hello, old chap.'

'Did *you* know that Peter Wimsey proposed marriage in Latin?'

Martha seems unsurprised by the line of questioning. 'I don't, as you might expect, wet my pants over Dotty Sayers as much as everyone else, but yes, I did know that. It's at the end of that book where nobody gets murdered, isn't it?'

'*Gaudy Night*, it's called, and yes. Your books are pretty murder-free, though; I wondered if you were inspired by it.'

'Listen, matey, plenty happens in my books, more than just a few Oxford lesbians losing their gowns ahead of High Table.'

'Touched a nerve, I see.'

'Don't flatter yourself. And don't get ideas of thinking you're in a novel when you finally propose to Livia.'

'Who says I was thinking of doing that?'

'Your smug face, one. And, two, the fact that you are – despite all the hippy posturing – pretty conventional really. You've been living in sin with a lovely lady, of course you want to marry her. And three, you're thinking about these dead women and it's made you a bit maudlin, you soft bastard. Four . . .'

Jake holds up his hands in surrender. 'Three's enough. And yes, it's the women I want to talk about. I do care, Livia cares. You care, obviously.'

Martha pauses for a moment, lets her tone shift, then nods. 'I do care, you're right. Of course I do. So, as soon as you dredged up that poor girl, I started looking into things.'

Jake settles back. 'Tell me what you've got.'

'Not much, my friend, but I'm still working on it. We

know the victim is Jade Fortescue, more or less a nobody from a law enforcement point of view – a cleanskin. She's from the area, went to uni, did law, qualified and came back to be a solicitor. Lived alone, her parents moved to France a few years ago. I've gone through her social media, and she seems to have liked long runs by the river, arts and crafts, loved country living. The reason nobody knew she was missing was her idea of a holiday – have a technology break, no emails, just look after herself. She must have gone missing three days in.'

'So no link to Claire?'

'Other than they both liked river runs, not so far.'

Jake scratches his beard. 'Is that something?'

'It might be, because it suggests a key location in common, a reason why they were near the water. But we don't know what happened to Claire yet.'

'We don't know what happened to Jade, for that matter.'

'Exactly, no obvious cause of death. But being stripped is suggestive. I tried to work out something from the amount of water they found in her lungs, but there was too much deterioration of the body. I wondered if we could determine whether she was unconscious or barely conscious, not awake enough to take in a big breath. There might be something there.'

'Do the cops agree?'

'From what it looks like, no they don't. The body was pretty waterlogged all over, they think it's all inconclusive.'

'Have you looked into Claire?' Jake explains what happened with Paul Sansom. Martha rolls her eyes, grabs a small bag of weed. 'This is becoming a real two-pipe problem.' She fills her little glass vial and lights it.

'I'm not sure that's what Sherlock Holmes meant by a pipe.'

'He liked cocaine, the dirty beast. Far worse for you. All right, I'll have a ferret around Mr Sansom's life, see if anything pops, but he sounds – like you say – as though he's just a common or garden thug. There's one other thing.' She puts her pipe down. 'Let me share my screen with you.'

A big satellite image of the river appears. 'The government does analysis of river flows from time to time, helps them work out flood risks.' She presses a button, and a series of colours is transposed onto the outline. 'Not to confuse your pretty head, but the different shades mean different speeds of water flow, and if you focus on one colour here, you see where the river gets snarled up, the flow slows, as it were. Now are you still with me?'

Jake raises an ironical eyebrow. 'Even I can grasp that.'

'What it means is that there are two locations, one upstream, the other downstream, where river detritus is likely to get stuck. Both below, in fact, the place where Claire's shoes and phone were found. One just up from where you found poor Jade. I think her body was originally there, and got partially dislodged and floated to where the cops saw it. The other spot is a bit further along and Claire could – sad to say – have bounced around and then got snagged there. You should take a look at that other place.'

'Won't the police have done that already?'

Martha clicks off the image, reappears on the screen. 'Your local force doesn't get access to this data without knowing to ask for it. The radar scanning they do is pretty hit-and-miss. I'll email the location to Livia, and you can go have a look. That's if you can be bothered.'

'Of course I can. You're a genius, Martha.'

'Wouldn't help me in a running race, dear chap. Let me know what you find. Out.' With typical abruptness, she blips off.

Chapter Thirteen

The next morning dawns warm but with a dampness in the air, the sky heavy with cloud. Jake has a printed-out map with the location of Martha's proposed site marked. As he leaves Livia's house, he hears the rumble of an engine. Ten minutes later, he hears it again. He's heading off the road anyway, and uses it as a prompt to slip through the hedgerow, get out of obvious sight. Is he being paranoid, he wonders?

He makes for the river, cross-country, pausing every few minutes to look around for any sign of people. The sky now grey as slate, sun completely enshrouded, the only movement the birds in the distance, hawkish, swooping and soaring. He tries to reorientate himself. The tin-roofed buildings in front of him are connected to a farm, which is thankfully named on his map, and behind it lies the river itself to guide him. In half an hour, he is at his destination, alone.

Here, he can see the sluggish flow of water, pondy, greeny-brown, sullen. The river bottom is heavily silted, giving off cloudy puffs when Jake pokes it with a stick.

There is a forest of reeds at the crook of the bend, four or five feet high. Jake slips off his pack, then his vest and flip-flops, feels the pleasant breath of the breeze. A swim would be no hardship in this heat. He debates going in naked, but doesn't really want to be exposed if some hiker wanders past. Or, God forbid, Dani, with her camera, her ironic sexuality. He can imagine her reaction. He shakes his head to clear the thought.

The water isn't quite cool when he eases himself in, but somehow soupy; it clings to his skin. The ground is soft, he can feel the mud between his toes. He can stand well enough, even ten yards from the bank, not far from the middle of the channel. But there, sudden, the bottom drops, the flow quickens, the colour changes from brown to metallic grey. Jake thinks it unlikely that anybody would get stuck out here. The opposite bank is less silted, there is a thin layer of vegetation, one or two overhanging trees. Jake swims across to them and clings to a branch, startling, gloriously, a kingfisher, a vibrant flash of colours, white and burnt orange and Caribbean blue. Something exotic and impossible. Jake has never seen one before, wishes he had someone to share the experience with.

No other movement to distract him. He pushes his hair from his eyes and looks around. The reeded area back across the way still looks his best bet. It is tangled, the water visibly slowed, signs of driftwood snagged throughout, glumly decomposing. He dives back in, letting the current push him towards it. In the middle of the river, he flips onto his back, makes himself still and heavy, corpse-like, feels the pull of the bank, watches as his body is manoeuvred inexorably towards the vegetation.

His feet are soon tangled up in clutching reeds, slimy

to the touch. He stands, and the water comes to his chest, leaving a line of dirt upon his skin. He pushes himself into the bank, on tiptoes, exploring with his hands, fingers lingering on fibrous roots, slick with mulch, all that riverine decay. For an hour he searches, until his arms are scratched and his hair is damp with sweat. The warmth of the day clings to his torso, his submerged parts now completely acclimatized to the water, which feels thick and unwholesome, like a bath gone tepid.

He leaps back and splashes into the main channel once more, enlivening, cleaning. He treads water and then finds an easy part of the bank to climb, shaking the moisture from his hair.

There was nothing here. No more than abundant nature, and its endless struggle of rise and rot. He thinks about drying off and leaving, frustrated, Martha wrong for once. As he squats on the grass, he idly watches a piece of driftwood bob in front of him. It is being spun by the current, and somehow avoids the centrifugal pull of his particular part of the bank, skittering and swirling in the centre of the river. To his right, the course bends faintly, before straightening once more, and the branch – which is thick and heavy, a limb torn from a substantial tree – spins towards a different patch of reeds a few hundred yards away. Soon it is enmeshed, caught in the toils of the vegetation. This is not where Martha thought he should look, but it is close enough.

Jake doesn't pause for long, eases himself back into the river. Cold again, a mild shock, an ache he feels in his core. He swims out and follows the line the branch had taken, feeling the current tug him anew. Soon he is standing, his ankles deep in sludge.

It is not a pleasant spot to linger. Flies buzz insistent,

there is slime and scum on the water's surface. He can stand at least, and moves crab-like along the front of the bank, arms plunging into the marshy fronds. He decides to make a traverse to one edge, then trace his steps back. After half an hour, he has got nothing, is ten yards from completing the second pass.

As he steps sidelong, he slips, the ground unstable. Strands, sharp and sinewy, scratch his face. His eyes close. His left hand shoots out to stabilize him, touches something solid. It is firm, it is out of place, it feels like an ankle.

Chapter Fourteen

The sun appears for a fleeting moment as Jake drags himself out of the water again, spilling across the ground as it chases the shadow away. It is welcome, because his body feels again the chill of his prolonged submersion. He looks around, then pulls down his soggy shorts, replacing them with a spare from his bag.

The field is flat, the grass soft and springy, freckled with daisies, and he runs sprints to warm himself up, feels the blood pumping around him. He repacks his bag, including the map, and heads back towards the road and the incident room, some miles away. He needs to tell the police as soon as possible, while the corpse remains secured. He had deliberately not interfered with it much, after he'd touched the ankle, beyond tracing the bone down to the foot, and pulling the whole thing tentatively forward. It certainly looked and felt like a whole body, and he'd glimpsed the neon pink of her shorts, a blobby mass of saturated hair, dark as the river bottom.

He hears the rumble of an engine before he sees the car.

The road here is narrow, the hedges close and high, massed with leaves and writhing branches.

The engine gets louder, as does the insistent beat that accompanies it, the thud of dance music. Jake turns, nowhere to escape to, and looks back along the road, which runs straight for a few hundred yards. A familiar red convertible, moving sedately towards him, its driver with wide sunglasses, long hair flowing pendent in the breeze. Jake huffs out a laugh.

It is Rose, looking every inch the local delinquent he undoubtedly is. Jake can identify him just from the music and the lack of speed. Most drivers of sports cars, in Jake's experience, like noise and swagger, the macho assertion of the over-revved engine: driving as bullying, imposing themselves on the road and other drivers. Rose likes cars, likes having the money to buy cars, but also prioritizes being as relaxed as possible at all times. Driving fast is stressful, so he avoids it. He pootles, he potters, those big engines deliberately under-used.

They had met in difficult circumstances: Rose was a scoundrel, a dealer in cannabis and so connected to various unsavoury types; he had also once unsuccessfully dated Livia. But he and Jake had come together in the tracking of a sexual predator, and become firm friends and fishing partners. This summer, Jake had come to know Rose's sister Lily, and he recognizes the bronze frizz of her hair in the passenger seat.

Jake moves to the middle of the road and waves, watches as Rose swerves the car delicately upon the verge, wing mirror dislodging a few elderberries.

'Fancy a lift, wild man?'

Jake for a moment has forgotten what he must look

like, shorts slung low on his hips, body still damp from the river, hair plastered against his head. There is a patch of mud drying on one knee where he heaved himself against the bank.

'Let me in, and I'll explain. I've found something.'

He clasps hands with Lily as he passes her, jumping into the seat behind. Next to him, crouched behind Rose's seat to avoid being seen, is Dani. She is wearing stone-washed dungarees with what looks like just a bra beneath. She sits back, triumphant. She mouths 'surprise' at him.

Rose looks over his shoulder as he starts the engine. 'You guys have met, haven't you? This is Dani, apparently a big deal on the internet. Lils here was quite starstruck when they met at the search. It's why we ditched you and Livia, actually. Lils thought Dani was more important.'

Lily slaps her brother gently but does not entirely deny the charge. She is sipping from a bottle of beer, her face a picture of repose. 'I'm sure you coped just fine without us, Jake. So what've you found? Dani will be keen to cover it.'

Dani looks across at him. 'Have you been in the river, Jake?' She leans over, pats his exposed chest, her palm soft, her fingernail sharp against his skin. It tugs against his hairs. She inhales deeply. 'I can smell the water on you, it's sort of half-fresh, half-sordid. Smells of life, you know?'

Rose has started driving, slowly. 'Jake always smells like that. Where can I drop you, man?'

Jake shifts a little away from Dani. 'That village hall, downstream from Westerby. I need to talk to McAllister.'

Nobody speaks for a few moments. The landscape passes in verdant blur. Dani looks across at him, studying. 'You've found Claire's body, haven't you, Jake?' She pushes herself back into her seat, wide eyes to the pale sky. 'How exciting. What's the state of it, Jake? Is it messy? Did you see her face?'

Jake is rummaging in his bag for his vest. He pulls it on, then ties his hair roughly in a ponytail. 'I've found something, but nothing to talk to you about. I don't want to see myself in a video in an hour's time.'

'Dear Jake.' She puts her hand on his, insouciant. 'You can't control the internet. You might as well just lean into it. Don't you think, Lils?'

Lily chuckles into her beer. 'Jake and the internet don't mix.'

Rose smiles vacantly, his head dipping in time with the music, which is – as normal – strange and spacy. 'Let's give the old man a break. Here we are anyway.' They are coming up to the village hall. The environs are quiet. Two figures sitting on the bench by the war memorial, murmuring into phones. The big trucks departed for the moment.

Rose pulls over and Jake gets out. He hears Dani asking Rose to park properly, so they can see what is going on. Inside the hall it is warm, soporific. A constable is sitting on a chair by the door, valiantly battling sleep. He stiffens when Jake approaches.

'Is the boss about?'

'In the office back yonder, not in the best of moods. Maybe you could cheer him up.'

McAllister's 'office' is a repurposed kitchen, two sinks running down one wall, an unplugged microwave, the smell of decades of boiled soup lingering. He is tapping away at a laptop, his face and shirt damp. The air is close, even with the windows open.

'Jake, you got something for me?'

McAllister clearly reads the answer from his face. He

sits up, energized, as Jake explains what he has found, and how. Jakes hands over the map and explains the reed bank as McAllister types a couple of furious messages, closes the laptop.

'I've got the team moving. You're coming too, aren't you?'

Jake had thought about it. 'There'll be a huge circus now, and you need to run it. I'll jog back to Livia's and be on the phone there if you need me. But you'll find it easy enough.'

'You think it's Claire?'

'I do. Pink shorts, cropped dark hair. Must be.'

Jake can hear movement outside, people gathering, the hum of activity building. He feels tired all of a sudden. He is used, he supposes, to dead bodies, but the psychic blow of dealing with them never disappears. He thinks of Claire's husband, the feral desperation in his eyes, that reek of despair. He thinks of their children, being kept busy somewhere by tense and over-polite relations, dimly aware of the absence of their mum, nobody quite explaining what it means or why everyone looks so broken.

McAllister seems to intuit something of what he is feeling.

'Don't walk back. I'll drop you off as we go, that way I'll know exactly where you are. Here, take my keys, avoid the questions out front there.'

Jake agrees, leaving the hall through the side exit. He sits in McAllister's Range Rover, the seat belt warm against his skin, watching as the activity spills out. All the urgency of a disturbed ants' nest. TV journalists straightening their clothes, other reporters on their phones, a couple actually running from the pub down the road, as the sheer osmosis of major news breaking – that oddly imprecise phenomenon – does its work. One woman dead, one family ruined, all this excitement nonetheless. Jake is rueful. What had Dani said? 'Everything is content.' It might be true, but what a shame it is.

Chapter Fifteen

It's drizzling when Livia gets home, the light having faded early, the promise of more rain to come. Jake has had a hot bath, cleaned the river from his hair and body, is swaddled in a jumper and trousers, his feet outstretched, bare and gnarly. He sits on the back porch to wait for her car. There are bats in the air above. At least he thinks they are bats: just little black shapes that shift and flit so fast you can never see them straight on; they subsist as specks on the periphery of your vision, soundless, darting away when you turn in their direction.

The car's engine fades, a door slams. Livia sits down without going into the house. She listens to his account of the day, looks tired.

'Well that's that.'

'Aside from how she got there.'

'And how her husband and kids will cope.'

'It's a story we'll never know the ending of. I'm sorry, Liv. I know you felt this one.'

Her phone buzzes. She looks at the screen, smiles

weakly. A message from Martha, which she holds up to show to Jake. Just three words: 'Fucking right again.' She puts the phone back in her pocket, reaches for the cider in his hand, then seems to remember her pregnancy, hand darting instinctively to her stomach. 'It's all so futile, isn't it? I cared so much about Claire, but no good came of it. And something else bad will always be happening somewhere else, some other problem.'

He takes a sip. 'Everything is content.' His voice is quiet.

'What was that?'

'Nothing. By the way, annoying that Lily seems to have taken a shine to that Dani woman.'

Livia stands to go inside. Diana will be dropped off any time. 'Annoying too that you got into a car half-naked with her.'

The next morning, Jake has been in Caelum Parvum talking to Jo. All of it off the record, explaining what he had found on the understanding she wouldn't credit him in public. He doesn't mind doing her a favour, giving the local press the information ahead of the online hordes. And McAllister has announced most of it anyway.

She goes off to file her copy, and he is sitting on the bench outside the church. A favourite location of his, quiet even by local standards, grass growing wild against the weathered stone of the graves that stretch away from him in serried lines. A yew tree, as ancient as the building, overhangs him, putting him in the shade, dropping its pines to the ground, its scaly trunk scratched and purpled. He is lost in thought. He looks up. Claire's husband, Steve, is standing in front of him, hand outstretched. Jake takes it. It is cold, bloodless, papery.

'I can't stay long. I've just been, you know, identifying Claire. They're driving me back home to see the kids, and I saw you sitting here. I wanted to stop for a second.' He sits down himself, tentatively.

His stubble has grown, gingery and uneven; the pallor of his skin has deepened, taken on an unhealthy taint, as if he has somehow absorbed it from his wife's body. Jake notices that his hand trembles when he rests it on his legs.

'I'm so sorry this has happened.' Jake's voice is graveyard low.

Two magpies stalk on a patch of grass. Jake touches his head reflexively for luck. Two for joy, wasn't it? Inappropriate here. Steve looks glassily at them. When he speaks he is addressing the air, staring forward.

'I woke up that day she disappeared, when was it, Tuesday? Thinking I had problems. Claire reckoned I was staying at work too late, not doing my bit at bedtime with the kids. She was sick of the hospital, all the stress of it, the futility. Our little one had tonsillitis, was sleeping in our bed. I was grumpy – shit, I even spent ten minutes looking at my head worrying about losing my hair. Not a problem for you, I know.'

Jake smiles wanly, lets him carry on.

'I wish, I wish I'd known that they weren't actual problems, you know? I wish we'd laughed more together. Everything had just become serious all the time. We'd even talked about it once or twice, the pity of it. Paying the bills, dealing with the kids, whatever, going shopping, all that. Life had all gotten so joyless. And Claire was a joyful person really; she loved to be happy. One of things I'd loved about her in the beginning.' His eyes implore the sky. Jake places a hand in consolation upon his arm.

Steve tries to gather himself. 'Anyway, I wish this'd never happened. And I wish I could go back in time. But at least now I know, I'm not wondering any more, I'm not making things up for the children.' He twists his body, red-rimmed eyes fixed on Jake's. 'And I'm grateful to you for finding her. She'd mentioned you were a proper detective, and you are. So thank you.'

Jake doesn't know what to say. He feels a flush of awkwardness, impotence. He clasps Steve's arm harder. 'I didn't do much, and I would give anything to have found her alive and well. You're a strong guy, Steve, you're going to be strong for your children. If I can do anything . . .' He lets the offer hang, well-meaning but manifestly empty.

Steve nods. He raises himself to his feet, walks out towards the lychgate, its covering age-stained and forlorn, and through to the street where the car is waiting. McAllister is standing sentry, and lingers until Steve comes past, before striding quickly to Jake's bench. He seems more flushed than usual, his sanguine expression replaced by something taut and distant.

Jake's smile of greeting is not returned.

'Don't get up, Jake. I just wanted to say I may've made a mistake letting you too close to this one. People are asking how come you found the body, when we couldn't. Steve there's been telling folk you've brought him peace, you were the one who found his wife. That's fine and all, but then that girl you've been chatting up is all over the internet singing your praises like you're some sort of wonder kid. And part of me thinks you love the attention. You must see it: it makes me look like a fool; it makes my job impossible.'

Jake stands, but McAllister is already turning to leave. 'We don't have time to get into this now, I need to get that poor feller home. But I wanted to tell you, Jake. I'm not happy.' He lifts his feet and hurries over the mossy cobbles and into the car, refusing to look back.

Chapter Sixteen

'What the fuck do you mean, you feel guilty about getting involved? You're not a saint, are you? I mean, you look like a sort of picture-book version of a holy simpleton, but still.'

Early afternoon, back at Livia's house, alone and brooding upon McAllister's words, Jake had decided to call Martha. She is forthright, bracing.

Her eyes glint with relished outrage. 'Mac's just sore because you've taken credit from him and his team.' Jake begins to demur.

'No, Jake, you have. Quite right too. And WE do deserve the credit because WE'RE better at all this than them. I'm the brains, after all. All brains, half a body. I don't blame McAllister, though. He'll be hearing it from his boss and the boys and girls beneath him. You can imagine it, can't you? "Thank God, for your friend Jake; you're so lucky to have him" – all that. And look, your flirt-buddy, the fragrant Dani with her hair and her boobs, is getting quite a bit of attention, on TV and radio now, and she's using you to help get it. They're all turning you into something you're not trying to be.'

Jake puts his chin on his hands. 'Can we not use terms like "flirt-buddy", which I'm not sure even exist, especially not near Liv. I'm not doing any flirting.'

'Course you're not. You're the first man in history to avoid flirting with a younger woman who says nice things about you. It doesn't matter. My point is that the chief will calm down when he hears your name a bit less. The actual question is how much he needs us now we've got here, and how far does he think his investigation needs to go.'

'What do you mean, and are you drinking milk?'

Martha has a pint glass in one hand, filled with thick white liquid. She belches softly. 'It's the best way of drinking bourbon in the daytime in my experience, takes the sting right out, protects the stomach lining.' He can't tell quite if she is joking.

Martha sips, continues. 'The thing we need to establish is: what, if anything, links Claire and Jade? Did they both fall into that river separately, coincidentally; or do you have someone down there knocking off women who's not yet been caught?'

'Is there an official view as yet on that?' Martha has access – semi-legitimately – to all police electronic files.

'Early view is that Claire drowned, probably while cooling off after her run. The autopsy is being finished now, but there was water in the lungs. Best guess is some sort of laryngeal spasm, reaction to the cold, breathing stops, game over. Jade could have been skinny-dipping and something similar happened to her, I guess. No sexual assault, no obvious blunt trauma, from what we can tell, though with both of them the river has knocked them about a bit.' Martha leans forward. 'Also, what do you think the bosses will want to happen here? Some sombre warnings about swimming in rivers because of two intrepid but unlucky gals; or the whole population panicking about riverside murder? No, my feeling is that this'll be allowed to go quiet.'

'And what do you think?'

She finishes her drink. 'Dear Jake, I don't know either way. But I think our job is to fucking make sure these people are doing their job properly, until we are sure. Now do you fancy sneaking into the morgue again?'

'I really don't.' Jake had been to the mortuary twice in the recent past, once pretending – with identification faked by Martha – to be an official called 'Rex Stout'. Once was with McAllister's blessing. There was an odd man running the reception there, who spent his days looking at pornography and writing a novel, and who probably would let him in if he needed to.

'I didn't think so. Actually, there's no real need for the moment. I'll get the reports when they're filed and we can take a look together. Aletheia is coming around for dinner tonight; I'll talk to her too. Stay out of trouble until then, especially around internet temptresses.'

Martha signs off as abruptly as ever. Jake decides to walk back to Little Sky, stretch his legs, clear his mind. He comes out of his house and sees a group of runners, male, topless, slowly making their way down the hill. They look like they spend more time on bulking their upper body than training their legs; their jogging motions are clunky and awkward. He vaguely recognizes them from the search for Claire, the local lads from the gym.

He is strolling away from them towards the river,

when he hears an engine. A car screeches up so quickly that one of the headlights actually clips Jake's leg, sending him to the ground. Two men in masks stumble out, both clutching thick pieces of piping. The closest to Jake raises his weapon and brings it savagely down, just missing him, a thud into the damp earth, a showering of muddy droplets on his face.

Jake throws himself to one side, gets to his feet. Another swing and he takes a shot to his right arm, a whomp of steel on skin, numbing him all down one side. He steps back. The other man has moved behind him, swinging wildly. Jake ducks and spins, comes up punching, a wild left hook, which connects against the man's temple, splitting his knuckle. Another jarring pain down his arm. The man falls to one knee, stunned.

Meanwhile, his first opponent is raising his weapon again. Jake launches himself into his midriff, shouldering the air from him, driving him into the ground. He can smell the sweat and the whisky on his clothes, hear him gasping for air behind the cloth that is slipping down from his face.

Jake pushes himself up from the ground, with difficulty. One arm is useless. Immediately he is kicked back down, a boot hard and spiteful in his ribs. He twists as he falls, looks up to dodge the next assault. The second man looms before the sun: a big body in silhouette, haloed by golden light, thick arms raised.

Jake flinches, raises his hands to absorb the initial punishment. No blow comes. He sees the eyes of his attacker turn. He hears the sound of young men baying in unison, sprinting towards them. The two masked attackers make for the car – one running, the other crawling. The car is driving away before the doors properly close. Shouts of derision, of challenge.

Jake blinks. A hand reaches down and helps him to his feet. He is sore, a little dazed. His left hand is bleeding where his own punch landed, his right arm stiff and unresponsive where it absorbed the hit from the pipe.

'You OK, boss?'

There are three of them, panting heavily, their bare chests flushed and damp. Hairless and heavily muscled, plucked like chickens. Jake shakes their hands, wincing. He pulls off his own shirt, sees the huge weal across his bicep, purpling and angry, flecks of blood like freckles.

'Better than I would've been without you lot showing up.' He tries to massage feeling into his arm, feels the pain flow down it as he does so. 'I'm Jake, by the way.'

'I'm Antonio.' This is the evident spokesman of the group, a little shorter than Jake, dark hair, wide shoulders, girlish waist, Italian colouring. 'The Black feller is Wayne, he's a boxer, so would've been useful if there'd been a proper tear-up.' Wayne grins in acknowledgement. He is tall and lean, acne scarring on his shoulders, raised and red marks on his dark skin. 'And the runt of the group is Michael.' Who flushes, raises himself a little bit on his toes. He may be smaller than the other two, but he is, if anything, even more muscled: vanity-gorged, huge arms and chest, excess definition chiselled into living flesh. He has a small goatee, hair carefully shorn at the sides, long at the back. His legs are thick, but short.

'You can call me MC.' The other two laugh gently. He ignores them. 'What beef did they have with you?'

Jake had recognized one of his attackers, he thinks, as Paul Sansom, from the shape of his head, that scent of booze and despair. 'I told one of them not to beat up his wife.'

'Yeah, you're that wild ex-copper we got around here. I heard of you. Glad you're intervening in a domestic.' This is Antonio, who pats Jake on his good arm.

MC nods. 'All the problems in the world, they come back to women in the end.'

Antonio pushes him. 'What you know about fucking women, man?'

'I know enough.' He looks up at Jake, appraising his body. 'You're in shape all right, but you could be bigger, stronger, then you wouldn't get pushed around.' His accent falls in and out of a gangsterish register, as if he is searching for a persona and has not yet found it. The others roll their eyes but seem to agree.

'Being fit is one thing, bruv, but size never goes out of fashion, you know what I'm saying.' This is Wayne, huge hand on Jake's shoulder.

'I'm old, guys, so I need to keep a bit of speed while I can. Listen, I'm grateful, you didn't need to run up like you did, and you got me out of a jam.'

'Damn straight.'

They pump his hand, the exultation of being top dogs. Antonio gives a final benediction. 'Our pleasure, bruv. And if you ever want to add some oomph to that skinny body of yours, you're always welcome to our gym. We're in Meryton; it's called the Boathouse. As you can tell, we're always there.'

Jake grits his teeth to avoid showing the pain as they jostle him farewell. He goes towards the glint of the river, heading home. It has not been a great day, however you look at it. Staring into the soul of a devastated man without being able to console him, being rebuked for vanity and attention-seeking, and then being rescued by the super-vain themselves.

When he gets back, he sits alone in the sauna, the fierce heat soothing his cramped and aching body, watching the bruise balloon out on his arm, spreading like an oil spill, stretching until all the kinks have gone.

Chapter Seventeen

In the library, alone, night having eased in. The light of the flames flicker orange, make his bruises black as coal. He has music on low: Chopin, one of the Nocturnes. In Livia's absence tonight, Jake has rolled a small joint and lights it from a glowing piece of wood from the fire. He inhales deeply, mulling over what to do about Paul Sansom. He can feel a gentle mist descend, which calms his mind and soothes his arm, but does not give him additional clarity. He could talk to the police about what had just happened, of course, but relations there are no longer great. And they couldn't do that much anyway: a warning, a wagged finger, easily dismissed. No doubt Sansom's friends could alibi him for that afternoon.

Jake takes three deep puffs in succession, gets a floating sensation and lies down on his favourite sofa, its cushions soft and misshapen. No, he will have to do something to warn Sansom off, really scare him this time. Jake idly wonders if he has the mentality to do it, the swagger, the cut-throat attitude. He will have to find a way to be convincing, if he is not to be looking over his shoulder forever.

He could also check whether Sansom has any connection to Jade, gives any cause to be a suspect in her death. That is a second problem to wrangle in itself. He closes his eyes, feels his wounds throb like living creatures. Should he carry on his interest in the two women, or should he accept McAllister's hurt feelings and leave him to it? He knows what Martha has to say on the subject, can imagine Livia still being on the side of intervention, given how much she has been occupied by all this. On the other hand, it is a problem that might solve itself – if Claire and Jade died naturally, then there is little more for him to do.

His instinct – and what is that really? A set of indeterminate feelings, scarcely interrogated – tells him that the two women did not die in the same way, despite the similarity of how and where they ended up. But that doesn't mean either or both of them died violently. He tries to put the problem from his mind, picks up a book from the floor, but soon gives himself up to pondering. In his heightened state, his thoughts and the music mingle, timeless, and he sits, immobile and contemplative, the only movement in the room the rise and fall of his chest and the insistent flicker of the dying fire.

The next day, Jake discovers he can't leave things alone, and sets off for the barges, semi-intentionally. He walks through the village of Greenwood, peers over the hedge into Paul and Louise's garden. She is by the house, putting some washing out to dry. She is wearing a peach-coloured vest and tiny shorts, which makes her seem somehow more naked. Her flesh tells another tale. There are more bruise marks on her upper arms, one of her eyes is half-closed. Jake tries to get her attention. She immediately drops the washing basket, and scurries towards the house. She looks back for a second, her face contorted with fear and mistrust and rage. A sound like a sob emerges, hanging in the still morning like an accusation. Then she is gone.

That was his responsibility, Jake thinks. He brought the further punishment upon her. And for what gain? To prove he could take on a bigger, angrier man in his home, to show to himself he was still strong and imposing? He keeps walking, finding the river path once more, hands clenched by his side, unresolved feelings of shame roiling.

Maud is sitting in the same place as before, using needles to worry at some knitting. She is with a couple, man and woman, probably in their late thirties. The man is tall and slender, pale flesh browned by the sun, a hint of pink beneath the tan; the woman is darker, some South East Asian heritage there, black hair the colour of a raven's wing, small gold earrings that glint. Maud waves a needle at him, the point sharp in her soft hands.

'Come in and sit a while. You'll have to tell me your name again, though I remember your face right enough. These are my neighbours Rajni and David, did I tell you they were doctors? Very useful pair to have around the place.'

Jake introduces himself, shakes their hands. She is warm and direct in her gaze.

'Don't mind David here. Had an all-night shift, should be in bed.' Rajni's voice is sharp and cultivated, full of girls-school briskness.

David smiles, but distantly. 'The worst thing about being up all night is that you waste the day snoring down below, missing all the air up here. The magic of the river. Seems like a crime somehow. Not a crime like you would recognize.' He looks across at Maud, who grins as her hands clack away. 'She told us about the bearded policeman, even if she couldn't tell us your name.'

'Ex-policeman, as I'm sure you can spot. And I do remember shift work all too clearly.'

He does, the good and the bad. The feeling of uncanny early-morning light soothing your tired eyes, your mind a beat off the new day's pace, a constant lag, like life is trapped in perennial slow motion. How the sleep that follows is deep and dreamless, but never satisfying; a container that cannot quite ever be refilled. But also the contrasting sensation of superiority in the smallest hours, of being awake and grasping reality while others slumber, the camaraderie of night workers who all share that same secret of stolen time.

Jake discovers Rajni has been part-time since the birth of the children several years before; both she and David work as consultants, though seldom together. Maud appears happy to sit back and listen. At one point, she hands Jake a coffee in an old ceramic cup, alongside a piece of ginger cake, which is dense and treacly and delicious.

Rajni moves the conversation to the women pulled out of the river. 'It's been a worry, since that Claire went missing. Then when you found the other one, we all thought, well, we thought someone might be attacking people near here. Do you think that's still possible?'

Jake swallows. 'It's possible, but I'm not sure it's that likely. Claire may have just drowned. Jade could've as well. Have you noticed anything odd?'

Maud looks uncertain, swallows the beginnings of

a sentence. Jake waits. He notices Rajni looking at her thoughtfully.

Maud coughs, self-conscious. 'I'm not saying I've seen anything. I don't startle easy, but you know, since all this, I've been having a look around at night, before I close up. And I've spotted a torch bobbing, yonder in the woods.'

David makes a faintly exasperated sound, checks himself. 'We get lots of hikers about the place, Maud.'

'Not at night, not stopping still for ten minutes in the middle of the trees, we don't. I've hallooed and got nothing back, and then I've locked my doors and said my prayers.'

David stares out across the river. 'A bobbing light isn't a murder clue.'

Jake tries to be sympathetic. 'You should always be careful of strangers hovering about the place in the night. But I'm not sure it ties to Claire or Jade going into the water.'

'She was in the nude, wasn't she, the young lass? Skinny-dipping perhaps?' A middle-aged man is addressing them from his boat, where he has just emerged from below deck, wiping his hands on a towel.

Maud gives him a broad smile; the other two appear a little more equivocal. She hands him a coffee from the pot by her feet. 'This is Vaughan, my old oppo. Vaughan, this is our new friend, Jake. Former policeman.'

He shakes Jake's hand, offers a toothy smile. He is well-groomed, grey hair tightly cropped, expensive coat and trousers all in pale colours, loafers with no socks. 'Less of the "old", if you don't mind, Maud. I heard you talking about our sordid crime wave, and thought I'd better find out more.'

Jake looks over his shoulder, sees the name of his boat,

The Playboy, shrugs his shoulders. 'If you were listening, you'd know it wasn't necessarily a crime wave at all. Two sad deaths, at least.'

Vaughan pulls out a long black cigarette, lights it expertly, drawing the smoke into his lungs. 'Sounds awfully coincidental for such a quiet neck of the woods, though. Losing one lady sounds like a misfortune, to lose two sounds like carelessness, if I've got the quote right.'

'Had you seen either of them around the river?'

He exhales, the smoke carried off downriver with the breeze. 'I'm not sure I have, though I do pay attention to some of the ladies who jog on the bank. All that exertion, that carelessness about how they look, just bouncing flesh and lycra. It's so intriguing.'

'Bloody hell, Vaughan, you don't need to try so hard to be creepy.' This is Rajni, rolling her eyes.

'*The Playboy*, eh?' Jake is wry.

Rajni responds in kind. 'I know, it's all a little too obvious. Don't get me wrong, I'm sure Vaughan here could be a genuine pest, but I mostly think it's an act. There's probably a good person, drowning in cologne, trying to get out.'

Vaughan appears unconcerned by the character assessment. He looks up to David, whose attention has drifted again, staring into the oily water below. 'So would you trust me with your wife, Doctor?'

'I trust Rajni with you, which is the main thing.'

'You're no fun, David. Half-asleep and still a match for me.' He turns back to Jake. 'In all seriousness.' He pauses grandly. 'Though who can trust someone who says that. "In all seriousness . . ."' He rolls the words around his mouth, eyebrows raised. 'I haven't got anything much to help your investigation, Jake. Especially if you're not sure there is anything to investigate. But if you change your mind, let me know. I'll do anything to keep in Rajni's positive esteem. Must head off, just wanted to say hello.'

They watch him saunter away, agile on the shifting decks, his feet never slipping. Rajni picks up his smouldering cigarette stub, and puts it carefully into a metal bin. 'You'll notice how David was "doctor" and I wasn't? He's not as much of a pig as he seems, though pig enough.'

'Now, now.' Maud is untroubled by the conversation. 'It's all just idle talk in the end, isn't it, Jake? Nothing wrong with that.'

Jake agrees blandly, stays a little while longer. David lapses into introspection once more, ignoring his wife's gentle nudges to rejoin the conversation. He seems exhausted, unmoved by stories of missing women and mysterious disappearances. Maybe it is the arrogance of being a doctor, a life-saver set amidst ordinary mortals. Maybe just tiredness.

As the conversation flags, David gives a sonorous sigh. 'Vaughan was right, at least. Why was the young solicitor nude? Was she with someone?' Jake hadn't mentioned Jade's job, though it had appeared in the news reports. He shrugs eloquently.

Later, Rajni helps Jake back onto the path. 'We all just want to know what happened to Claire and Jade. I want to be free, and for my kids to be free to wander safe.'

'I know. But I'm not sure anywhere can guarantee that. I'm keeping an eye on this, though the police don't want me to. If you see anything that worries you, you can get me at the Jolly Nook.'

Dusk is starting to fall as he makes his way towards

home, or rather, as he soon realizes, first towards the village of Greenwood and the home of the Sansoms. It draws him back, despite himself. His body is still sore, each bruise throbbing like a pulse. And he is uneasy, bitter at the thought that he has left a provoked man within easy reach of his chosen victim.

The path is quiet and gloomy, made narrow by overhanging trees. Jake hears footsteps behind him, moving swiftly. He stiffens, looks back, can make out little in the encroaching murk. The pace is steady, unrelenting, the thud of boot heels on leaf-litter. He moves to the edge of the path, where there is an old stump to crouch by. It smells of wet wood, rot, the bark peeling to reveal pale, peach-toned strands of tree flesh, softened and weakened by invisible creatures.

The steps get closer, a shape emerges from the dusk. It is Martin George, the man from outside the bookshop. He cuts a solid figure, marching as Sam Fryer had foretold, as Jake has seen before, face fixed in relentless frown. Jake makes no effort to intercede, and Martin passes without a glance, quickly clasped again by the shadow. Jake feels unsettled by him, by his sheer relentlessness, his restlessness. He seems – and this might be just because of his story, of that tragic mistake that cost him his family – a purgatorial figure, not quite fitting in the world, too uncanny and disconcerting, especially as night comes.

Jake follows Martin's route, but slowly, allowing the sound of his footsteps to disappear from hearing. He then cuts off across a field and reaches the patch of lights that is the village. There is nobody about. In the distance, he can hear the hum of a car on an invisible road, heading away. Somewhere a radio plays softly, the words inaudible.

He leaps the small gate and stands outside the Sansom property. Lights are on, and curtains not drawn. They would be confident in their privacy simply because of the location. You couldn't see into any part of their house from the road.

Most of the places round here have that sense of isolation. One of the reasons, he thinks, why abuse could – and did – happen so often, furtive and insidious. In the countryside, he thinks, nobody can hear you scream.

There is an apple tree in the small front garden, heavy with foliage and fruit, and he leans against it, now almost entirely obscured by the shadow. He sees Paul amble between kitchen and living room. He is wearing a pair of shorts and nothing more, his body a vast barrel of pallid flesh, thick pelt of hair, big muscles coiled beneath a rolled coating of fat. He carries a can of Guinness in one hand, scratches his balls with the other, keeps an eye on the TV.

If he is a beast, Louise is a bird, flitting uncertainly, not resting. She brings food, another beer, empties an overflowing bin, stares at her phone, her thumb rolling endlessly downwards. It must be nearly seven. He wonders if Paul will leave the house. He doesn't really want to do anything in front of Louise, if he can help it. He needs to get him on his own, ideally somewhere unexpected.

They both settle down on the sofa. Paul's hand goes to the back of her neck, big paddling fingers stroking the fretwork of hair there. She leans in like a cat, eyes still locked on her phone. Jake knows from long police experience that abusive relationships are often like this: moments of peace and pleasure, reliance. That is why the punctuating periods of violence get explained away. Jake thinks of the bruises on Louise's face and body.

No, he realizes: he cannot bring more violence into this household. As he goes to leave, Paul switches off the television, starts kissing Louise. She stiffens then responds, shifting herself on top of Paul's spreading bulk. He begins to remove her clothes, roughly. Jake, feeling every bit the unwilling voyeur, the inadequate meddler, hurries away into the night.

Chapter Eighteen

Livia's cottage is welcoming, more so than ever, lamps casting a warm glow. The smell of cooking hits him as he opens the door, something meaty and wholesome.

Diana is at the table in the living room, which had been remodelled last year after a car was driven into it. Seamlessly done, really, Jake thinks with pride: you can't see the join between new and old. Diana is doing homework, which seems to involve an inordinate amount of glue and glitter, winking under the lights. She gives him a greeting, then resumes concentration.

Livia is in the kitchen in a denim boiler suit, the zip pulled halfway down. He stands at the doorway watching her, stirring a big bubbling pot, huffing her hair from her eyes, rising and falling rhythmically on tiptoes. There is music on, Taylor Swift, he thinks (Diana has been giving him a steady education in modern pop music, which he is mostly refusing to allow to settle in his brain).

She looks up, eyes the colour of old Coke bottles. She

wiggles to the music, as she puts a wooden spoon to her mouth to taste.

'Hello, lovey. You've caught me doing my moves.'

He moves forward to kiss her. 'That smells great. What is it?'

'Rabbit stew, with some of the prunes and apples. Rather French, I thought. I've got some bread in the oven too.'

'Is Di eating that?'

'What do you think? No, she's chosen to have my lovely bread in the form of cheese and cucumber sandwiches.'

'That sounds nice too.' Livia grips him tight, and he winces, pain shooting in arm and rib.

'Are you OK? What's happened?'

He explains the incident with Sansom and friend, his wanderings since. She moves to close the kitchen door. 'I wish you'd told me before. I hate thinking of you on your own when stuff like this happens, asleep in that big old bed up there.'

She undoes his shirt and takes a look at his bruises, which are still as purple and ugly as before. 'They look sore, Jake. I might have something in my bag that can help.'

'I don't want horse ointment, thank you very much.'

'It's all the same chemicals involved, you know. Let me run you a bath after dinner, and I'll fix you up. We were going to speak to Martha as well.' She swears and runs to the oven, pulling out small, steaming loaves, which are just on the turn towards being over-cooked.

'Let's get Di fed and in bed, then we'll get going.'

Two hours later, Jake is in the bath, revelling in the steam and heat. He has his eyes closed, and so is pleasantly startled when Livia joins him with a splash, her body slipping under the bubbles, flashes of brown curves and smooth skin. He can feel her thighs squeezing against his, firm and rubbery, watches her face flush pink, the water collect at the base of her neck, that pocket of flesh above her jutting collarbone.

Afterwards, she rubs his upper body briskly with a liniment that comes, suspiciously, from an old bottle with no label. It burns hot, too hot, for a second and then settles to a thrumming, efficient sting, not unpleasant. They both pull on soft robes, while Livia makes the call on her computer.

Martha answers almost immediately, and winces.

'Love-birds. Don't tell me you've been bathing together? Disgusting. So unhygienic, especially with a man like Jake.'

'Don't listen to her, she's just been too bitter for too long. Hates to see people in love, or clean for that matter.' They both recognize the voice, as Aletheia sits down next to Martha, two martini glasses in hand. She passes one to Martha.

Jake's friend and ex-colleague, Aletheia is one of the stable influences in their lives. She is taller than Martha, ampler, her shoulders broad and strong. She has her black hair in a thick braid, and Jake notices that it – like his – has begun to be flecked peppery-grey. Her skin is of a woman much younger, the colour of ebony, lacking in any wrinkles at all, like it has been delicately sanded. She is an expert desk officer, but Jake has seen her practical, physical side, too. He knows she can be formidable. He's seen her grapple, in more than one desperate situation, with men Jake's size.

'Al, what are you doing there?' This is Livia, who likes Aletheia very much.

'Didn't Jake mention? Martha here asked me for dinner.'

'How generous. Just think: she might do that for me one day.' Jake's voice shows he is not serious.

Martha finishes her drink. 'No chance, Jake. The last time you came over, we got wasted and I'm too fragile these days for that.'

He remembers. There had been martinis and spliffs, and stories and songs and general camaraderie. The next day he had got an important clue to help him identify a killer. Jake looks back to Aletheia, who has barely touched her martini, taking mouse-sized sips as she surveys the screen. 'Al, have you been officially roped into this missing woman thing?'

She puts the glass down, easy transition to her professional demeanour. 'No, no chance. The evidence that's been seen by all the senior bods is that foul play, while possible, is quite unlikely. They're announcing tomorrow that the investigation is suspended, pending a final coroner's report.'

'McAllister gets off the hook for it.'

'Yeah, Martha mentioned he'd got in a grump about you being a glory-hunter. I'm a bit surprised by that. He's done all the right things as lead in this, pursued all the angles. Though I've seen some stories about you on the internet, Jake, in which you're discussed in a very flattering fashion. Maybe he got jealous.'

'Al, can you believe, Jake's been hanging out with some influencer whore, trying to become famous?' Livia's smile shows that she's not joking.

'I saw it. Very showbiz, I thought.'

Jake tries to get them back on track. 'You've looked at the evidence, both of you, what do you think?'

Aletheia answers first, eyes half-closed in concentration.

'This has a feel of coincidence, to me. The river is the common theme, but water's a relatively common killer, especially in hot weather. Now, you wouldn't expect two in such a small area in such a short time, but the same goes for two murders unless there's a serial killer at work. And I see no real sign of that.'

Martha nods. 'I've looked at Jade's movements, gone through all her social media and references to her on other people's. Nothing jumps. One thing is she *was* interested in the initial story about Claire going missing; someone posted a pic and I got a glimpse of her actually attending one of the searches very early on. But I'm not sure that means a great deal. As you know, everyone was interested in Claire's disappearance where you are.'

'What about her body, anything else show up?'

Martha is clicking her mouse at something. 'Just the nakedness. Which looks odd. But definitely no evidence of sexual assault we could confidently recognize; no battering.'

'Do we know when and where she went in?'

'Excellent questions, Liv, which these so-called police experts should've asked sooner.' Martha shoves Aletheia playfully; Aletheia rolls her eyes. 'And the answer is we don't know with Jade. We can see where Claire left her shoes and phone, and can postulate that was where she entered the river, and then where it all went wrong.'

'Postulating already, are you? Feels early.'

'Put a sock in it, Jake. You don't want to get on my bad side. It's harder to tell with Jade. The time of death is unclear but the best guess is now the Friday night, three days after Claire. But that could be anywhere between six and midnight, and maybe even a wider time-frame than that. There are places upstream from where she was found where she could've been on her own and unseen, but nobody's produced physical evidence of where she went in.'

'Do we buy skinny-dipping, really?' Livia looks unconvinced. 'I mean, she knew a woman was missing, probably in the river. Would she then suddenly decide to leap in alone, naked?'

'Was she necessarily alone?' asks Jake. 'Could she have been skinny-dipping with someone who's not come forward? You could maybe see that happening.'

Martha nods. 'All sorts of things *could've* happened. It could've been a moonlight dip, she gets into difficulty, he scarpers. But is that likely? It looks like she might have had sex in the previous twenty-four hours, but we can't be sure of that.'

Jake leans forward. 'But that implies a boyfriend, or some sort of partner. Any sign of him in the record?'

Martha grabs the mouse from Aletheia, starts pulling documents across the screen. 'Not that I've seen.'

'So maybe a mystery man.'

Aletheia tries to stop the momentum on this. 'Maybe, but the physical evidence is corrupted, and there's no obvious cause of death that points to a third party. Look at this the other way. If Claire had never existed, would we be worried about this case, beyond the tragedy of a young, slightly wild swimmer turning up dead?'

Livia sits forward, signalling agreement. 'And the point about Claire is that there's almost nothing suspicious about her death in itself, beyond the mystery of how long it took us to find her. Both bodies cast suspicion on the other, but not enough to make a solid case either way.'

'Expertly summarized.' Aletheia beams and Livia

responds in kind. Jake can see the flush of pleasure. She seems to feel a thrill when her role in this odd, hodgepodge team is recognized, given her comparative lack of experience in policing. 'My feeling is that we should leave it, let Mr McAllister's ego recover, and enjoy what's left of the nice weather.'

Martha lights her pipe. 'I'd tend to agree, with two provisos. One, Jake, remember the house you saw near where Jade's body was found? It's owned by a pair of downsizing potters – very fucking chi-chi – and my internet trawl shows they were giving Jade pottery classes. Something she mentioned very briefly, but I'm sure it's them. Jess and Emma. It's a little connection, probably nothing. If this were an efficient investigation, though, you'd chase that down, so maybe it's worth one conversation.'

'Do we know that McAllister didn't already look into it?'

'There's nothing in the file, and his lot probably spoke to them before Jade was even identified, and never went back. Al thinks he's done a solid job, and he has, but this is a slight loose end.'

Livia slaps her legs with energy. 'I'll come with you, Jake. I was thinking of taking up pottery, you know, a hobby to have as I slow down with work. Something which'll no doubt be taken from me as soon as the baby is born.'

Nobody speaks. Aletheia and Martha are grinning at each other.

Martha breaks the silence. 'What was that, dearie?'

Jake takes Livia's hand, squeezes. 'Yes, what was that?'

Livia is clutching at her mouth, half in horror, half in humour. 'Oh fuckety fuck. Jake, I'm so sorry. Guys, we weren't going to tell anyone until it was as far gone as possible. Not because of you, but because of us.'

Aletheia puts her hand against the screen, a show of solidarity. Her palm is pinkish, a thick life-line etched into her skin. 'Liv, I hate to break it to you. But we'd realized this already. You are not that subtle a couple. Plus, I always knew something happened at the dig that you didn't want to talk about, where you had to go to hospital, but which seemed to turn out OK. Since then there's been all the non-drinking, or smoking, the little dreamy love-bug looks between you and the old man there.'

'Plus that boiler suit screams late-life switch to lesbianism.' Martha looks genuinely pleased. 'Or bo-ho pregnancy. While I'd sympathize with the first one, given . . . well, given Jake, the second's always been more likely.'

'The main thing.' Aletheia is sincere, flicks a warning glance at Martha. 'Is congratulations. What a lovely family you are.'

'Cheers to that.' Martha swigs her drink.

Jake leans over and kisses Livia, near her mouth. Her skin smells of cocoa. He feels a surge of happiness, glad that this secret of theirs – clutched so tight, cherished like a fragile object that only both can stop from shattering – has been shared. Livia seems relieved too. She kisses him back firmly, with the forcefulness of joy.

Martha coughs. 'There was a second proviso, remember? Before you two get soppy. None of this solves your problem with that wife-beating animal you were just spying on, and who tried to beat you to death with an iron bar, Jake.'

Chapter Nineteen

The conversation about that lasted some time. It continues the next morning, as Jake and Livia walk towards the spot where Jade's body had been found. They agree to wait to see if Aletheia can offer some way of helping deal with Paul as a threat to both Jake and his own wife.

It's a little cooler again, the wind flicking their hair, colouring their cheeks, making the water beside them foam, spittling at the edges, as it rises and falls.

Livia sets the pace, keen to prove she is as strong as ever, not disadvantaged by pregnancy. They now see the evidence of the police operation in the chewed-up land around the bend of the river. A piece of crime tape flutters, an intrusion of man-made colour amid the countryside pastels. The van has left tyre tracks, thick lines patterned into the damp turf, a patch of oil where the engine had been left running for hours. The water is sludgy, the colour of camouflage, studded with stiff and lifeless reeds. For all the largesse of the season, it feels a pretty morbid place.

They walk up to the cottage, which looks occupied, the smoulder of smoke from the chimney, faint noise of music being played. Its name, 'Talboys', is written in weathered, looping writing inked on a small sign. Livia knocks on the back door, which looks out onto a well-tended garden, lines of staked vegetables, contrasting with exuberant splurges of colour in semi-wild patches of flowers: Dahlias and veronicas and clematis, pinks and purples, soft spheres and delicate stars and prominent points.

A woman answers, wiping her hands on a stained rag. She is tall and slender, her red hair pulled up in a high ponytail, exposing her long, equine face, slightly freckled, with prominent cheekbones. She is impressive-looking, rather than conventionally attractive. She has on a potters' apron, split down the middle below the waist, mottled with clay spatter. Beneath it, jeans and a faded yellow T-shirt.

'Hello, can I help you?' Her voice is strong and clear.

Livia is warm, bold in her subterfuge. 'Hello, I read that you offered pottery lessons? I'm interested, but I've never done it before. I wondered if you could tell me something about it? I'm Livia, by the way. This is my husband, Jake.'

She gives him a sly wink as she speaks.

'My name is Jess.'

They shake hands. Jess's are cold and damp, the fingers slender and strong. Sculptors' hands. She appraises Livia quickly, before turning to Jake. 'Are you interested in a class as well?'

'No, I'm just here with Liv. You don't want my shambling efforts.'

His smile is not returned. 'Probably not.' Jess turns sharply and walks down the hallway, calling over her shoulder. 'Come this way, and I'll show you the space.'

The cottage is old, the ceilings low, the scuffed wooden floor warped, cambering gently into the centre. Jake stoops through a doorway into a large, well-lit room, daylight pouring in through a series of long windows, all open to the morning breeze. The incoming freshness contrasts with earthy smell of clay, which is thick and damp and hovers in the air. It is not a pleasant scent, Jake thinks. It cloys, it feels heavy, like the unhealthy weight of a tomb.

There are three potter's wheels in a line, two of which have been cleaned and stand motionless. Sitting at the third, on a low milkmaid stool, is another woman, sleeves rolled up, hands shaping a mass of what looks like wet mud. The wheel turns, and a rough spherical shape starts to appear. She is utterly focused, determined. Jake can see the sinewy tension in her forearms as she squeezes and pulls.

'That's my partner, Emma.'

'It's a lovely place,' says Livia brightly.

Emma appears to be the physical opposite of Jess. She is small, a bob of dark hair, a roundness to her face and body. She is in overalls, also freckled with old clay, taut around her bust and hips. She has not looked up yet.

There is a record player in the corner, turning in sympathy with the wheel. The music is jazzy and louche, muted trumpets, throbbing bass. Jake can see the sleeve propped up on one side: Miles Davis, *Kind of Blue*. An album even he's heard of.

'Emma.' Jess's voice is stern, has a way of piercing through the ambient sounds. Emma looks up and smiles broadly.

'One second. Our last guest had to go early, and I couldn't bear to waste the material.' Her hands seem independent of the rest of her, as each subtle piece of pressure they bring to bear draws further detail from the clay. Jake is mesmerized for a moment. It is like it is being pulled into life, its shape revealed in the form it was destined to be.

'Emma would just do this all day if you let her. It's charming, but no way to run a business.'

Emma snorts softly to herself, but offers no denial.

Jess guides them both to some soft chairs in the corner. She goes to the stove on the other side of the room, where a coffee pot bubbles. The coffee is served in beautiful mugs that have clearly been made in this room: bone-coloured, ridges thumbed neatly across the curves, the handles dainty as ears.

Jess explains their history. They had both worked in the city in office jobs (lawyer; pharmaceutical executive) and met at pottery classes, where they discovered a talent and a passion at similar times.

'We wanted a different life, so we merged all our savings and assets, and struck out for here. We don't need the business to make a ton of money. Just enough to keep body and soul together.' Jess looks across the room fondly at her partner, preoccupied once more, head bobbing faintly to the beat of the drums, the bowl – as it now is – nearing completion.

Livia talks about her interest in a new hobby, how it might fit into the second half of her pregnancy.

After a while, the wheel stops, and Emma stands, stretching her back.

'Did you get the family history?'

They both nod. Jess is staring quietly at Jake. 'I was just about to ask Jake here about his own past, which I reckon is not that different to ours. Leaving an over-privileged, morally questionable job in the city to bury himself in the countryside mud.'

'You are direct, aren't you?' Jake puts his mug down.

'Come on, you're not exactly an anonymous figure around here. I saw you sitting on that stump outside when that poor woman was pulled from the river. I've seen your story on the internet since.' She looks at Livia, a flutter of annoyance on her sallow features.

'So are you pretending to want lessons, just to have an excuse to sniff around?'

'Jess, you're such a blowhard.' Emma still looks amused, says it with something approaching affection.

Livia is unfazed. 'No, it's a fair enough point. Cards on the table. I am interested in lessons, which is why I'm here. But Jake's been looking into what happened to Claire Davidson and to Jade. She's the woman discovered in the river out there, and you guys knew her. So we thought we'd come together and have a chat.'

'And why the interest, Jake?' Jess's tone remains suspicious. 'You're trying to play the hero? I've seen that fatuous fright of a TikTok girl around the place, and she seems rather taken with the idea.'

Livia raises her eyebrows, archly. Jake doesn't look at her. 'I've got no interest in being a hero. You might not believe it, but I came here, like you, to get away from things, to find a bit of peace. But I've also got some experience of . . .' – he mulls over the phrase – 'dealing with crimes that are hard to detect. And so I've been drawn in once or twice, like now.'

'Do the police like it when you get "drawn in"?'

'Usually they're doing the drawing. But not this time. No, they don't want me to be a hero either, told me not to bother.'

Jess nods. 'I've no special time for the police, who never

seem to be looking after the right people – especially the right women – in my experience. But you used to be a policeman, and yet here you are. Does that mean you think the women were murdered?'

'It means I want to make sure. We want to make sure. Liv has as much interest as anyone in not living in a place where women are unsafe.'

Jess finishes her coffee. 'I thought for a horrible moment you were going to say "as a father of girls". Man, that's a tell. It's such a desperate misdirection of the closet misogynist.'

'I'm not a father of anyone. But as you know we're hoping that's going to change.' A glance at Livia, hand poised lightly on her belly. 'I have to say, though, that everything points to an accident, or rather nothing points much to something sinister. That's what we're checking.' He pauses, feels the room is as with him as it is going to get. 'So tell us about Jade Fortescue. Please.'

Emma looks as if for permission from Jess, before joining the conversation. 'I taught her. She was lovely. Young, kind of innocent. She'd come up with the idea of self-growth, some sort of nonsense she'd picked up somewhere about the need always to find ways to make improvements in her life. Laudable, I suppose. Anyway, she thought pottery might be something.' She wrinkles her nose. 'She wasn't terribly good at it, and she could tell. But she was game for a while, paid for her six lessons and did them all. The last one was a week ago. I've not seen her since.'

'Did she mention what else she was into?'

'She liked exercise, running. I've half an idea her next big thing was going to be wild swimming. She kept talking about the spirituality of the water. I didn't disagree; I'm all for spirituality. We all need to find it where we can, is my philosophy. You should see this one when she's gardening.' Jess stiffens, but looks pleased.

'Any sign of a relationship, a man in the background?' This is Livia, leaning forward.

Jess exhales noisily through thin lips. 'It always has to come to that, doesn't it? Who's the man directing operations.' She folds her arms.

'If this wasn't an accident, do you think a woman would be as likely as a man to have killed her?' Jake is watching her reaction.

'I thought we were talking about a relationship, not a killing? No woman is AS likely as a man to be a murderer. I've no doubt women can kill, but we just don't do it very often, probably because we're less violent and more sensible. Don't have testosterone coursing through us. Don't have that sense of entitlement and arrogance. Though you're not looking for all killers, you're looking, perhaps, for just one. And why shouldn't that be a woman?'

'Would it suit your politics more or less if the killer was female?'

'Who's to say I've got any relevant politics in this area at all. That's just your assumption.'

Emma chortles, slaps her hands on her thighs. 'You two are going to get on famously, I can tell. But there's no need to squabble like dogs over a bone today. Jake, I'm glad you're taking an interest. Livia, you too. But you need to be honest with us: did you really come here for pottery as well as murder?'

Livia welcomes the release of tension. 'I really did. Let me sign up now, so you know I'm serious. I can just see myself giving this a go. I love the room, the clay, even the music. Jake here can't quite get jazz, though he has tried. It's what all hard-boiled detectives have to listen to if they can, but sadly he's been a miserable failure.'

Emma loops a companionable arm around his waist. 'Let me lend you a record or two, then, get you going. I can't bear it when people are put off by jazz, it's such a waste of one of the world's great gifts.'

'Be careful.' Jess allows her tone to be softened by irony. 'She'll never let you out of her grip now. She's always looking for someone to lecture about music. It's not just clay she wants to shape.'

'I'm happy to surrender.' Jake picks up the record sleeve, reads some of the notes on the back. 'But before I do, is there anything else you can tell us about Jade?'

Emma is now burying herself in a box crammed to bursting with records. Jess is contemplative. 'We talked once about relationships when she was cleaning up. She was shy, I think. Told me that she liked men who were shy at heart too, even if they pretended not to be. I just had a faint notion she was talking about someone specific, but I have no idea who.'

They stay for another twenty minutes, leaving with a lesson arranged and several carefully wrapped records under Jake's arm. They walk out through the garden, the plants shimmying left and right as the breeze takes them, and right into McAllister, who is standing, eyes fixated upon the river.

He turns to face them, face stony. 'Morning, Jake. Though maybe I shouldn't be too surprised to see you near a crime scene.'

Liv hovers by his arm. Jake is unmoved. If McAllister is not going to make amends, he isn't going to make conversation any easier himself. 'I hope you're not checking up on us, when you've probably got more important things to be doing.'

McAllister exhales, and as he does, his face opens a little. 'I'm not checking up on you. I don't know what to do with you.' What seemed like hostility slides into something more like despair. 'Fact is, I've got a problem. Dammit, you're going to find out anyway. Late last night we found another body, another woman, in the river. Dead.'

Book Three: Upstream

I ain't one of the supposing sort. If you'd got your living to haul out of the river every day of your life, you mighn't be much given to supposing.
    Charles Dickens, *Our Mutual Friend*

Chapter Twenty

Another day, another trip to the mortuary. Jake has no fondness for the place. Its obscene proximity to the life-prolonging bustle of the hospital; its sterility and pallor, drained of colour like the bodies within, neatly stacked in steel drawers, an absurdist version of a filing system; the smell of disinfectant that never quite eliminates the iron tang of blood or the sewerage stink of voided bowels.

McAllister had dropped Livia at home and driven them both here. He hadn't slept, and anyone could tell that much from a glance. Face blue-black with no shaving, shirt crumpled, eyes pinked around the edges. The journey silent, sullen.

At the hospital, McAllister raggedly parks his car across two spaces, and they stand for a second outside the steel-grey doors of the anonymous building.

'Why did you come find me? I thought I was trying to steal your glory.' Jake isn't entirely willing to let this go.

'Let's just say I thought you were a bit too pleased with the attention.'

Jake thinks this over, thinks of the ignoble flutter of

pleasure he feels – and conceals – when someone describes him in heroic terms. 'I might be able to accept a bit of fault there. I probably didn't think of you enough. I'm sorry.'

'Ach, you don't need to apologize. I'm also being too damned sensitive. Point is I know you can help me, and I reckon I'm going to need help. Three deaths is a problem, a huge problem. I can keep it quiet for mebbe twenty-four more hours while we work, but once the ID comes in, we'll be in the circus again. Plus, there's no way I'll be allowed to keep hold of something as big as this myself; I'm going to get given reinforcements whether I want them or not. So I tried to get ahead of the game. I called Aletheia this morning, she's agreed to come in and help, and she'll want to have you on board. Christ, I'm happier with you on board myself.'

'I wondered how you'd found me.'

'She mentioned your plans to speak to those potting ladies, yes.'

Aletheia's status meant that she could be seconded – on rare occasions – to local forces, and had been with McAllister before. She would be part of the team sent from the city to support the investigation, and he knew she could do that without taking over entirely.

McAllister pushes the doors open with vigour, a surge of anger, which he soon controls. He turns back to Jake. 'The autopsy's being hurried, but probably won't happen until a bit later. I wanted to get a look at the body, see if anything leaps out to get us started.'

'Do we know anything about the victim?'

'No ID on her, I don't know much else. It was dark when she came out the water.'

Jake recognizes the man at the desk, as he thought he

would. John Dennis, idle and unwilling hospital employee, user of online pornography, amateur writer of post-apocalyptic spy novels. Tubby and unhealthy-looking, he is wearing a greying shirt, a blue ribbed vest peeking out between the straining buttons. His hair is straw-coloured and thinning. He has the self-protecting facade, the sort of visible arrogance, of the regularly mocked.

'Hi John, how's the book going?'

He beams, as if unsurprised by the interest. 'Not far from the end, thanks for asking, boss.' He looks blank for a second as he tries to remember Jake's name. The first time he had called himself Rex Stout, the second time Roderick Alleyn.

Jake reaches out to shake his hand, which is smooth and damp, like the underside of a rock. 'You remember me, I'm sure: Al Campion.' He decides to stick to a fictional detective, rather than a famous author.

A doubtful pause. 'I do. And I remember your colleague too.' He favours McAllister with an unrepentant scowl. 'Not his name, just his abrupt, stereotypically Scottish manner.'

McAllister seems content with that. 'And I remember you, my portly chum. No fucking help, you spent your time staring at that screen, enjoying yourself with all sorts of pornographic material. No respect for where you are. Now, we've got some official business here, so open the door quick before I get "stereotypically Scottish" and clock you one on that big heid of yours.'

Dennis allows a beat pause, turns back to Jake. 'Yes, the book's going pretty well. Coming close to the showdown between my man and the shadowy figures controlling the government.'

'Can you open the doors, before my friend here has some sort of coronary?'

'Seeing as you're so polite, Al.' He casts another withering look at McAllister, who is visibly sleep-deprived and irritable. 'Of course I can. I know from last time you're both cleared to come in.' He presses a button, and there's a click from the double doors behind him. 'The pathologist'll be here shortly with his team. They just dropped the body.'

The outer room is cleaned down, and silent bar the ticking of the clock. It is sterile, the bright yellow lights intimidating, jaundicing all they touch. McAllister throws a pair of surgical gloves and a mask to Jake.

'We won't interfere with anything, but put these on just in case. They're moving ahead with this even quicker than I thought.'

Jake inhales as he goes through the further doors, holds his breath, the mask sealing his mouth damply. The inner room is harshly lit like the outer; the cleaned surfaces bounce the light back, plastic and metal gleaming. The centre of the room is dominated by a long table. On it is a woman, or what used to be a woman.

Jake can tell she is fresh – if that is not too obscene a notion – from the water. Her brown skin looks tacky, her hair, long and dark, almost black, is matted and wet. She is mostly naked, just a pair of purple knickers clinging damply to her hips. Her toenails are pink. She has a necklace, silver, adding a further winking glint to the shine of the room.

'Was she dressed like this when she came out?' Jake presumes he knows the answer. Nobody would interfere with the body ahead of the post-mortem.

'Aye, she was, poor thing.'

Jake is conscious of being a man, with another man,

alone in the room like this. He wants to pull a sheet over her, cover her up, protect her dignity. Not that she cares. Her chance at awkwardness or embarrassment or outrage gone forever.

'No sign I can see of obvious trauma.' Jake walks to her head, lifts it very gently.

'She doesn't look like she was in the water long to get bounced around much.' The river smell is present, a muddy, peaty note. 'The pathologist on the scene wouldn't be pushed, naturally, but offered the last twenty-four hours as his initial take. We'll find out more soon enough.'

'Her skin is naturally dark, I see. Very modest tan-lines. There's not many folk of colour round here, might help the ID.'

Her face is in absolute repose, no sign of stress or terror. She could be in dreamless sleep.

'Where was she pulled out?'

'Upstream of the other two. She bumped into a boat with a chap fishing on it. Startled all hell from him. He thought she might be alive, pulled her carefully on board, then saw what was what.'

'Any thoughts on him?'

'Nothing obvious, but we're checking him out. We don't technically have a view on cause of death here.'

Jake feels weary all of sudden, the room airless and oppressive. 'Three dead women, one river, less than two weeks. What the fuck else is going on?'

'An excellent question. I'll try and answer if I can.' This comes from the doorway, the clipped voice of a middle-aged man in a white coat. He addresses McAllister. 'I don't need to worry, Chief Inspector, about you interfering with the body, do I? I'm sure not. Well, let me get going, and

I'll see if this young lady can give us anything useful from beyond the grave. Would you like to stand in and watch, gentlemen?'

McAllister is sidling past. 'I'll wait outside until you have something, Doc, thanks all the same.' A masked assistant passes them, and he and Jake step into the outer room, pulling off their own masks, their gloves.

McAllister grabs a chair from a corner and sits down, hands on his knees. He looks exhausted, a traveller on an endless journey. 'You sticking around, Jake?'

'I'd better see Livia, work out when Aletheia's coming. She'll stay with me, I guess. We'll use Little Sky as a base, and you can come when you need to get away from it all. Which may well be soon, and often.'

'I appreciate that. I've got a terrible feeling about this, you know. It all feels outside my grasp somehow.'

'They all feel like that, Chief, till you solve them.'

Jake walks out, so quietly Dennis doesn't see him go. He is hunched over his computer, flicker of screenglow on his smeared glasses. It could be the draft of his novel, or something altogether less savoury. Jake can't tell.

Outside, the breeze whips his hair, replaces the dead air in his lungs. He hears his name called. Aletheia is standing in front of her sports car, maroon and shiny and needlessly flash. He's pleased to see her. If it's another messy situation to deal with, at least it's good to have the team back together.

Chapter Twenty-One

The library at Little Sky, night-time, the first council of war. The weather has shifted a little. Rain is sputtering against the windows, the air the coldest it has been for months. Cyprian the cat is asleep in front of the fire, a marmalade coil of relaxation.

Aletheia has packed for a longish stay and brought a whiteboard, which is now propped against one of the bookshelves. Lee Child and Michael Connelly on one side; Dorothy Sayers and Margery Allingham on the other. Fiction meeting reality. Jake is playing one of the jazz records provided by Emma, softly: Miles Davis, *Sketches of Spain*.

Aletheia is bustling around the table, setting up a screen. She is in pyjamas and a kimono, a sign she feels at home. 'Is this jazz, Jake? Don't tell Martha, she'll think you're getting above yourself.'

Jake explains their meeting with Jess and Emma.

'This isn't pure jazz, anyway. It's a bit classical, a bit world music, a big old messy mix. Like us.' This is Livia, also pyjama-clad, resplendent in racing green, reclining on a sofa.

Jake is next to her, looks surprised. 'How do you know that?'

'I know a little about music, Jake. I just don't wang on about it like you do.' She slaps his arm. 'You won't believe it, but I actually went through something of a pretentious phase at uni. The full polo-neck. I grew out of it, hence slumming it with you. But I had this album; it's lovely. I'm not surprised she got you started with this one, as a newbie with no sophisticated tastes.'

'Is this the fucking *Late Review*? What's going on?' Martha has blipped onto Aletheia's tablet, the screen propped against a stack of books in the middle of the table.

Jake goes to the table and sits down. He has a bottle of beer in his hand. 'Evening, Martha, glad you could join us. It's always a shock to have a screen working here.' In normal circumstances, Jake can have no electronic communication at Little Sky, but Aletheia uses special government kit that establishes signal more or less anywhere. It is useful, especially on days like this, but an intrusion still, a reminder to Jake that the real world cannot be resisted successfully forever.

Aletheia is writing on the whiteboard in the corner. She stands back, and the three others read what she has written, Martha squinting with the effort: 'FIRST QUESTION: HAVE ANY OR ALL BEEN MURDERED?'

'Let's look at what we know about the three women. McAllister now has some details about victim number three, which I'll get to, but let's go in the order they went into the water, which is not the order they were discovered in.' She draws three columns on the board, fills in detail as they talk.

'We'll start with Claire Davidson. She leaves her stuff behind on Tuesday afternoon, at a place called Westerby. We think she must have run there, as part of planned exercise. She takes off her shoes and socks, leaves her phone, keeps the rest of her clothes on. Why?'

Martha waves her own beer bottle. 'A paddle, or a swim.'

Aletheia nods. 'Maybe a paddle to begin with. At some point, she loses the dark running top, leaving her in pink shorts and a crop top, which is reasonable swimwear for outside in September, if you're not an exhibitionist.'

Jake puts his drink down. 'She starts out tentative, decides to take the plunge. Takes off her outer top, maybe leaves it on the bank, then it falls in later. In any event, something happens. Maybe the cold-water shock. She drowns and we find her over a week later.'

'That's the innocent version of events.' Martha is cynical as ever. 'What about: she's getting ready to jump in, and someone bashes her. That would still look the same.'

Jake is flicking through one of Aletheia's files. 'The body's in no real shape to tell anything concrete after all that immersion, but there's no obvious trauma beyond stuff you could explain from the action of the river. She definitely was alive when she went in, looks like water in her lungs.'

'OK, so much for Claire. We'll come back to her.' This is Aletheia, brisk, running the show. 'Jade Fortescue, enters the water on Friday night, three days later. Another degraded body, but again signs she was alive when she went in. The key difference is that she was naked, which means what?'

Livia's eyes are wide, candlelight flickering against their deepening green. She still seems troubled, emotionally engaged by these sad events. 'Could mean skinny-dipping, alone or with a man. There's the possible evidence of recent sex, and Jess's testimony that she liked someone – what did she say? – "shy". Though nobody's come forward. A guilty man in all this? Could mean she was killed and stripped, I suppose.'

Martha is smoking her pipe. 'I don't think so. If she was dead when she went in, there'd be no water in the lungs. She could've been drowned and then stripped, I suppose, but not killed away from the water.' She expels a plume. 'The fact she was naked is crucial, I agree, but I'm not sure how. And you know how much I hate not being omniscient. To go back to teacher Aletheia's point: she may not have been murdered at all.'

Aletheia moves to the other side of the board. She looks at her screen in one hand. 'Let's keep things going. Third victim. The PM is back, and she was in the water for much less time, probably twenty-four hours. So her body's in good shape. Water in the lungs, so again alive when she went in. No obvious blunt force trauma. And we have an ID, as of a couple of hours ago. Boyfriend reported her missing. Her name is Isabelle Abbas, a Frenchwoman, partial Algerian descent, here on holiday visiting a feller who works in the city. Found just in her knickers. Rest of her clothes not yet discovered.'

Jake moves to sit next to Livia, an idle hand on her thigh. 'None of this makes sense though, does it? Three women: middle-aged, married nurse; young, single professional; foreign holidaymaker. Different stages of undress, no signs of violence. It looks so . . .'

'Random.' Martha's expression is serious. 'Which

means either this is the sort of strange thing that happens naturally, can't be explained, and will stop as abruptly as it began. Or someone is brilliantly creating the impression of randomness, and we're in trouble.'

'Why was Isabelle near the river, do we know? You think people would be cautious with all that's been going on.' Jake drums his fingers as he thinks.

Aletheia checks her notes. 'Maybe she didn't know to be cautious. If you were on holiday in Provence, would you know about any suspected drownings in the area? And what would you do about it?' Jake concedes the point with a shrug. Aletheia continues. 'Here's all we've got so far. Jade and her boyfriend – his name's Philip Carr – have a row. She says she needs time to cool off. He heads back to the city and work. The last he sees her is going out for a long walk to clear her head. He hears nothing for a couple of days, makes the report.'

The record has finished, is hissing. Jake goes to the corner, picks up another sleeve from inside the opened wrapping. Another Emma recommendation. He turns back and sees everyone looking at him, smirking.

'What?'

Aletheia's voice is wry. 'Just wondering what the great jazz guru's going to give us next.'

Jake reads out the title. 'It's *Blue Train* by John Coltrane. From 1957.' Stately drums and piano fill the room, brassy tones wailing above them.

'Are you trying to copy Harry Bosch now, Jake?' Martha is unimpressed, and always likes to bring things back to fictional detectives where she can.

'I don't know, just trying new things. I enjoy music while we work. Shall I switch it off?'

'No need for a grump. Just stop fiddling over there and come back to the table.'

He doesn't mind doing that. They need some sort of plan. He sits down heavily, turns to Aletheia. 'So what's our thinking? We need to talk to this Philip chap, get a read on him. I keep coming back to the problem that these could be three separate events, and it's just a weird twist of fate that unites them.'

'A weird twist of river.' Livia is thoughtful.

'Exactly. They'll be looking for evidence of where the second two women went in, but it's a huge stretch of bank to cover. We should get a map of the water and keep a track of where things get found.' Aletheia makes a note. Jake turns to Martha, who is sitting, glassy-faced. 'M, can you look for any trace of our vics on the record anywhere in the hours before they disappeared, any CCTV, anything?' He holds his hands up to forestall the objections. 'I know, I know, we live in the middle of nowhere. Just adds to the challenge. Al, can I come with you to see the boyfriend, if that's not too intrusive?'

'I think the chief has got over his little fright about being outshined. So, if he doesn't mind, yes.'

Livia stands up. She stretches and yawns, a feline glimpse of her pink mouth. 'I've got to work in the morning, and then have my first pottery class. I'll see if I can get anything further on Jade from those ladies. So, if you don't mind, I'm going to get to bed now. Night all.' She squeezes Aletheia's waist affectionately, blows a kiss to Martha and hugs Jake hard, her arms reaching around his broad shoulders, lingering a little. He kisses the top of her head, which is soft and sweet-smelling.

'Get a room.' Martha's reaction is inevitable; Livia's response is a lurid hand gesture. She then glides out, serene.

Aletheia is tidying up her files. She looks up. 'Do we need to talk about the Paul Sansom threat?'

Jake had let that go out of his mind, with all the excitement of the third victim, though the bruises on his body are still very much present. 'I guess he looks even less likely as a serial killer, able to cover up his own role in three women's deaths.'

'I agree he's not much use to us on the investigation, but he could still cause us problems if he comes looking for more revenge.' She pauses. A lugubrious saxophone wails in the background. 'It'd be wrong for me to become too involved in a private disagreement, but I've carefully voiced a suggestion that he be discouraged from interfering with you, and us.'

Martha giggles, refills her pipe. 'Ah, a Thomas à Becket job.'

Jake is picking up empty bottles. 'What are you talking about?'

'You know, "who will rid me of this turbulent priest?" Al can't order anyone to go round and rough this loser up, she can just imply it's necessary for the good of the state.'

Aletheia pretends to be covering her ears. 'I never said anything about "roughing anybody up". Maybe just allowing someone to make an appeal to his patriotism, the need for law and order. An intervention from authority, let's leave it at that.'

Jake feels an ignoble sense of being protected. 'I don't need battles fought for me.'

'Oh do get over yourself. You need to help on this. You don't need to be looking over your shoulder the whole time. You can go fuck him up when this is over. Martha out.'

Aletheia lingers at the doorway. 'Not how I would've

put it, but basically she's right. And it'll keep him careful about how he treats his wife too.' She looks mournful for a moment. 'I have a bad feeling about these other women, Jake. There's a hidden shape here I don't like.' She purses her lips. 'Good night.'

Chapter Twenty-Two

The rain clears at some point in the watches of the night, leaving a dawn landscape that feels washed anew. Jake is the first awake. Livia a dense, dark shape to his side, snuffling and warm, an arm in front of her face, a long leg out of the covers. He pads out without disturbing her, pauses outside Diana's room, listens to her steady breathing for a second.

He runs, soon warms, his mind on the dead women, the river a thin, pale reflection of the endless sky. He feels safe and secure on his land, which takes him almost all the way to one of the water's endless loops and passages. The isolation, though, is unmistakeable. He can be out, like this, for hours without seeing anybody, without hearing a voice, or sensing a presence. He keeps coming back to that point. What might be done in the cover of the dusk in a place like this, or behind shielding trees even in the middle of the day? To kill without exciting comment at all, in front of nothing more than the indifferent natural world, to whom one less human is neither here nor there.

He makes the turn homeward, feels the pleasurable ache

in his legs that he knows can sustain him for hours. He follows a stream back, a tiny tributary of the main body of water, one of the countless capillaries that connect to the main artery. It has taken the colour of the surroundings, vivid green, as if the trees have been turned to liquid. A heron stands on one of the nearby rocks, immobile, sage-looking in its scholarly grey cloak.

Most living things die foreshortened deaths, the victims of circumstance and ill luck. The imprudent dart for food that attracts the hawk's eye; the rabbit mauled by a fox; the tiny creatures whose life-span is measured in hours, sucked up and consumed without notice. If these women had died by similar accident, by malign fate, that would be one thing; it's the still-nagging sense that some extra agency or action, something impious and unnatural, has become involved. Discovering that is what has always driven him, still drives him now.

Jake increases his pace for the last mile home, breath ragged and sweat flying. Deliberately drives the thoughts away. No good comes from running and philosophizing, he thinks.

They have a family breakfast together, outside beneath the arbour. A big white ewer of steaming coffee, home-made crumpets carefully fried so they emerged bubbly and soft, a central platter of eggs and mushrooms. Just the other week Rose had taken Jake mushrooming, partly – he said – to further Jake's belated rural education. They had tramped in the late summer dawn, through Agatha Wood and beyond to some fields that had been left wild, full of humps and dips, swamped with ferns and brackens. Rose had been oddly expert in that offhand way of his, his eye picking up the various outgrowths even though their mostly bony greys and brown colours, their muted mottling, made them blend into the landscape. They found all sorts on a long march, Rose passing on their names each time: Medusae, with their triangular scales, a sort of fungal leopard-print across their broad caps; blushing wood mushrooms, whitish and anonymous, bleeding eerie red when broken; and armfuls of field mushrooms, which even Jake recognized, their flesh firm, the gills underneath like ornamental buttresses. At one point, Jake moved to pick some that looked similar, and Rose checked his hand with unaccustomed severity. They were death caps, well-named and lethal, heads like parasols, an ornamental tint of green upon white. 'One of the best ways to kill people quickly in the countryside,' he said grimly as he kicked them away.

Aletheia is eating hungrily after her morning exercise rowing on the lake. Jake tells her where the mushrooms came from, and she smiles ruefully.

'How is Rose?' The two of them have met a few times, socially, though nobody is allowed to use the term 'date'.

Livia is bustling, putting food on Diana's plate. 'I thought you'd tell us, Al. Aren't you an item?'

Diana is reading at the table, a usually forbidden pleasure, not paying much attention to anybody else. She raises her head. Her hair has been brushed conker shiny. 'Is this gossip?' she whispers hungrily. 'Gossip' being the highest award possible for any new information.

Aletheia steals a mushroom from her plate. 'You get back to your book. And you' – this to Livia, who is drinking coffee and trying to look innocent – 'stop being naughty. I've only seen Rose once since my last time here, and we're certainly not an item.' Aletheia was hurt, quite badly, in their last shared investigation, a blow to the head that left her hospitalized and unconscious. Rose scarcely left the hospital until she was out of danger.

'And how did that go?' Jake is glad to talk about something other than drowned women.

Aletheia sits back and drains her mug. 'Not that it's any of your business – even yours, Di – but it was weird.' She leans confidingly towards Diana. 'Boys are weird. No, it was as if he'd worried too much about me when I was hurt and didn't know how to treat me now I was better. And, as I've told you before, we can't go out as a couple: he's a probable criminal, and I'm an agent of the state.'

The 'probable' part of his criminality is a fiction they all maintain for Aletheia's sake. Rose is certainly a dealer in cannabis, illegal still, though broadly tolerated in the area. Indeed, Rose's ad hoc assistance to Jake in solving the occasional and serious criminal matter is somehow understood to offset his ventures elsewhere. He and McAllister keep an aloof distance, and Jake always makes sure not to cause a diplomatic incident.

'He's handsome, though. Rose . . .' Diana remains faintly intrigued.

'Did you know your mum kissed him once?' Jake is mischievous.

'Jake! Di does not need to hear about my romantic misadventures before I found true love.'

Diana's face turns sombre, as if she is announcing news of considerable moment. 'Mum has had sex twice, Jake. Once to make me, and once to make the baby in her tummy.'

Nobody really knows what to say to that. Aletheia devotes amused attention to her eggs. Livia is weighing up options carefully. She adopts a brusque honesty. 'I've had sex more than twice, Di.'

'Don't be gross, Mum.' A pause descends, without anyone being keen to fill it. Aletheia stands, relieved to have the attention taken from her.

'As it happens, I'm seeing Rose for a coffee this morning. Just for everyone's information, and now we've stopped talking about sex. And then, Jake, we're seeing Mr Carr, the boyfriend, at eleven. You come meet me at the Nook, and I'll drive.'

She takes her plate inside, and Jake can hear her washing it. She is a very easy house guest, neat and precise. He knows without looking that her bed will have been made, her room aired, her possessions packed away. Rose is a much more chaotic, undisciplined figure, a muddy-booted wanderer and poacher. A bit of that might be good for her.

Jake spends the morning in the gentle, mindless housework he has come to rather welcome. He scrubs down the sauna, leaving the door open so it can dry in the blustery air. He goes to his workshop and sorts and cleans his tools. He's back in front of Little Sky, washing out the outdoor shower, when he sees movement from down by the lake. Someone approaching from the direction of Parvum and the river. He wipes his brow, wanders down to meet them, moving in happier expectation when he sees it is Jo, their friend from the *Shire Gazette*.

She looks uncomfortable with the exertion. She is wearing dark jeans and a pale T-shirt, carries a lumpen shoulder bag, her neck and face a little red from the day's rising heat. She hugs him and her body feels warm and damp.

'Jakey, can you spare a drop of cold drink for a horribly out-of-shape, oldish woman?'

'Of course, of course.' He goes to the kitchen, turns down the music, Nina Simone warbling inexplicably in French. He brings a jug of iced tea from the fridge, made the American way by letting tea bags steep all afternoon in the warmth of the sun. He adds crushed ice and fresh mint to long glasses and carries them outside. Jo is on a bench in the shade, frowning at the sun as if it were trying to do her personal damage. She accepts a glass and takes a deep glug.

'That's better. You can keep your lingering summers, Jake. I'm ready for some cold mornings and crackling frost.'

He sits down companionably. Cyprian emerges from a pool of sun and clambers on his lap, kneading at his chest, claws snagging on his vest. He pets her hard head for a moment, as she purrs and leans into his hand, then gently shoos her off.

Jo seems a little uncertain. 'Hey, I've brought you another serving of our most ridiculous headlines, perfect for the journalism connoisseur.' She takes her job seriously, but they both enjoy the cosy absurdity of some of the minor stories that are used to bulk out the paper occasionally. 'Get ready for a new top three, Jake: "Grass growing fast after rain", "Postman beaten by lavender bush", and, my favourite, "What are the odds? Man receives five identical birthday cards".' She chuckles softly to herself, sips her drink.

'Magnificent. All important stuff too. Who says journalists don't make a difference?' He watches as Jo worries the frayed denim of one of her trouser legs. 'Is there something you want to tell me, Jo?'

'It's like this. I want to find out about these dead women, and you do too.' Jo turns to face him. 'You wouldn't go talking to that TikTok woman instead of me, would you? My boss says he's tired of learning about our patch by watching dumb videos with tinkly music under the dramatic bits. Though I suspect he knows plenty when it comes to making his way around internet videos, if you know what I mean. That's not the point. Look, I hate to be a dick about this.'

Jake gives her arm a push. 'Jo, don't be ridiculous. You're the second person Dani seems to have annoyed, or made me annoy. McAllister's no fan either. I promise: I've done nothing to help her out, nor would I. If I know anything I can share, I'll share it with you.'

Jo looks unconvinced, seems to be searching for words to articulate what she is feeling. 'I know I'm just the local hack; I've been doing this for what, twenty years? Part of the scenery, a quaint hangover from the past, like an old pub. Jake, it's fucking miserable being unimportant sometimes. You know that – you've been at the centre of things, and you've been on the margins. And we can laugh about the stupid headlines, and I do, you know I do, but look at the future I've got in front of me: it's young upstarts like Dani with their videos, not relics like me. But I'm forty-five, not seventy. I've got to cling on for a while.'

Her voice has become bitter. She looks down at herself with a spasm of loathing he has not seen before, before fixing her eyes upon him with the same unforgiving stare. 'So I'm not kidding around when I ask about you and Dani, specially since Rose tells me how you've been talking to her. I value our friendship, Jake, but I'm not going to be dumbly loyal about it. This is my career.'

He nods. These deaths, this intrusion of attention upon their little patch of countryside, has unsettled everyone.

Jo slaps her hands upon her thighs. 'So *do* you know anything more? We got the ID overnight – Isabelle Abass, isn't it? Is it connected, is there something big going on?'

Jake pauses while he balances his own loyalty to Jo with what he thinks McAllister would say about inviting her in further. And his own desire, ignoble, to be at the centre of things. Then he leads her off the bench and guides her to the library, where the material from last night is still laid out. It is cool and gloomy in the room, smells pleasantly of old fire. Jo looks at the whiteboard, nods. 'We're about to report that reinforcements from another force are coming. We won't name Aletheia. I don't suppose we should mention you?'

'I'm helping as a consultant, but nothing more. You could say that if you have to.' All of a sudden there is too much ego in all this, he thinks. Jo wants a story, he wants credit more than he should. A whiff of ugliness between them.

'I think I will, it gives me something new to write. And you think there is a connection between the three women?'

'I can't see one. But it's one hell of a coincidence otherwise. What do you think?'

'I can't remember multiple river deaths in one summer, ever. In fact the only really notable drowning I've reported on was that school teacher, I don't know, a decade ago. Jill Hayes. Nobody could work out why she'd gone in. The whisper was suicide, but it was never properly established.'

She hands Jake back her empty glass. Her voice is bright, perhaps falsely so. She is trying to re-establish the normal tone of their relationship. 'Thanks for the drink, and I do appreciate the chat. Just let me know if anything happens. As a woman who lives near the river, I'm interested personally as much as professionally, if you know what I mean. Love to Livia.'

He puts the glass on the table. He walks her to the door, and she slips on a pair of sunglasses. 'And I'll be nice about you if you get a mention, I promise.' She walks off into the haze of the morning, the sun shimmering behind a curtain of gauzy cloud, rising above her.

Jake finishes cleaning up, slips on a shirt, some light cotton trousers and locks the place up. He wishes he had a concrete answer to the question of what exactly was going on, and he supposes he better get out there and start finding one.

Chapter Twenty-Three

Jake enters the Nook, grabs a ripe apple from a tottering pile, crayon colours of red and green, and winks at Sarah. She nods to the open door at the back, through which he can see Aletheia and Rose together. They are sitting on the grass, glasses of some sort of cordial to their sides, talking easily. The Nook is mainly a shop, but it also serves as a sort of café in the day, pub in the night, its garden at the back a place for people to eat and drink in clement weather.

There are a several picnic tables, old and weatherbeaten, scattered across the lawn, which is thick and lush from the late summer rains. Earlier in the season it had been hard and sparse, scabbed with patches of dried earth, so much so that you might reasonably wonder if the grass would ever return. It always did.

Sitting alone on one table in the corner is Dani, staring at her phone. She is wearing tight denim shorts, a black vest, and an outsized lumberjack shirt, open at the middle, bare feet, blue-white against the green beneath, an incongruous pair of wellies next to them. Jake moves back quickly when he spies her, but too late. Sarah follows his line of vision. 'Ah, she's a bit of a rum'un, that one. Constantly jabbering into that phone of hers, stuff that baffles me. But you know . . .' Sarah turns her kindly eyes upon Jake. Her hair is in a tight bun, smoothing her forehead. She looks her age, mid-fifties, but no more; the hard work of her life (first on a farm, now here) has left her robust. 'You know, I think she might be a bit lonely. She's been in and out all week, and I never seen her have a friendly chat with a single person. I gave her some shortbread yesterday, cheer her up, and she just started taking pictures of it.' She shakes her head. 'Then she tried taking a picture with me, her standing there, with her tongue poking out. I said I was a bit old for that.'

Dani has indeed spotted him, put her wellies on and waddled through the doors, hips swinging. She gives Sarah an awkward smile and hugs Jake, wrapping her arms around his body as he stands, rather stiff.

'Jake, hello. So what do we think? Another body found, must mean something, right? Someone with a vendetta against women?'

'So you don't think it's a hospital patient any more?'

'Jake, I had a theory, I shared it, people were engaged. Nothing wrong with that. Now tell me: my sources say that the lady . . . well, that lady of colour over there, is a high-up policewoman. Is she part of the team? I have to say, that's a triumph for diversity.'

'She's someone who tends to stay in the background.'

Dani slaps his arm. 'I hope that's not you trying to hold her back, because her heritage and success threatens you.'

He holds her gaze. 'No, I'm not doing that. It might be

easier for her to work if she's not broadcast all over the internet, though.'

Dani slips some gum in her mouth. 'Security, I get it. Well, I'll ask her before doing anything.'

'Like you did with me?'

'You're just a local eccentric. The hot hippy. No reason not to take advantage of you.' She puts her face close to his. Jake can smell the peppermint on her breath, see the dots of concealer on one cheek. Sarah chuckles to herself. He can hear her muttering the phrase 'the hot hippy' with quiet glee.

Dani rises on tiptoes and gives him a peck on the forehead. 'Anyway, I've got to go, I'm filming a river walk, an evidence hunt, see if I can work out where those unfortunate women went into the water. Could find something that breaks the case. Let's swap info if we have it. Ciao.'

With that she swishes from the shop, shirt-tails soaring in her wake. Sarah hands him another apple. 'See what I mean. She's lonely, wants to feel important. She'll grow out of it.'

'You're a kind and generous woman, Sarah.'

'So I keep telling folk.'

He waves to Aletheia and Rose, who are standing up, brushing themselves down. They walk into the shop, and Aletheia pauses to wash up the glasses. Sarah spots her. 'Oh stop that, you daft thing.' She bustles over, and the two men walk outside.

'Nice chat?' Jake is solicitous.

'Very nice, you cheeky bastard. And no, I don't want to talk about it. I'm glad she's here, though. I worry a bit about Lils, who's always wandering around and about, near the river, headphones in, like she owns the place.'

'Is she being careful?'

'She says she is, but who knows? She's my sister, which means she shares the family trait of irresponsibility.'

Aletheia has come out to join them. 'Lovely to see you Rose, and love to Lily.' They hug, not awkwardly, Jake notices, and as Rose lopes off down the dusty lane, Jake gives Aletheia a knowing smile.

She punches Jake's shoulder. 'Shut your mouth, and let's go.'

Aletheia's car is fast and silent, and she drives with the windows open. She has spoken to McAllister, who – like them – feels there is some shape to all of this, just one out of their current grasp. He has confirmed he is happy to have Jake on the record as a consultant.

She drives expertly, minimal turns of the wheel, the car shifting around corners smoothly each time. 'The first two bodies, we don't know much, beyond they were probably alive when they went in. Isabelle is different, and yet it's also somehow unhelpful. Body in good condition, no signs of trauma.'

'Ah, but the absence of evidence might be the evidence of absence.' A pause, while Jake smirks and Aletheia wrinkles her nose.

'Tell me what you mean, and try not to be annoying.'

'There's no evidence of trauma on Isabelle, so maybe there was no trauma, against her or any of them.'

'So how did they end up in the water, drowned?'

'I don't know.'

'I told you not to be annoying.' Aletheia turns her attention fully back to the road. 'And I knew you wouldn't listen.'

Isabelle and her boyfriend Philip had rented a cottage

a few miles downstream of Westerby, really just an old fisherman's hovel, tiny and twisted, squished down into the landscape by the forces of time and weather. Jake and Aletheia park on the verge outside and walk up. The river behind the house has a mercury sheen to it, its surface quicksilvered by the returning sun.

They knock, and a heavy-set man lumbers along to meet them. He is in his twenties, burly, perhaps the legacy of an athletic background gone faintly to seed, piercing blue eyes, nicely cropped hair. He is wearing scruffy, expensive clothes: a brown shirt and dark jeans, brown deck shoes, no socks. For all his readily apparent grief, he looks wholesome and attractive.

'Mr Carr?' Aletheia takes the lead. 'We spoke on the phone. I'm Aletheia Campbell, and this is Jake, who does some consulting with the police. We'd like to speak informally if we can.'

'Come in.' He shakes their hands, his grip meaty and warm. 'I googled you, man, saw you've done some good stuff, found some bad guys.' His accent is a strange mid-Atlantic medley of New York and Paris.

They sit down and he leaves them while he goes to the kitchen. The room is clearly a holiday let, but on the higher end of the scale: artisanal, antique furniture arranged elegantly, minimal clutter. Carr brings coffee on a tray, in small white cups.

'Ridiculous, I know, but I can't travel without my espresso machine. It's the only way to guarantee good coffee, especially in the sticks. Isabelle used to laugh, but she'd see it was needed now.' He pauses, sighs, looks away.

Nothing is said for a moment. Jake sips his coffee, which is indeed excellent. 'Where's your accent come from, Mr Carr?'

'Call me Phil. I'm a mongrel. American dad, Parisian mum, English school, but home in France in the holidays. It's where I met Issy. She was in grad school, history of art, still working out what she wanted to do. I came over here to work in the city last year, and she'd come for visits.'

'Why were you out here, in the sticks, as you say?'

'A holiday. I work pretty hard, and she fancied a break from the city, so we hired this place for a month. She was here, painting and walking. I came up to stay when I could, mainly at weekends.'

Aletheia puts her cup down, looks at him appraisingly. 'Tell us about the argument you had before you left.'

He sighs again, almost sobs, his hands behind his head. 'Stupid. All our rows were stupid, and we both knew it. I thought we might go back to the city, go out, you know, party a bit. She liked it here, where it was quiet. She told me to give her space, so I did. Man, I wish I hadn't.'

'Did you not worry about those other women who'd been found in the water?' Jake is looking for tells of guilt, and sees plenty, but over what? Killing his girlfriend, or – far more likely – just leaving her to her fate? Philip looks defeated, the air driven from him. He sags.

'I don't follow the news, apart from the markets. My life in a bank is pretty full on, because I'm so junior. I don't pay attention to much else. Issy used to say it was a waste of my education.' He grins bitterly. 'She mentioned the girls, in fact she'd been on a search for the first one – Claire, I think. I didn't pay it any mind; I thought it was just Brits getting excited by the hot weather and jumping into dangerous water.'

Jake sits forward, a flicker in his eyes. 'She definitely went on a search for Claire?'

Philip nods, leans back and lights a French cigarette. The smell, which instantly overwhelms the pleasant aroma of Colombian coffee beans, is dense and acrid. 'Yup. She liked walking, wanted to help. She might've even gone twice, I think.'

Jake is remembering Jade, who'd also been involved in the search. Coincidence? Yet another one makes the whole idea of coincidence harder to swallow.

Aletheia is looking through her notebook. 'Phil, Isabelle was found in the water in just her underwear. Did she swim much? Was she likely to spontaneously go in the river like that?'

He stubs the cigarette in an ashtray. 'Issy was a free spirit, but she wasn't much of an exhibitionist. Maybe her Arab background. At home, she was, you know, pretty physical, but she wasn't the sort to go swimming half-naked. No, I don't think she would've done that.' His voice has thickened, as he appears to remember the sensual reality of Isabelle, alive and dead.

'And swimming generally?'

Phil cracks his knuckles. His shirt is slightly too tight and bulges when he moves. 'She thought English rivers were as dirty as French ones. It's nice here, but she was still suspicious of it. She never mentioned wanting to go in.'

Jake has a vision of the body in the mortuary. 'She had a silver necklace, was it worth anything to a thief?'

'It came from her Algerian grandmother, but I don't suppose it was worth a great deal. She wore it for sentimental reasons. Generally she didn't like ornamentation, you know, make-up or earrings or anything like that. She liked to be natural.'

Aletheia closes her notebook, a gentle slap in the quiet

room. 'I know you'll have told the police all this, but what was she wearing when you saw her leave after the argument?'

He winces at the thought of it. 'A white dress, knee-length, sandals.'

'That purple underwear?'

Phil puts his head in his hands. 'I guess so, I think I remember them from earlier in the day. She had a matching bra. She made a joke that it was a bit bright for the dress, but nobody would see it out here.'

'I'm sorry to keep asking questions, but her phone and purse, not left here?' Aletheia's voice is gentle and coaxing.

'She left her purse here, and you guys have it, but had her phone with her, like we all do. It's not been found, just goes to answerphone.' Phil lights another cigarette, inhales slowly.

Jake stands. 'Would you mind us having a quick look at her room – your room I guess too, but hers when she was on her own?'

'Sure. This is a small place. Head upstairs. Main bedroom on the left.' He makes no move to escort them, but sits, staring into space, the cigarette smouldering unheeded in his fingers.

They pad up narrow stairs. The room is dark, with half-closed shutters, a pleasant breeze coming through an open window. There is a small table facing the bed, on which Isabelle's meagre cosmetic supplies are lined up. Moisturizer, a bottle of vanilla perfume, a miniature vanity mirror. On the wall above it, she has hung a poster, perhaps a reminder of home. Jake reads the inscription at the bottom: *A Summer Landscape*, Georges Seurat, 1883.

Aletheia is looking at it too. 'Do you know it?'

'Never seen it before. It's beautiful, though, isn't it?'

And it is. The landscape teems from the canvas, as if blurred by an insistent wind. To the right, what looks like a cornfield looms, smudges of sandy yellow. The foreground is wilder, grassland maybe, with cerise flowers running into nearby greens. A huge tree, blue-black, is silhouetted against the skyline, which is a smear of blue and cloudy white and a pinkish sunset that seems to borrow something from the flowers below. The most striking thing about the picture, though, is the figure, striding away from you, all in black, featureless.

Jake stares at it. It now seems to stand as a reminder of what they are looking for. A shadowy and faceless presence, an unknown danger in a world that is otherwise soft and gentle and giving. Is there a killer in the real fields, moving remorselessly, even now, to his next victim?

Chapter Twenty-Four

Aletheia heads back to brief McAllister. She drops Jake at the river, and he wanders down towards the bend where Jade had been found, close to where the potters live. There is something nagging in his mind, something he has seen that connects the victims, or seems to, but he can't get a grip on it. He concentrates on breathing, walking, letting the sensations around him fall upon him. The rippling of the water, the smell of the hedgerows, the harsh mutter of the unseen bird.

Halfway down the path, there is a bench, usually empty and forlorn, apart from the fall of yellowing leaf and purple blossom from the tree above. Sitting on it today is Martin George, in stasis for once.

Jake sits down next to him, but not close. Martin is staring vacantly into the water, his backpack by his feet. It is open and Jake can see a tumble of clothes inside, a paperback book on top. It's a Morse novel by Colin Dexter.

Jake gestures towards it. 'Good one, that. I've read it,

the one with the Swedish girl. All the Morses are good, aren't they?'

Martin's voice is faintly strangled, high in pitch. 'I'm working my way through them. Sam sells me them cheap, and no, they never seem to disappoint. I even like the way he starts sections with quotes from random chunks of literature. It's clever.' He picks it up and turns it over. 'I've seen you in Sam's bookshop. The one with the silly name.'

'Books Do Furnish A Room. I don't get the reference myself.'

'It's from a book by Anthony Powell. I just don't understand why he's used it, beyond the obvious. It's too much of a mouthful for a shop. I try not to mention it to him, because it only winds him up.' A brief smile, the first time his features have been animated at all.

Jake holds out his hand. 'I'm Jake, by the way. Sam told me you're Martin.'

Martin shakes it, his grip firmer than expected. 'I'm sure he told you my tale of woe too.' He looks up at the heaving sky, his expression cynical. 'Well, it's true enough, and I don't hide from it. I fucked things up, and this is my life.'

Jake lets the statement settle, watches a sodden duck emerge from its dive, scrabbling and shaking. He tries to imagine how it would feel to have an intruder enter your home, ravage your family. 'Can you find pleasure in life still, at all?'

'Nobody's ever asked me that, you know. They just assume – maybe rightly – that I'm a wreck.' His eyes are dead, set deep, the irises mottled gold. There is no fat or excess upon him, and while his body is thickened with a fair covering of muscle, his face is drawn, the skin shrunk upon the skull. Jake can see the outline of his orbital bones, jutting and hooding. He looks like a sculpture of a religious martyr.

Martin talks to the river more than anything else. 'They're probably right. But I've found a sort of pause, if not quite peace. I stay in shape, keep on the move, bury myself in this place. It's not how I wanted to be, not how I saw myself, but there are times I feel almost settled.'

'Could you do something about it, get back to normal life?'

He turns his face, and Jake sees an expression that is glazed, deadened. 'Now I do get asked that one quite a bit. I'm sure I could get a proper job, start socializing again, slowly build up from a bedsit to a bigger house, maybe try to meet someone special.' His voice drops. 'But the thought of it exhausts me, maybe even disgusts me. No, Jake, this is me. I can't be trusted to have more than this.'

'What disgusts you?'

'People disgust me, *I* disgust me, Jake. Even this experience, pleasant though you are, disgusts me. I'm sorry to say it, but it's true. And there's no water in this river enough to wash it clean.'

Jake suddenly feels like an intruder himself. The way Martin's voice has changed startles him, that shift from gentle musing to something so aching and angry. This is a man on the brink, permanently, in constant battle with himself and the world. A throb of energy beside him, full of destructive force. Jake stands, and reaches out his hand once more. 'I won't trouble you any more, then. One question before I go. Three women have gone missing on this river in the last week or so. Have you seen anything suspicious?'

Martin stuffs his hands in his pockets, looks forward

again. 'I see things that are innocent and suspicious the whole time, and sometimes I feel I lack the discrimination to tell the two apart. I see lonely women, and I've seen a steady parade of searchers, I see couples arguing, and I've even seen them making love on the riverbank, like animals. But I've not seen anything I can share with you.'

He hunches his shoulders. Nothing else to say, Jake walks on. When he looks back, he sees Martin hasn't moved, the late afternoon sun glinting on his shorn head, the course of the water moving inexorably past him.

An hour later, he waits outside the cottage called Talboys. Through the window he can see Livia at the pottery wheel, guided by Emma who is standing at her shoulder. Dusk is approaching, the sun now dipped half beneath the horizon, leaving a trail of bruises in its wake. He can hear music, a female singer, her voice dense and deep, effortlessly rising and falling. In front of Livia, spinning, is a malformed piece of turned clay, endearingly wonky. He can imagine her face, puckered in concentration, enlivened by the challenge.

The river snakes away from him, becoming black, and then disappearing entirely into shadow. As the end of the hour approaches, he waits underneath the light at the bottom of the garden.

She spots him as she emerges, that charming note of recognition, her face suddenly wreathed with a smile that shines even in this light. Jess is walking her out, acknowledges Jake with something closer to a frown.

Livia walks into the warmth of his hug. 'Why are you here? I was going to meet you at home.' Jake feels a tug of pleasure at her use of the term to describe Little Sky. 'Aletheia is cooking curry with Di. She's made special "curry night" signs and everything.'

Jake points at the water, visible only in the milky sheen that sits atop it. 'I was worried about you near the river at night, to be honest.'

'That's nice, although my car's just here. I promise not to go wandering along the bank when I come here. I know you're not paranoid or anything, but please don't worry.'

'I'll trust you to stick to that promise, and then maybe worry a bit less.'

At home, there is brightness and activity. The smell of cooking hits them as they enter the kitchen from the courtyard outside. Diana is kneeling on a stool, making unleavened bread, flour everywhere, a white puff across her black hair. Two pans bubble luxuriously on the stove. Aletheia is trying to tidy up around her. Then there is the welcome flurry of domesticity: noisy communal eating and washing up, some books and a screen, bath and bedtime. Jake is not tired of this, and hopes he never will be. The fleeting thought occurs that a squalling baby will make certain parts more difficult.

In the library, the team gather again. Jake has gone back to his classical collection for the background music, Mozart's Piano Concerto No. 21, which – he remembers – features in the Morse book that Martin had been reading. He'd checked the reference while the others were getting ready.

Aletheia and Jake begin with their interview with Phil Carr, and as she speaks she goes to the big whiteboard. Under the title, 'Common characteristics', she writes in big block capitals: SEARCH PARTY.

'We're looking for a possible thread here, and this feels like something, doesn't it?' She scratches her nose with the back of the marker pen.

Martha makes her own note. 'So we know that after Claire goes missing, Jade and Isabelle both were there looking for her. Does that make a thread? I mean, lots of women were bothered about Claire disappearing, these women both live in the area, wouldn't you expect them to be there? Liv here went on a search, for example, so did that elderly shopkeeper of yours.'

'That's true.' Jake had been down that route in his mind. 'But how many people went on the searches? The one we saw was maybe twenty or thirty, maybe slightly more than half of them women. A hit rate of two from that group is not nothing.'

'So what's our inference? They were killed for looking for a missing woman? I hate to be all disabled Sherlock Holmes on this, but there's a risk we start theorizing without the facts, which – as you know – he advised very strongly against.'

'It's definitely a lead, though. We need to find out who took part in the searches, don't we? Will that be easy?'

Martha shrugs. 'The police who handed out the maps will know some of them. I think some of our social media chums will've filmed bits of the gathering, so we can maybe get IDs of those in the background. That feels like a split between you and me to run that down, Al. The breeders there, as ever, doing nothing.' She exhales smoke, which fills the front of her hood for a second, making her look demonic.

Livia has been largely silent until this point. 'Presumably, nobody's gathering together any more, are they? Not now there's nothing to search for.'

Aletheia moves to the table. 'Good point, which reminds me.' She pulls out a copy of the *Shire Gazette*, Jo's paper.

'We'll move past the picture of Jake on page four, and Jo's description of him as the "brilliant local resource".' Martha's smoky laugh sounds more like a choke. 'And look here: there *are* some small-scale patrols down the riverbank at night. A quote from our friend Dani: "this is rural women refusing to be intimidated by the possibility of a killer targeting them. People can join in, show their support. There's a hashtag to follow if you want to get involved, it's called #reclaimtheriver. I hope the community can come together on this."' Livia rolls her eyes nearly out of her head, but says nothing.

Martha is typing. 'I'll keep an eye on that hashtag. I'm already following Dani, which I've got to say is doing nothing for my hatred of modernity. It's like watching a dim child chase attention.'

'Sarah thinks she's just lonely, needs a bit of love.' Jake offers this thought gently.

'Love from you is the last thing she needs. Or rather the last thing she's getting.' Livia's voice is flinty.

Aletheia brings them back to the point. 'Anyhow, it's something we can look at. Jake, you spoke to that strange man, Martin George?'

Jake has been trying to parse that conversation in his mind. 'He's a pretty nihilistic chap, even more so than Martha over there. He mentioned witnessing the searches, and seeing women on their own and in couples. He's unsettling, talked about the river as a cleansing place, which may be a red flag. I didn't really get much of a solid read. But he unnerved me. If there is a killer, he's someone you'd want to take a look at.'

They wrap it up soon after, the night advancing, the moon up and high. Aletheia and Livia head to their beds,

Jake remains alone among his books. He goes to the Sherlock Holmes section and pulls at a heavy volume. There's a creak and the secret compartment opens, one of his uncle's minor eccentricities built into the library, less useful than the beer fridge, but more evocative. Jake keeps his shotgun there, alongside documents and keepsakes.

The conversation with Martin has unsettled him. The idea that Martin is little more than a piece of wreckage, life's flotsam, that he fell to such depths, unsalvageable, when his family was taken from him – it nags at Jake's mind. It brings out the contradiction within him. On the one hand, he believes in the pleasure of renunciation, in shucking off the claims of his past relations; on the other, here he is on the brink – beyond the brink – of starting a new family himself. There is joy there, but pressure, the need to preserve and protect, the grim prospect of failure.

He has a wooden box he brought with him to Little Sky all those months ago. He reaches for it, family on his mind. In it are the small number of possessions that had followed him from his old life, including a handful of photographs of him with his parents: the proud baby in the hospital, the well-wrapped toddler in the snow, first day at primary and secondary schools, a final late-teenage shot notable for his corkscrew pose of adolescent awkwardness.

Jake's parents had died as he entered adulthood, together in a car accident, a late-night smash in terrible conditions. He doesn't think about them much. They had been loving, and in love; they had been important in his life, but they had also prepared him for the world, a place where he would have to exist without them. The gift of loneliness, or – perhaps put more positively – of unremarkable solitude. As an only child, he had always learned self-reliance, and that had become a central part of his identity the moment he left childhood behind. Which had indeed been a definable moment: coming as soon as the grave policeman had broken the news of their death.

His parents had left him money, not too much, but enough to get him started on the property ladder. He had not kept many of their possessions. He had left their wedding rings on, at their sentimental request, and they were buried in them. He has their engagement rings in this box, his mum's favourite necklace, and that is about it.

He holds the jewellery now in his hands, in his quiet farmhouse in the middle of nowhere, his newish family sleeping silently, unseen.

Chapter Twenty-Five

Jake gets up the next day with a domestic project in mind. He has some time alone: Livia is at work, Diana at school, and Aletheia putting in a shift at the police station. There is little to be done until she and Martha come back with some information on the search parties.

The day is clear but cool, long-sleeved-shirt weather, his morning swim just this side of comfortable. He is in the back of his workshop, formerly just a storage room for his uncle. He had discovered there an antique zinc bathtub, giant and unwieldy, the colour of an old penny. It stands on four feet shaped like lion's heads and was clearly a relic of the old farmhouse. The idea of an outdoor bath, a complement to the courtyard shower, appeals to him. He is no plumber, but knows he can connect a hose to the nearest sink in the house, and fill it from there.

Jake carries the tub on his head, with difficulty, out back, past the arbour and fire pit. He sets it down on a miniature hillock of grass, on which he has lined up some offcuts of treated pinewood. Behind it, falling back away to the flat ground, is a rockery, tufted with wild flowers. Beyond, a view all the way up to Poirot Point, a quilt of land and dense hedge and trees silhouetted against the blank-page horizon. He goes to fetch wire wool and cloths and hot water. He scrapes and cleans, removing centuries of rust and muck a small patch at a time. Soon it begins to gleam, the inside revealed to be a contrasting cream colour.

His mind returns to Isabelle. If she had been attacked, where were the telltale marks? The same went for any forcible drowning. It is very hard to stop someone fighting for their lives, harder still to obliterate the evidence of them trying to do so. She had no bruising on her at all. If her boyfriend was correct, she wasn't likely to have stripped down, out in the open, to her underwear and just jumped in. So how did she get there, and how did she lose her clothes?

Jake fixes the hose up, burying it under the topsoil, so it is invisible as it snakes to the house. Then he arranges some old plant pots around the bath itself, filled with autumn flowers from the garden, fuchsias and Michaelmas daisies, half camouflaging it into the background. He steps back to examine his work, satisfied. It is idyllic, charmingly offbeat; he hopes Livia will enjoy it.

At lunchtime he grabs a cheese-and-mustard sandwich, contrasting yellows, and goes for a walk around the lake to stretch his legs. At its opposite end, he walks far enough past to get a glimpse in the distance of Sherlock Beech, bordered now with a soft mist as damp makes its descent upon the day. This is his favourite tree in the county, in the world, because it is an important part of his relationship with Livia. They have never been able to communicate using a phone, so from the beginning they had arranged to meet by leaving a bright cloth hanging in its branches, a signal that the other should visit as soon as possible. Today, the mist is unhelpful, dimming the colours, but he sees fluttering something definitely out of place, a red-and-black shirt on one of the lower limbs.

The sign did not necessarily mean an urgent problem; it could simply mean an invitation for coffee. At one point, earlier in the year, it had meant a summons for a hasty attempt at impregnation, sordidly biological but nonetheless thrilling. Jake's heart leaps a fraction, as it always does, and he continues his walk onward towards Parvum.

As he gets to the river and the road, the bend before the village itself, he sees Dani sprawled on the grass, taking photographs of the clouds with her phone. She sits up as soon as she sees him.

'I can't believe it. It worked!'

Jake frowns. 'What worked?'

'Your cute little message system. Lily told me about it, but I didn't believe it. Sounded too hokey even for a romantic like me. But look, here you are.'

'You didn't interfere with my private thing with Livia, did you?'

'Oh tush and hush, you silly man. How can hanging a cloth on a tree be private? I just wanted to try it out. Don't get grumpy about it.'

Jake is glad Livia isn't around, feels a throb of guilt he cannot quite explain. Dani pats the ground next to him in invitation, and he squats, keeping a sensible distance. She shows him her phone. 'Look what Detective Dani has uncovered.' It is a picture of a riverside scene, long reeds growing at water's edge, a small black box in the foreground. 'I showed it to that charming, if perhaps a little gruff, policeman, and he thinks it might belong to Isabelle – the third woman, you know – it might be her phone. Which means this is where she went in, or was pushed in. Go on, admit it, I'm good at this.'

He hands her phone back. 'That is something. Anything else at the site?'

'They have forensic people there now. Look, let me show you where it is on my map, and you can go and take a look. Or, even better, jump on my scooter and I'll take you there now.'

He is torn between curiosity and scepticism about Dani. 'I'll come, but you have to promise not to use the tree again. It's something special I have with Liv, and I don't want it . . . I don't know, taken from us.'

Dani gets up, punches him lightly in the stomach. 'All right, Mr Serious. I'll never use it, unless it's an emergency.' He looks warningly. 'All right, I'll never use it.' Dramatic pause. 'Unless I really really have to. Come on.' Her scooter is parked by the roadside, bronze and sleek and conspicuously trendy. She swings her legs over, shorts riding up dangerously high. 'You'll have to hang on to me, I'm afraid, Jake. But don't worry, I won't take advantage of you.'

He sits behind her, as far back on the seat as he can, warm leather between them. She grabs his hands and puts them around her middle, which is soft and giving. He can feel the line of her waistband. 'Don't let go, whatever happens.'

With that, she purrs the engine and sends the scooter shuddering into the road's centre. She is a skilful rider, fast and precise. Jake feels his hair shoot back in the wind, his hands tighten as they turn the corners. It is too noisy to speak, and he concentrates on the scenery flashing past, blurred colours like hurried brushstrokes.

He sees the activity at the site ahead, and Dani slows, parking a few hundred yards away from the river itself. As they walk up the verge and into the nearest field, she thrusts a proprietorial arm through his, and waves at the group of people standing nearest to them. One of them is McAllister, who acknowledges them with a semi-wave.

'Chief Inspector, look who I've brought.' Dani is bright and confident.

Jake detaches himself from her arm, under McAllister's ironic gaze. 'Chief, this looks like progress.'

'Aye, it is. But we don't know what we've got yet. Miss, you can't go through there.' This to Dani, who is trying to get closer to the search area. 'It's now a potential crime scene.'

She does not look fazed. 'Hear that, "potential crime scene", Jake. All thanks to me.' She walks away from them, back near the opening to the field. 'I'll film my stuff here anyway, have you in the background. You can't stop me doing that.' They watch as she kicks off her shoes, feet flashing white, and strikes poses for her camera.

McAllister draws Jake away, towards the river. He has men carefully examining the grassy area, and the reed-studded bank. A diver is in the water.

'I guess I can't stop her for all that, but why in the name of God did you bring her?'

'She brought me. Look, it doesn't matter. What've we got?'

'We have the phone, switched off, but not quite dead. It's Isabelle's all right. There's a scrap of disturbed ground, but nothing I'd like to call a clue. We're still looking.'

'Where was the phone?'

'According to that mad lass, she saw it in the middle of the reeds, just above the surface of the water.'

'Which is not where you'd leave it voluntarily. That might mean something.'

'If she's telling the truth, and not just making stuff up for the internet.'

They watch the bustle of activity for a moment. 'Did Al tell you about the search party connection?' asks Jake.

'She did, and I like it as far as it goes. She's getting the info about everyone we know who joined the search from my people, and has sent folk out to get witness statements. She and your mysterious friend Martha are going to create a master list. But I've got to tell you something, Jake. My boss, and her boss, keep coming back to this point: none of the post-mortems point to anything suspicious. At some stage, they are going to call this all off, call them accidents, and issue a campaign to stop people wild swimming on their own.'

'You happy with that?'

'Nope. You?'

'Nope.'

There doesn't seem to be much more they can say.

Chapter Twenty-Six

Martha cannot make the nightly gathering until very late, for reasons she has no interest in disclosing, so Aletheia decides to take Diana out in her car for pizza in Meryton. Jake knows almost nothing about her view on having children herself, whether she has abandoned hopes of her own or never harboured them in the first place. She is brilliant with Diana, at least, treating her seriously, almost like an adult. To Diana, Aletheia is little short of a superhero.

Jake and Livia make pizza, a little treat for themselves. In the greenhouse, Jake strips some plants of tomatoes, grabs chillies and a handful of basil. He makes a fast sauce and lets it putter on the stove, becoming more concentrated. Then he takes a smoked, peppered sausage that normally hangs down from the beams in the kitchen and slices it very thinly. Meanwhile Livia has some pre-worked dough – which she had removed from the freezer that morning – and kneads it with practised hand, thudding and pounding until there are two large, circular shapes on the board.

Jake builds the fire outside, and while Livia is still in the kitchen runs hot water through the hose into the new bath. It thunders in, a rolling crash against the metal. Livia, a Mahler symphony on loud, hears only trumpets and tympanis. Jake pours in some lavender oil, then lights lanterns and places them around the bath, so their gleam shimmers on the sleek surface. The water steams mysteriously, a witchy broth, like the Roman hot spring on the plateau a few miles away.

He goes inside. 'I've got a little surprise for you, but I should warn you that it involves you being naked and outside.'

Livia turns and smears flour on his nose. 'I've warned you before: I refuse to have sex on a zipwire. It's neither dignified nor safe.'

'I'll wear you down in the end. OK, naked under a robe, while we wait for the fire to die down.'

'It's a good job I trust you.' She is wearing a chocolate-brown jumpsuit, which falls from her shoulders to the ground. She steps from it, wriggles from her knickers and stands, half-shadowed and defiant. He hands her a robe, which he has warmed above the stove. Her eyes appraise him. 'Your turn.'

He performs the same operation, somewhat less elegantly, and takes her by the hand towards the back door. Before he opens it, he removes the belt from around her waist, sliding it out with a silken whisper. He gently ties it around her head, covering her eyes.

'Are you sure you still trust me?'

'Hurry up, I don't get to eat pizza without a child that often. I trust my desire for carbohydrates above everything else.'

He opens the door and leads her out. The scene is dream-like: the pulsing fire, the bath banked by flowers, the swirling fog above the water, the pool of light that dies quickly into darkness. He pulls the belt from her eyes.

She squeals, then puts her hand to her mouth. 'Oh Jake, I love it. It's beautiful. I know one day you'll want indoor plumbing, but I'm glad it's not tonight.'

'May I?'

'But of course.' He slips the robe from her shoulders and they walk up to the bath. The grass is cool, daubed with early dew. Livia turns and looks back at him. 'Why am I the only one naked again?'

'Give me a second.' He puts his hand in his pocket, clenches it around two hard objects, which he holds so tightly he can feel their outline, adorned and annular, scored against his skin. Then he drops the robe and follows her.

Livia is standing in the bath, half crouched, as she gets used to the heat. Jake lets the sight take the breath from him; she looks like some sort of nymph or goddess, the lamplight turning her skin the colour of rust, her body all curves wreathed in steam. 'I'll just dip in and out. It's not too hot, but I'm being careful.'

'I know. I could've made it hotter.' She slips in, up to her collarbone, moisture beading her face, and he slides in beside her, making the water roll and slop a little down the sides. She grins, finally squirming into a sitting position. He takes her by the hand, his other held out of the water.

'Liv, I want to ask you something. Now, I'm not asking this because of the baby, or because of what's expected of me. I'm not trying to dazzle you with romance.'

'You could've fooled me.' Her cat eyes gleam.

'Liv, I want you to marry me. I want to be indivisible

from you. I want to be with you forever. I don't need a ceremony to prove anything, but I want to do everything that shows how close we are. I love you. And I know this is in English not Latin, and in an outdoor bath not in Oxford, but I wanted something that is only ours forever to remember. In our wide and lovely land, in the night, nothing between us.'

'Yes.'

'I haven't got to the asking bit yet.'

'Yes, yes, yes. Of course, yes. You don't need to say any more.' She reaches out, hands slippery, and grabs his head, pulling it to her. Forward she slithers, until she encompasses him all around; he feels flesh on flesh, the familiar dips and patterns of her body. He takes her hand, and puts on the ring; the stone is emerald, matching her eyes. She does the same to him; his is white gold, the surrounding light made solid.

And then they kiss, as the wind rustles the trees behind them and provokes the fire to spit and soar.

Chapter Twenty-Seven

Later, rather a lot later, wrapped in towels, their bodies tingling, they sit by the fire and cook pizzas, which rest on a wire rack barely an inch above the now-whitened coals. Jake grabs two empty plant pots, and places them over each base, so the heat will circulate and melt the cheese on top.

Livia is staring at her ring. He leans over. It looks different on her finger.

'It was my mum's. They're almost the only things I brought to Little Sky, the rings. She'd have thought it was a good idea, I reckon. She and my dad didn't really need anyone else but each other, but she'd have loved you. I could've gone to get something bigger and better, I guess.'

Livia's voice is soft. 'Oh Jake, there's nothing better. And there's no better way of asking than you did. I'll never forget that.'

Jake lifts one pot with a stick, sees the pizza is not quite ready. 'I didn't actually get round to asking, if you remember.'

'Well I was overwhelmed, and plus I couldn't sit marinating there all night. You need me to hurry you along occasionally.' Her teeth flash white in the now total gloom, the lamps casting an orangey animating flicker upon them. Jake knocks the pots off, pushes the pizzas onto wooden boards and carries them into the kitchen. They eat in silence, ring-clad hand in hand, content. And that is how Aletheia and Diana discover them, entering boisterously a short while after.

They celebrate, noisily this time. Jake watches Diana's reaction carefully, trying to see himself through her eyes. He must be a startling figure – this giant, bearded stranger – who had entered her world unbidden and changed it utterly; he would understand if there was reticence or jealousy or lingering suspicion. He finds none for now. At one point, amid the flurry of babbling conversation, she places a hot hand inside his, and smiles. His heart lurches. She dashes off to ask Livia for a drink, to join the toasting, unaware of any effect.

Later he pulls out a chocolate cake he had asked Sarah to bake especially. The room soon reverberates with the joyous sounds of family. Sugar-powered sounds too, of course, so it is very late by the time Diana is washed and in bed, and midnight by the time they break the news to Martha, when she appears on the screen in the library.

She beams with genuine affection and pleasure, makes a generally inappropriate speech, and soon brings the meeting to order, brings them all back to a far more sombre place.

'There were two official searches for Claire, and, look: Jade attended the first and Isabelle attended both.' She pulls up on the screen a picture from the first occasion, the two women, separate, circled, faces intent and serious. 'In fact, there is quite a bit of replication of names who attended both, at least of those I've managed to identify.'

Aletheia coughs gently.

'I should say "we've managed to identify". Al harnessed the efforts of at least one PC Plod, which helped. Names coming up now.'

Jake stares at the list, recognizing some acquaintances. Rajni and David, the doctors, along with Vaughan from the barges. The gym boys. Dani Jones. Rose and Lily. At least two of Lily's friends from the dig, whom he had met earlier in the summer. Sarah from the Nook. Clifford, the malingering mummy's boy who lived next to her. Jess and Emma, the potters. Sam Fryer from the bookshop had attended the first search, but not the second. Martin George was not named, but he may have been there, lurking on the margins, or marching resolutely through.

Jake is drinking coffee, black and bitter. Too late for it, he knows, but the food and occasion has made him slow and sleepy.

'What do we do with this?'

Martha is also drinking coffee, from an outsized mug, decorated in pinky-peach tones to look like a breast, complete with nipple painted on the base.

'We pick some names, and find out if anything happened on the searches, anything suspicious at all. Jake, you could try the barges again. Al could talk to her boyfriend, Rose.' A strangled snort from Livia. 'I actually think that Dani might be useful. She records a lot on her phone. Jake, she seems to think you're as hot as a bastard, maybe use your masculine wiles on her.'

'Is "hot as a bastard" a phrase?'

'You tell me. You're the hot one.'

'Can we stop discussing the hotness of my fiancé?' Livia rolls the phrase around her mouth, the first time she has used it. There is relish upon her features. 'And can we stop driving him into the floury arms of the TikTok lady?' Her voice rises in pitch to show she is kidding, which Jake understands to mean she is not.

'Did Isabelle's phone offer anything?' Martha herself moves on, briskly. 'Jake, you were there.'

Livia runs a finger down his back, sleepy. 'You didn't mention that.'

His voice is a little thick. 'I didn't really find anything to report. There wasn't much physical evidence, beyond the phone. Did that change, Al?'

Aletheia shakes her head. 'The grass near the water was a little scuffed up, but nothing to help us. There is one thing, though. The phone was hers, but it was very hard to switch on and it had been pretty badly damaged.'

'The water?'

'It looks like it had been caught in the reeds above the waterline. It could have gone in and out again, I suppose, as the river rose and fell.'

Martha is looking interested. 'Can you send me the specs? I'll take a look. Could it have been on her and hit hard? It might even give us a time of death.'

'Take a look, M, it could be something, could be nothing. Meanwhile, the next step is definitely talking to the searchers. It might not get us anywhere, but it's pretty much the only thing we can try.'

'You're so inspirational, Aletheia. It's why I love you.' Martha drains her cup. 'I'm also going to trace movement patterns on the searchers too, see if any interact with the vics. But it's all very needle in the haystack.' She conceals a gentle belch. 'Let's call it a night. I'm sure the smug marrieds there want to celebrate their union with a bit of already-overfamiliar bonking.'

'I built an outdoor bath, Martha, actually. Just to freshen things up.'

'You disgust me, Jake. I want you to know that. Martha out.'

Chapter Twenty-Eight

The next two days were long, and felt largely fruitless. The weather shifted abruptly, rain fell in chill and unrelenting sheets, the temperature dipped, the sky and land were joined in sodden union.

Jake walked for miles, a notebook in his back pocket, talking to whoever he could readily find in the area. Rajni and David welcomed Jake to their boat, which was snug and low-ceilinged, a haven from the wetness that surrounded it on all sides. They said the searches had been conducted with goodwill, a sense of togetherness, bar two incidents. In one, a woman – 'tall and a bit bossy' – had given a speech about the danger of men to women, which had left some members of the group angry. The atmosphere had turned from camaraderie to one of tension and mistrust.

'She was right, I'm sure,' said David. 'But it felt like it was the wrong time to raise it. Some of the locals are pretty traditional, and they weren't hugely up for being part of a war between the sexes.'

Rajni nodded her agreement. 'I'm as solid a feminist as you'll find, and – if I'm honest – I did suspect, I do suspect some terrible man's involvement in this. But why shout at the men who were there to help? What change was she really going to create?'

The other contretemps was between locals and 'intruders', especially the journalists and online influencers who continued to cover the searches. Rajni recognized a picture of Dani, and remembered her being hectored by a man, who reduced her almost to tears. 'He called her a voyeur, said she didn't understand the pain she was reporting on. It was awkward. I mean, he might've had a point but you could tell it rattled her.' When pressed she couldn't identify the man, who'd been facing away from her. 'I was terribly English, and looking at my feet throughout.'

Dani herself was hard to find, the very reverse of Jake's normal experience of her. She whizzed up on her scooter once, water spraying from the tyres, to boast about following 'a hot lead', but he did not manage to stop her disappearing immediately after.

Jake had been standing outside the Nook at the time, from which Vaughan Mitchell, Rajni's neighbour from the barges, had just emerged. He stood companionably beside Jake, clad in rustling waterproofs, reaching for a cigarette, watching Dani depart.

'You know I've always found something sexy in the sight of a woman on a bike of any kind. I think it must be the thought of being the lucky seat.' He chortled and coughed bluish smoke at the same time. 'Oh, cheer up, Jake. The problem with your generation, if you don't mind me saying, is that you take everything so sodding seriously, including sex. Thank God I'm old. The things I used to say to women would get me shot these days.'

'That's progress for you.' Jake has shifted slightly away from the smoky plume, which is hanging heavy in the still air.

'Is it, though? I'm being serious for once, Jake. You can't compliment a woman on her dress or her hair or her nails any more without being seen as some sort of putative rapist. It used to be good manners, saying how nice a girl looked. Now it's oppression. I don't get it.'

'I reckon it's how you say it, maybe. Women have always been good at spotting creeps. Depends what you're looking to get from it all, I guess.'

'Don't be a prude, Jake. We all of us want the same thing when it comes down to it. And thank God we do.' He killed the cigarette, and patted Jake on the shoulder, letting his hand rest gently. 'Keeps the species alive. Women know that, deep down. Least they should do. Nice seeing you, anyhow.' He walked off towards the river path at a jaunty clip, head bobbing as he went.

The next day, Jake couldn't find Dani at all. He was intrigued by her concept of a 'lead' and even borrowed Livia's phone to look at what she had been saying on her social media. Dani hadn't posted for twenty-four hours, a rare absence for her. When Livia retrieved her phone later, she may have looked at his searches; her eyes blazed fierce and she talked loudly to Diana about her homework, addressing him only in terms of frigid politeness. Even when she isn't there, he thinks, Dani has the power to cause trouble. He tries to put her out of his mind, unsuccessfully – where might she be, and why does he care?

That evening, Jake is in the outskirts of Meryton.

Aletheia has given him a map, which marks the location of the Boathouse Gym, and he walks up to it, a square block of ugly pre-fab on a patch of scrappy land near to the river. It is already dark despite the early hour, the sun abandoned behind a smear of grey cloud, the rain spattering, receding only to return again. The lights inside are on, and Jake can see a large hall-like room, a line of treadmills facing towards him, red-faced souls huffing miserably, going nowhere.

Inside, there is a small reception desk, a bored-looking woman in her early twenties, hunched into her tracksuit, the collar raised up over her ears. She is chewing gum loudly.

Jake gives her his warmest smile. 'D'you mind if I take a look around the gym?'

She points to a sign, which says 'Day membership, £20, available 9–5pm'. He can hear the click of her jawbones, the gentle salivary squelch each time she chews. 'It's five thirty. You could come back tomorrow.'

'I actually just want to have a chat with some people who might be inside.'

'You need membership to go on the gym floor. You need induction. You can't go in without an induction.'

'What would happen if I did? Do you have machines that nobody's ever seen before?'

She is stubborn. 'You need an induction.'

Jake is pondering his next gambit when the door opens, a scurrying blast of wetness with it. He recognizes Antonio, who is wearing long shorts, a tight vest, and an orange beanie that has been darkened by rain. He pulls off his headphones. He seems pleased to see him.

'Jake, right? We was just talking about you the other

day. Whether someone as skinny as you could still be strong as all that. Want to come in and prove it?'

'He needs an induction.' The receptionist is obdurate, pointing to the sign with her outsize, blood-red nail.

'Come on, Jaqueline. He's with me. You trust me, don't you?' Antonio pats her arm. She smiles, chews a little slower.

He turns back to Jake. 'You fancy it, man? MC has been looking into you. Says you're some sort of hero copper, know how to look after yourself. Want to show us youngsters how we don't know nothing about being tough?'

Jake doesn't take long to mull it over. 'Why not? I've not been in a gym for years.' He peers at Jaqueline. 'Not that I need an induction.' She is already looking at her computer, chewing stoically. He nods at Antonio. 'Sure, I'll come along inside.'

'Hero. You're dressed OK for it. For an old man.'

Jake normally wears clothes you can safely exercise in. Today, he is in shorts, flip-flops and a waterproof top. He shrugs it off with a rustle, has a vest on underneath.

Antonio fake-whistles. 'Safe, safe. You're not looking bad for your age, though those bruises are ugly enough. What do you think, J? You know I rescued him from a beating the other day.'

She is appraising his body with the air of a connoisseur. 'Very nice. Not big. Not properly big like you, Ant. But nice.'

Jake thinks he better move on before he develops a complex. Antonio shoulders the door into the changing rooms, winking at Jaqueline as he goes. Inside, it is damp and cramped, little pools of water on the floor, a smell of must and man, of mould and soggy towels.

Antonio explains his weight routine while he gets changed. He is unselfconscious, standing nude, gesticulating widely, his body massive and gleaming, hairless as a baby rat. Soon he is escorting Jake into the gym which looks and feels like every gym he has ever been in: bright lights, scuffed floors, loud and senseless dance music just about overpowering the grunts and clanking equipment.

The boys have commandeered a corner in front of the big mirrors and next to the free weights. An indisputable centre of machismo. Jake watches one woman, lithe and clearly strong, sneak in to grab a weight and move off elsewhere. Wayne whispers something to MC, who explodes with amusement, checking himself in the mirror, how his triceps bulge when he laughs.

Antonio greets his friends with handshakes and half-hugs, makes a big show of bringing Jake along. They seem pleased to see him, which they demonstrate in the firmness of their grips, the percussiveness of their backslaps.

They are well-practised in their routines, determined and precise for all their showiness. They pick outsize weights, of course, but only a little more than good form and sense would dictate. Jake slips easily into their circuits, but with smaller weights, and soon they are conducting an efficient progress around the different stations. He realizes that he is aerobically fitter than them, can cope with the pace of the exercise without too much effort.

As they rest between sets, Jake talks to them about the search for Claire. Wayne remembers the woman who gave the speech about the evils of men. 'It fucked us off, right? And not just us; there were all sorts of people moaning about it. We were there to help, we were being pro-female, and we get told we're the problem.'

MC starts pumping a weight furiously, his huge biceps like four-litre milk bottles, squarish and lumpen. 'Yeah, some beautiful girl gets lost, we want to find her, and we get treated like scum.' He shakes his head, looks for a second, Jake thinks, like a little boy. 'It's impossible to be a guy these days. You know it. However sweet we look after our women, we still get called creeps.'

Wayne rolls his eyes. 'MC and his women. Your man here likes to worship girls, doesn't actually get round to nailing them.' MC flushes, keeps pumping.

Jake is non-committal. Their talk makes him think a bit about what Vaughan had said to him, and that it wasn't just old men who were complaining about the brave new world.

'Did you ever talk to the two women who died after Claire?' Jake carefully brings the subject back to what interests him. 'They were at the search.'

Antonio is serene, a bead of sweat trickling down his face, which is shaved close and blue-black. He is, Jake has observed, the de facto leader of the group. 'That Jade lady came in here once to use the treadmill. We spoke to her, well I did, just to be polite. But she wasn't interested much in a bit of rough like me. I appreciated her form sure enough, but no more. When I saw her on the search, she pretty much blanked me.'

Jake looks at MC questioningly, who is pulling down a weight between his shoulder blades, elbow locked. He shakes his head. As does Wayne, mid sit-up. 'The only thing we got out of going on that search was Toni there being filmed for TikTok. What was the name of the girl, T, who filmed you diving into the water?'

'Dani. She knew you, Jake. She liked seeing me in just

my shorts, bruv, her hand was shaking when she used her camera. I got wet, she got wet, you know what I mean.' Guffaws all round. Jake lets them settle. He is on biceps now, each move slow and controlled, each rep the same as before. 'What do you think happened to the women, then?'

MC shrugs, weights in hand, either in confusion or as part of his routine. Wayne is lifting up his vest to examine his stomach in the mirror, thick slabs of muscle, scored lines across his flesh. Antonio puts down his weight. 'Either they went swimming and drowned, or somebody pushed them in. Hey, maybe it was that woman who wanted men to look bad?'

The conversation turns to protein shakes and supplements. They are baffled by Jake's refusal to try the heavier weights. They want him to understand he could make himself bigger, more cut, if he tried. When he demurs, he senses them growing bored with him. He finishes his final set and tries to get them back on the subject of the missing women. 'You guys were on the search. You've lived around here forever. You didn't see anything at all that might be suspicious?'

Antonio sidles over to him, face wreathed in his perpetual grin, but now tense, somewhat intimidating. He stands too close to Jake, who can smell his deodorant, its sweetness sharpened by the sour scent of the exercising male.

'I'm beginning to feel like we're being interrogated here, Jake. And I'm not sure I like it.'

Jake plays it nonchalant. 'We're only talking, aren't we? I'm just interested in working out if there's been a problem. Something happened on that search, and you lot were there.'

'I tell you what, we'll tell you all we know, we'll remember whatever there is to remember about what we've seen and heard. But you've got to win it from us first.'

'What does that mean?'

Wayne is now on Jake's other side, close as well, two fleshy bookmarks. His grin is also mirthless. 'Show us something, bruv. Prove yourself. Be a man. Or maybe we don't want you in the gym at all.' He slaps Jake's shoulder a little too heavily.

Jake weighs up the situation. 'Are you challenging me to some sort of contest?'

Wayne nods. 'Guys used to have to pass tests to belong, right. That's when men were men. We want you to show us you're a man.'

MC and Antonio nod enthusiastically. Jake swallows, ponders.

'All right lads, I'll tell you what. Let's see if you can do more than just ego-weights. How about a pull-up competition?'

Antonio flexes his shoulders and grins. 'You're on, old man. Our brains if you can beat us. But we need something else too, don't we, boys? A forfeit to punish the weakest.'

'Money?'

'Nah, where's the fun in money? We need something a bit, you know, tastier. You win, we'll help you with being a sort of cop.' His eyes glint. 'But the loser gets a tattoo chosen by the winner, right?'

'Boom!' The other two leap about excitedly, hugging each other, a tumult which ends with Wayne shoving MC into the wall by the drinking fountain. Jake thinks about what Livia would say if he came home with a tattoo selected by one of them. On the other hand, this was a way of keeping in with the group. Maybe they knew something, maybe they didn't. And maybe he wanted to prove he could beat them anyway.

He commits himself. 'All right, deal. Full pull-ups, hands shoulder-width, arms straight at the bottom, chin to the bar at the top. And, because I'm old, I get to go last so I know what I need to beat.'

Antonio lets the moment build, the bright lights still reflecting in his pupils. 'Let's do it, bruv. I'll get things going.' He moves towards the bar at the top of the bench press area, slips his top off and crackles his shoulder muscles. He looks at himself – his perfectly triangular torso – in the sepia reflection of the giant window, through which the lamplight glows, now blurred by a million droplets coursing down the pane.

The gym is nearly empty. Jaqueline is picking up towels, but has paused to watch. The three young women who have been running on a treadmill are looking their way, glad, no doubt, of a distraction. One of them has removed her headphones.

Antonio is big and strong, but he clearly does not regularly do pull-ups like this. After ten, his body is swaying with effort, making each raise harder to control. He has grit at least. Jake watches him clench his jaw and keep going, arms shaking, body slick with sweat. At thirty-one, he can go no further, hangs grimly for a second, then drops to the floor. A scattering of applause. Jaqueline hands him a towel, starts dabbing at him with one of her own.

Wayne is next, now also stripped to the waist, a line of acne scars against his shoulders like whip-marks, angry and red. He is quicker, a little more lithe than Antonio and looks like he will easily beat him. He falters, though, towards the end, dying slowly as he hits twenty-nine.

'MC in the house.' Antonio keeps up his joshing attitude towards the evidently junior member of the group. MC tries to keep his T-shirt on, but they make him remove it. He is astonishingly muscled, heavy with muscles that hang off his frame like too-ripe fruit overwhelming a tree. When he lifts himself his shoulders and back ripple and writhe. But he struggles from the beginning: not enough flexibility or give, too much ballast, he has to jerk his body up each time, an explosion of new energy. After twenty-three, he is done, a howl of anguish as he falls to the floor.

Antonio, his status in his own pack now confirmed, is relaxed. He turns to Jake. 'So twenty-four keeps you away from the tattoo of a dick on your face. Can you do it, bruv?'

Jake feels the competitive surge rise in him. 'It's thirty-two I'm going for. And don't call me bruv.'

'All right, Jake. Shirt off and get to it.'

'I'm keeping my vest on, I reckon.'

'Nope, rules of the game. Gotta show us what you got. Right, J?' Jaqueline shrugs, smiles half-coquettishly.

Jake pulls off his vest, looks down at his body, still holding the pinkish-brown tan of the summer. He is different-shaped to them: no excess bulk, but trim and honed. He also has hair where they have none, bleached pale by the sun on his chest, a few scattered grey tufts merging in; a darker patch leading from stomach to groin. These guys have ten years on him, but he has spent the last three years making his body useful and strong and proportionate. He does countless pull-ups on the big tree by his house at Little Sky almost every day. He swings himself up, feels the ease in his arms as he pulls on the bar, the surge of adrenaline, a sudden sensation of ceaseless strength.

It carries him through. At twenty-five, he is steady, at

thirty-one he can still feel the power lingering in his muscles. He gets to forty, then holds position, his body locked, taut. Then he blows a kiss to Antonio and drops to the floor, the sting in his arms peaking and seeping away. He looks out the window as his breath returns to him. A scooter parked, a glimpse of blond hair under a hood. A woman standing in the rain filming him.

Chapter Twenty-Nine

Livia chuckles as Jake tells the story, as they walk past Chandler Lake the next day. 'I would've loved to see their faces when the old man showed them a thing or two. Why did you bother, though?'

'Vanity, obviously. They're all quite a bit stronger than me, and they were letting me know it. And we're looking for some detail that explains this all, aren't we? It's worth an extra effort trying to find it. They were at the searches, they've been around.'

'Did they know anything?'

'A little bit when they finally talked. Antonio was interesting. He seemed conflicted about the women: on the one hand he liked the thought of rescuing them, on the other he felt that the attention they were getting would be used to criticize men like him. He didn't like how the story was being reported, especially by people like Dani, skewed against men, he thought, and the locals and the village more generally. Clearly the searches weren't the cosy gatherings they seemed to be on the outside, there was a lot of tension there.'

'You mean Jess's speech?'

'That's one thing. I showed them one of Martha's pictures in the changing room afterwards, and it was definitely her.'

'I figured as much. She's said something similar to me when I went for my lesson. Not sure it means anything.'

'I've got to the point where I don't know what anything means. They described the guy who shouted at Dani, and it sounds like it was David, the doctor from the barges. Most of the locals are annoyed at her and her lot for being so intrusive. And you'll be pleased that I've not spoken to her in days.' Livia grimaces, says nothing. 'Now, Aletheia says the scale of the official investigation is going to get reduced because there's no confirmed evidence of foul play in any of the bodies. She'll stick around but not for much longer.'

'Meanwhile, we don't know whether it's safe to be near the river at night.'

They are walking, hand in hand. He can feel her ring against his palm, a physical reminder of what had so joyfully happened back at Little Sky. They stroll past Chicken City, stand and watch the birds fuss and peck, the sounds of soft croonings and grumblings. They are planning one final session in the library that night, to see what lines are left to explore, if any. Ahead of that, the morning feels like stolen time, Diana at school, no place to go but their own land.

'Did you agree a tattoo for that poor boy? What does he call himself? MC?'

'I did feel sorry for him. It's weird, he almost wants me to go through with it, so he can prove himself to the others. They tried to get me to agree to all sorts of horrors. I said I'd think of something, and get back to them. He told me he'd keep patrolling the riverbank, make himself useful, and come see me when he had something to report. He said he wanted to prove not all men were awful.'

When Livia walks, she cradles the outline of her stomach in one hand, as if she has to keep touching the bump to ensure it is real. Since the night last year when they found spots of blood on her legs, there have been no panics. She keeps telling Jake how she is strong and healthy, even if they can never be entirely free from worry. On days like this, though, the world teeming all around her, she has somehow become an aspect of nature, part of an outpouring of life, of life renewing itself, irresistible and everlasting.

They make their normal circuit, bending around back to the house when Livia stops.

'Jake, is that an old message for me? It's not your usual colour.'

A flutter of colour, Barbie pink. A sign on Sherlock Beech.

Jake hesitates for a moment, and then explains what happened with Dani, how she had summoned him with her shirt. Livia looks appalled. 'Are you saying she's stolen Sherlock Beech from us?'

'Of course not. Lily told her about it, and she was doing it to be, I don't know, provocative. She wanted to tell me about finding Isabelle's phone. I told her not to do it. I mean the phone thing was useful, and she took me to see where it'd been found, but I said using the tree was totally wrong.'

Livia is scuffing the ground with her boot. 'Hang on, she took you to see it? How?'

'On her scooter.'

'You two sharing a seat, pressed up against that little fat bottom of hers? Why on earth didn't you tell me?' There are tears in her eyes.

'Maybe because you're reacting like this.'

'No. No. Don't do that. I'm reacting like this *because* you didn't tell me. I'm merrily plodding along, fucking pregnant, celebrating being engaged, buying all your romance, your candlelit fucking grotto bath, and you're touring the countryside with some young thing who's constantly telling you how hot you are.'

'Liv, Liv, what did you want me to do? Ignore her?'

She shoves him in disbelief. 'That's precisely what I wanted you to do then, and what I want you to do now. She's trouble, she's trying to insinuate herself not only into all our worries about missing women, but into our lives too, Jake. Jesus. Everywhere you go in the last week, she pops up, simpering. It's disgusting.'

Jake turns and grabs her arm, holding her to him. He can feel her heart race, her body pulse with anger. 'Liv, slow down. I adore you. I adore nobody else. You must know that. Just tell me, what do you want?'

'I want you to humour me, and keep away from her. However unreasonable you silently think it is, I don't want to know. I want you to acknowledge that you're not free to flirt with someone who is flirting like that with you. Can you do that little thing?'

He thinks. He had been flattered by Dani, more than once; he had let himself be flirted with, enjoyed the little rub to his ego. He knows, ruefully, that there have been times in this last week where he's chased that feeling of being young again, part of the world of excitement and uncertainty, of banter and unfamiliarity, of competition. It was there in the gym too. He feels the ache across his shoulder blades where the pull-ups had left their mark.

He kisses Livia on the cheek, slight tang of a salty tear. 'I do get why you're angry, though I also want you to know I've done nothing and would do nothing with anybody else, however flirty they are.'

She kisses him on the mouth, fervent. 'That's what I wanted to hear.'

Something nags at him, though. A thought passes through his mind, visible to Livia in his eyes. 'So what is it?'

'She said she'd only use the tree as a sign in an emergency. She was half-joking, but still. I think I should check on her, just make sure she's OK.'

Livia half-shrieks. 'Jake, don't be such a moron. Of course she's OK, of course it's not a fucking emergency. She wants to get you running to her, to prove she can. If you go, it'll show that everything you've just said is untrue. If you go, it'll humiliate me.'

'What if she's in trouble?'

'She *is* the trouble. Seriously, Jake. You can't go running to her. Or you can, but don't expect me to be here when you get back.'

Livia starts for the house at a crisp march, refusing to look back. It takes him a few seconds to catch up with her, his hand outstretched to interlock with hers. A whisper in her ear. 'You're right. I don't owe Dani anything. She's been making mischief since she got here. I know why it's annoyed you.'

Livia doesn't reply, the flush to her cheeks revealing her emotion. But she slows her pace, allows her hand to relax into his. Together they go back to the house. The mood is heavy, tension still pools and simmers, but – like with the sky outside – there seems to be no longer the danger of an immediate outpouring. Jake and Livia are excessively polite to one another, and glad when Diana returns to be boisterous and distracting, to relieve the strain of the two of them alone.

That night, Aletheia misses dinner, and is not back by Diana's bedtime. Jake and Livia head to the library for the meeting with Martha.

They sit together on the sofa, waiting for her to come online. The fire is crackling, the cold evening air sauntering through the window in pleasing contrast. Mendelssohn's Hebrides Overture is playing softly, gentle drama in the quiet.

They hear Aletheia before she gets to the library, bursting into the kitchen, door slammed, her boots loud and swift on the stone-flagged floor. She walks through the door just as Martha's screen blips on. Martha looks troubled. Aletheia looks worse.

She strides to the middle of the room. 'I've just come back from the station. They've found another body in the river, dead. Hell, I don't know what to say. It's Dani.'

Book Four: Downstream

But the majestic river floated on,
Out of the mist and hum of that low land,
Into the frosty starlight.
        Matthew Arnold, 'Sohrab and Rustum'

Chapter Thirty

Back in the mortuary once more. Dawn encroaching outside, bringing faint colour to grey outlines. Jake is standing with Aletheia in the outer room. They both look drawn, feel bleak. He can taste sleeplessness, bitter in his mouth.

Their meeting, late the night before, had gone long. Livia had gasped at the news, squeezed his hand so hard it hurt. Aletheia's summary was terse: 'We're lucky to have found her so quickly. She bobbed up here.' She pointed to the map pinned to the wall. The site was between the barges and Talboys cottage, in yet another curve of the river. 'Two birdwatchers saw something floating late this afternoon, raised the alarm. We pulled her out here.' She gestured to another spot. 'The pathologist's initial view was that she'd been in the water for not much more than a few hours.'

'Not killed at night like the others,' Jake murmured to himself.

Livia had been silent, paled. She and Jake had seen the

sign on Sherlock Beech earlyish that morning. Jake kept his hand in place, stroking her arm with one free finger.

There was silence. Martha peered into her camera, scornful. 'Come on, people, we shouldn't just be staring at our shoelaces. Those of us lucky enough to have shoelaces, that is. It's another victim, another part of the puzzle. What does it tell us?'

Jake looked up. 'It tells us coincidence has now been stretched beyond breaking point.' His voice was weak, feathery.

Livia came to sit heavily at the table, head in her hands. 'There's more. She tried to tell us something was wrong. We – which is to say, I – ignored her.' Her throat pulsed in a suppressed sob. Jake explained what had happened with the tree.

Martha, to her immense credit, Jake thought, refused to palter. 'You reacted how any of us would've reacted. Her death doesn't make her any the less annoying. All it means is another point for us to consider. It's evidence. Everything is evidence. Dani was the very definition of someone involved in the other cases. It was her life. She was on the search. It proves a thread of connection between the victims. Terrible though it is, this'll help us find out what happened to the other women.'

Livia stood. 'I see that. I just can't help with it now. You work through stuff. I need to be by myself.' She shrugged off Jake's solicitous grab, walked out of the house. Jake could see her make it as far as the lake, sit down on the bench, stare into the blackness of the water beyond. She was uplit by pearl-toned lamplight, a mournful and sterile glow.

He kept an eye on her as they spoke, compared notes

on the various other people who had been involved in the searches with Dani, set Martha off on an electronic hunt through all of Dani's online activities. As they wrapped up, Livia returned, faint grimace on her face, and took herself off to bed. At the first glimmering of dawn, Jake wrote her a tender note and headed out for the hospital. The post-mortem was scheduled for that morning, but they wanted to observe the body for themselves, see if it could tell them anything before too much time had been lost.

Aletheia is the first to open the doors to the inner sanctum. Her pass had enabled them to get past the uniformed police waiting outside. Jake follows her tentatively. He feels a sadness within him. He had liked Dani, in spite of the problems she'd caused. She had been somehow trapped – victimized even – by much of the modern world he had largely escaped from. Sarah had noticed something else, something he had instinctively felt too: her loneliness, how much she wanted real connection and affirmation.

She has none now. Her body is in the middle of the room, a lifeless and unfeeling slab, the whiteness of her skin catching the jaundiced tone of the lights above. There are no marks upon her. Hardly any bold lines at all, as if she were made from deathly pallor alone, soft merging curves and ash-blond hair, darkened faintly at her eyebrows and pubic area. Her feet, which Jake had seen flashing upon the grass by the river in gleeful dance, are thick and swollen. She smells of the river.

Jake recoils as he thinks of her as she once was: a living, unassailable force, the way she touched him, insinuated herself towards him, the way he had been intrigued, even tantalized by her despite himself. It was what Livia had sensed. And that force of life was now spent, that potency gone. Jake walks around her, head lowered in thought. A tiny flash of colour strikes his eye. Pink varnish on her toenails. Pink like the cloth on Sherlock Beech that could have summoned him to her.

An idea strikes him hard, so hard his knees buckle. He turns to Aletheia, who is looking at a file. 'Al, I need to check something. Can I borrow your car? I'll be back before the autopsy's over.'

She flips her keys to him immediately. 'What is it?'

He hesitates. 'Quick, pass me those files first.' He flicks through them. Aletheia has brought the records of all the victims with her, and he races between each physical description of their bodies. He holds photos up to the light. He can feel the pulse in his temple throbbing. He takes a sheet from one file, folds it in his pocket.

'Have you got a phone?'

Aletheia looks like she is going to make a joke, but thinks better of it. She hands him her device. He stabs at the screen, finally accesses Dani's YouTube page. He leans against a cupboard as he watches the most recent video: Dani on a patch of sun-stroked grass, talking about her latest theory. She is feverish with energy, one protracted shot taken from above her head down the full length of her body, her feet clawing the green turf so it sprouts between her toes. Jake exhales loudly, kills the screen, tosses it back to Aletheia.

'Yep, I need your car. I'll look after it.'

'Go, and come back and tell me what the hell you're thinking. I need to stay here anyway, wait for the PM.'

He hastens outside. It is a little lighter now, the cool of the night still lingering, the car park empty, a scrap of litter fluttering and forlorn. One of the main hospital buildings looms over him, a tessellation of square windows, most of them brightly lit. He watches the figures, uniform-clad and brisk, flitting within, bustling around beds or marching up the stairwell. Hospitals don't ever sleep, but this one is definitely waking up from its quietness.

Jake presses the key and the car comes to life. It is all a little flashier and faster than he is used to. When he pushes what used to be called the ignition, the whole dashboard of electronics lights up, blinking symbols and figures, a horde of superfluous options. He just wants to move from here to where he is going, and for a moment can't quite work out where the 'drive forward' function is.

He switches the car off, composes himself. Tries again, clicking off every extraneous feature, and then moves a lever so the screen confidently illuminates the letter 'D'. No roar of an engine, just a serene surge forward, which is all he is looking to do.

Half an hour later, Jake is through Westerby and coming up to the cottage Isabelle had rented with her boyfriend. Jake hopes above everything Philip Carr hasn't cut his losses and gone back to the city. The drive has done him good. He feels energized, magnetized almost; determined to stop being so passive, to uncover the secrets that have sat so frustrating over the last few days. He couldn't save Dani, but he could avenge her, or at least explain her death, something she certainly would have wanted. Her story told. *Everything is content.*

Jake parks the car by the side of the road, experimenting with buttons he hopes will keep it in place, then runs down the short lane to the cottage. Morning has broken. There is warmth in the air, the seeping quiet of night has gone, and the trees and hedgerows are alive with movement. The sun is low and clementine-hued, a pair of jays flap and joust with one another in an apple tree, chit-chattering.

Jake bangs on the cottage door, loudly and hopefully. He is rewarded by a twitch of a curtain in the bedroom. Jake bangs again to keep Phil motivated to get up.

'It's Jake, I need a word. Something important.'

The door opens, and Phil's head emerges, hair tousled, eyes heavy with disturbed sleep. 'What is it, man? It's the middle of the night.'

'Look at that big ball of fire in the sky. That makes it morning in my book. Look, I'm sorry to disturb you, but I need to ask you a question. There's been another death.'

Phil looks startled. 'Come in, I'll make coffee.' He is wearing blue-and-white-striped pyjama bottoms, an old, shapeless T-shirt. He switches on the machine, and looks for clean cups.

'Phil . . .' Jake is twitchy, eager to speak right away.

'I can't talk before my coffee. Then I'll be as chatty as you like.'

Jake remains tense as he watches the man down a double espresso, brewing another one for them both. They take their drinks to the living room and sit opposite each other. The room smells musty; there is a full ashtray on the table, two empty red wine bottles.

'Drowned my sorrows a bit last night. I'm paying for it this morning. Now how can I help?'

'Something you said when we spoke last time. You mentioned that Isabelle didn't like jewellery and make-up; she wasn't keen on "ornamentation". I think that was the word you used. D'you remember?'

'Sure, man. It was a good thing she looked so beautiful, you know, natural. She never needed to bother with much, and preferred everything simple.' He sighs deeply. 'Shit, I miss her.'

'This is important. Did she wear nail varnish on her fingers or toes?'

'I'm sorry?'

'Humour me. It's a simple question. Painted nails. Did she have them?'

Phil is making every visible effort to think carefully. 'No, I'd say not. Never when she was with me. As I said, she didn't like stuff like that, natural beauty was one of her things. I'm positive.'

Jake hands him the photo taken by the forensic team, which he has folded in half just to reveal Isabelle's lower extremities. Sure enough, it shows two feet with neatly painted nails, pink and artificial-looking.

'I guess I didn't look there when I saw her to ID the body. She had a sheet over her then. But I'd swear she had no coloured toenails when I left her, nor any time before that. And I've never seen that colour on her. Not her style.'

'Would you say that under oath?'

Phil swells, aggressive. 'Of course, it's the truth.'

Jake reaches out and shakes his hand. 'I'm so grateful. Thank you.'

'Did I help, are you on to something?'

But Phil is talking to Jake's back, as he makes for the door. Soon he is hurtling around the narrow lanes back to the hospital, mind alive again. Back at the morgue, he bursts into the outer room, Aletheia now standing with McAllister, neither smiling.

Jake is almost out of breath. 'Toenails, guys. We need to look at their toenails.'

Chapter Thirty-One

An impressive silence ensues. Aletheia breaks it. 'What are you talking about?'

'Come here.' He feels excited, his blood hectic in his body, the thrill of the possible breakthrough. He kicks open the door. There are two masked and robed figures finishing up their examination. The sight stills Jake briefly. Dani has been examined, turned inside out. However undignified she had looked when he left, now it was worse, her body ribboned with cuts and sutures, her viscera removed, blood drained. She has moved from being dead to being a corpse, a travesty of itself.

The pathologist, whom Jake had met before, senior to the doctor who had performed the autopsy on Isabelle, raises his hands in warning. 'This is an autopsy. You cannot simply kick the door in, Mr Jackson. In fact' – he looks at McAllister, who is in the doorway – 'it's not clear to me that you have authority to be here at all.'

Jake can barely hear him. He waves Aletheia and McAllister over. 'Look at Dani's feet. I can swear that when

I saw her, what – a few days ago? When I saw her, she had no nail varnish on her feet.'

The pathologist drops an instrument noisily into a steel basin. 'That's the revelation? I fail to see how it justifies this sort of intrusion.'

Aletheia hushes him with a gesture. 'Go on. Why couldn't she have put it on since?'

'She could've. But my theory is she didn't. And I just checked her latest YouTube post, which is more recent: no varnish there either. Now,' he exhales, pauses, 'now look at the description of Isabelle's body in the file: "bright pink toenails". And I remembered her boyfriend telling me that she didn't like make-up or cosmetics. She had none in her room. She didn't wear nail varnish.' He turns to look at McAllister. 'And he told me this morning that the last time he saw her, the day she died, she'd had none on.'

There is a cynical snort from the doctor. McAllister's eyes flicker, reptilian, in his direction, then narrow dangerously. 'What about Jade?'

'Glad you asked. Her body had degenerated, but, again, check the file, evidence of pink nail polish on her feet. Three women who all searched for Claire, three women, all with pink nail polish, the same shade, three women all dead.'

'I've had enough of this. I'd like you to leave my examining room.' The doctor is sternly officious.

'I'd like you to shut the fuck up.' Jake seldom, if ever, allows himself to lose his temper, but he can feel gall rising within.

'How dare you?' The bluster bubbles forth from behind the doctor's mask.

'He dares. Leave it at that.' Aletheia ushers Jake away

before he can pursue the point further. Her tolerance for prissiness is similar to Jake's but she sees that nothing can be gained from a row here. The three of them walk back outside, into the air, which feels fresh and bright, the wind's bluster a welcome cleansing.

She points through a small gate at one end of the car park. 'There's a picnic area over there. Let's sit down and talk.'

You would only picnic here in desperation, Jake thinks, perhaps awaiting the news of a loved one's operation. It is a hardscrabble bit of untended landscape, kicked and scuffed and littered with cigarette butts. But it is empty. They arrange themselves at a table.

Aletheia takes the lead. 'So walk us through the theory again.'

'The theory is not much of a theory, yet. We're looking for evidence of intervention, aren't we? The bodies are all too clean, too untouched, there's nothing to point to a murder, or a murderer. And yet they're piling up.' He swivels to McCallister. 'Chief, do you accept that we're dealing with a serial killer?'

He is typically cautious, slow in his response. 'I accept that not all of the women can have died by natural causes, and I'm suspicious that they share so many things in common.'

'And that's where I'm headed. The three later victims share three things in common, in fact. One, dead in the water with no marks. Two, they were all involved in the searches for Claire. Three, they all have pink nail varnish on their toes, despite evidence that we know at least two of them didn't wear it themselves.'

McCallister nods. 'Four, they were all in some stage of

undress: Jade naked, Isabelle in her underwear, and Dani was naked too, actually.'

Aletheia is tracing her long fingers on the scarred wooden surface. 'So the theory-that's-not-a-theory is that someone killed them, stripped them, painted their toes and left them in the water.'

Jake is undeterred. 'That's it, yes.'

McAllister leans back. 'Dear God, Jake. You want me to go to my boss, to the fucking press, with that? Don't most women have painted nails?'

Aletheia shakes her head. 'No, they don't, and not the same colour. It's well beyond coincidence.'

'So you both want me to go to my boss with your feeling of a bit more than coincidence?'

Jake puts his hand on McAllister's knee. 'I don't want you to do anything, Chief. I'm only ever half-official at best. I can look at things you can't, but you just need to keep this going as a murder hunt. And then I'll try to convince you that I'm right. If I'm right.'

'I agree.' Aletheia is siding with Jake. 'And it's not like you have a better theory, or any theory.'

McAllister grimaces. 'Ain't that the truth, though.'

Jake is deep in thought, the conversation almost incidental to him. 'There are still problems, which I want to work through tonight, with Martha. One, how did they die? They were alive when they went in the river, because they have water in their lungs. So I guess my theory would have to be: they were made unconscious in a way that left no mark, undressed or mostly undressed, their toes painted, and then pushed into the river to drown. Does that sound possible?'

'Two, how does this fit in with Claire?' Aletheia now

has her pen out, scratching notes. 'Not naked, and – I just checked – no painted feet.'

'Aye, Jake, that's the thing,' complains McAllister. 'The whole point of this is to connect everything all the way back to her. This doesn't.'

'I wonder if Claire is connected, but not part of the chain, if you like. What links the other women is the search *for* Claire. Her death seems to have started things off: the concern spreads, you get the search, then you get the following three deaths. What happened to her is set to one side, somehow; it's the beginning, but not the main event. Does that make sense?'

'It does.' Aletheia is encouraging. 'But, looking at the chief's face, I can see how it doesn't help him make the case clear to other people.' She turns to McAllister. 'What's your plan now?'

He stands. 'You can come watch. I've got to do a press conference, in which I'll say that we're treating this death as connected to the other three, that we're following active leads, and that women especially should not go near the river at night, or in the day on their own. Dani was killed, or died, in the morning.'

'Do we know when?' Jake thinks immediately of Livia.

'Not yet, and I'm not sure we'll get a really clear timing to the nearest hour.' His phone bleeps. He looks at the message. 'They've found her phone, washed to the edge of the water. It's back at base, come on – we should go check it out.'

He strides across the ground, and Jake and Aletheia, filled with a shared sense of purpose, leap up to follow him.

Chapter Thirty-Two

Two hours later, they are sitting in the shade of an ash tree by the village hall near Westerby, watching the press set up for McAllister's statement. There are plenty of cameramen, heavily burdened, red-faced, shuffling about. Even more journalists, either tired-looking veterans or impossibly young newbies, on their first gigs, working for the minor networks or websites that seldom can afford people older than twenty-five. Almost everyone is on their phones, and there is a hum of expectation. Jake half-recognizes a news presenter, holding herself aloof in well-tailored clothes and immaculate boots, her skin over-taut, like it has been stretched over a drum. Dani would have enjoyed the crowd, he thinks, would have felt she was as important as anyone there.

He yawns. Neither he nor Aletheia have slept. He lies back, head against the trunk; she remains erect, her back stiff, her movements still precise.

'Al, I meant to ask about what happened with the wife-beater. You know: Paul Sansom. I've not had a whisper from him.'

She leans back on her elbows, so her head is level with him. 'One of my lot paid him a visit. Explained he was on the radar, would be in trouble if he meddled any further, or did anything that drew our attention, including anything that threatened his wife. I'm sure it worked; my guy would've been pretty persuasive.'

The phrase 'my lot', Jake thinks, could mean a range of people within the security apparatus. And he has no doubt that it would involve some extremely intimidating characters. 'Thanks for doing that.'

'My pleasure. I've obviously got no fondness for blokes like Sansom. Thick and weak and hurtful. He was endangering our investigation too. He never looked good for it, though, did he?'

'No, but we only checked his alibi really for Claire. We should try it for the others as well, just to be sure.'

'I'll get one of McAllister's team to do it. Another visit from the coppers will scare him even further.'

The hubbub increases, as the sense arises – by that strangely tacit form of communication which happens with all crowds – that proceedings are about to start. Jake sits up, stretches his tired arms, smells the sourness of his unwashed body. 'How are they treating you, the locals?'

'Because I'm an outsider from the city who outranks them, or because I'm Black, or because I'm a woman?'

'Any, or all of them. I don't know, I was just making conversation.'

'Well, to take your attempts at conversation seriously, Mr Jackson, I'd say that I'm granted respect but, with some exceptions, not much warmth. And I'm sure unkind things are said behind my back. But I can't entirely ever know what bit of my strangeness they're objecting to.'

'Does it bother you?'

She pats his knee. 'Jake, I wouldn't have got here if I let things like that bother me. I reckon I still feel it as a blow, at some level. It also makes me realize I'm lucky to work cases with people who treat me right, like you and Martha. And Liv, of course, though she's not in the business. I appreciate it, I appreciate you.'

He covers her hand with his own. 'Right back at you, Al. Now let's listen, McAllister's here to show off for the press.'

He has put on his suit jacket, buttoned his tie. His voice is clipped and serious. He sounds impressive, projects confidence, leaves the audience believing that, even if he doesn't have the answers, he is on the way to getting them.

The questions come after his terse statement, everyone keen to get a line that emphasizes the scale of the problem, that will create news. 'Is there a serial killer on the loose?' 'Have you ever seen a case like this before?' 'Are women safe on the river?'

On the final point, McAllister leans forward, seizes the opportunity. 'I want to be crystal clear on this. Until we have identified any perpetrators, nobody, especially women, should be near the river after dark, and no woman should be alone there at any time. We will get justice, but we need support and common sense until we do. Thank you.'

The hum rises as he walks off. That last answer is a good one, a line that will travel, be clipped for the bulletins, be used as the basis for studio discussions and phone-ins: modern Britain, where you can't take a walk at night in the countryside because your life might be in danger, where women are warned not to go outside without accompaniment, where men can't be trusted; a country in crisis. Plenty for the press to chew over, take aim at. Jake knows that McCallister's bosses, like the mayor in *Jaws*, want him to preach a message of calm, but honesty like this is safer. He could have ducked the issue for an easier life, and he chose to do the right thing.

They wait until the crowd has cleared, reporters filing copy on laptops in their cars, correspondents doing two-ways standing on the bank, the river shimmering brilliantly, ink-blue in the afternoon sun, now a central character in this great drama. 'Police are investigating what led four women', one journalist is solemnly intoning, 'to drown in the river that lies peacefully behind me. The sun may shine on them today, but these are now regarded as . . .' A portentous pause. 'Dark waters.'

In the hall, there is a great deal of bustle and activity. Jake and Aletheia are ushered into McAllister's office. He is taking his tie off. 'How'd I do?'

'Like Rebus himself.'

'Never heard of him. Now.' He grabs a clear evidence bag, with a phone in it, its outside striped black and yellow. 'Look at this. We think it's Dani's phone, because the case is fairly distinctive. But we can't open it. Something has gone wrong with it. Which reminds us . . .'

Aletheia finishes his sentence. 'Of Isabelle's phone. Martha was interested in that too. Are you sending it to a lab?'

'It's about to be put in a car now. I'll make sure she gets access to the results.'

'That's kind, though she'll get access to them anyway.'

McAllister frowns indulgently. 'I don't need to know that.'

After digging through statements for a while, Jake leaves Aletheia – who seems to have struck a second wind – to keep working. He wants a swim, and a sleep, and to make sure Livia is OK. He finds her, outside her own cottage, about to get in the car.

They hug, but she is distant, tightly wound, a little too much in control. 'Di has gone to Jo's house for a play with her kids. I thought I'd do some potting. I need to do something with my hands.'

'I won't make the obvious joke. I'll come meet you after and then we can pick up Di.'

'Jake, you don't need to escort me from a house to a car. I'm not weak.'

'You're the opposite of weak. But these are strange times, and by now hardly anyone will want to be by the river.' He explains what has happened that morning, his theory of the painted toenails.

She listens distantly. 'That sounds like something you'd come up with. And I can sort of see it.' Her voice drops a fraction. 'Did you find out when Dani was killed?'

'Not yet. We may never know accurately.'

She swallows, says nothing.

'Liv, it doesn't matter when she died. Even if I'd gone looking for her when I saw the sign, I would've had no idea where she was, or what she was doing. She could've been already in trouble, already drowned. We had no chance to save her, whatever we did.'

Livia is crying, tears milky on her face, her chest heaving. 'I fucking *hated* her for using Sherlock Beech, and for flirting with you. And now she's just . . . gone. She'll never do anything, become anything. And I wanted her gone, that's the thing I can't shake, I would've pressed a button to get rid of her, I thought terrible things. What sort of person am I?'

She leans in to him, and he holds her tight, feels the very sinews of her shoulders, her muscle shifting beneath his grip. 'Liv, you're a wonderful person, my favourite person. You can't be judged for the thoughts you have in anger. Everyone's guilty of that.'

She speaks into his jumper, he can feel the seeping moisture of her breath. 'I didn't just think it. I did something. I stopped you even having the chance of finding her. Because I didn't trust you not to be swayed by some young thing who thought you were great.'

'She thought I was at the centre of something that excited her. And, look, I made you feel jealous, I enjoyed the attention a bit too much. I could've told you about her sooner, I could've reassured you more. We're none of us ever perfect.'

She holds the clinch tight, her fingers digging into his skin. 'Thank you, lovey. But I still feel hollow, like I don't trust myself any more.' She looks at her watch. 'Listen, I've got to go, I booked myself in with Emma for a session. See if that woo-woo stuff is real, shall we? And I wouldn't mind you meeting me there, of course I wouldn't.'

'Would you mind me asking Jess a few questions about her speech during the search?'

'I'm not sure she'll co-operate, but you can ask. Otherwise, it's a nice enough afternoon, you can have a snooze while you wait.'

At Talboys, Livia is welcomed effusively, Jess ushering her in to the studio. Jake is not asked over the threshold. He can hear Emma greeting Livia, sees the kiss planted on her cheek. There is jazz music playing, as ever, staccato drums, the bray of vibrato trumpet. Jess returns to fill the doorway. She folds her arms, winces her mouth into an approximation of a smile.

'Are you going to wait outside?'

'Is that a bit like the Scottish phrase: "you'll have had your tea"?' He gets nothing back for this. 'Are you inviting me in?'

'We find that an audience inhibits the creative process.'

'Sounds awful. Why don't you come out and talk to me for five minutes? And then I'll go and wait somewhere else, just so I don't accidentally inhibit the creative process.'

Jess sighs, and closes the door behind her. She is wearing a black jumpsuit, her skin pale and freckled, her frame taut; her hair gleams fiery in the sun. They walk to the river, sit on the wide stump there. A barge slowly passes them with nobody aboard in sight. There are no joggers or dog-walkers on the path. The current picks up speed here, and there is a pleasant rill of running water.

'Hard to imagine anything bad happening when it looks like this.' Jake is purposefully bland.

Jess's glance towards him is austere. 'And yet bad things happen in beautiful places all the time. I heard on the news about that woman Dani. Devastating. I suppose she must've been murdered.'

'I think so. We can't come up with a cause of death, but there are good reasons to think this wasn't an accident.'

'Some angry, inarticulate, frenzied man, at a guess. Who can do nothing other than desecrate beauty, spoil it.' It is a statement, not a question.

'There's no sign of frenzy, but all experience would suggest it was a man. It normally is.'

She shrugs as if to accept the truism as not even worth saying. He perseveres. 'The three women who died after Claire had all been involved in the search for her. That's a possible link.' He stretches his legs out, so his toes touch the damp edge of the water. 'You were on the search too.'

'Does that make me a suspect or a potential victim?'

Jake doesn't answer that one. 'You made a speech, ruffled a few feathers . . .'

She chuckles, scornful. 'It was scarcely a speech. From memory, I simply stated the truth that Claire was likely the victim of male anger and violence. Even if she'd killed herself, there would've been a man behind it, a man who limited her life somehow.'

'I met her husband, who was completely bereft. I wonder if you'd have been so bold if you'd seen the grief on his face.'

'His grief doesn't alter my basic point.'

'But why bother making it at all? Who were you going to convert?'

A flush of anger, mottling her neck. 'I bothered saying it, because it needs saying. Otherwise, these things happen and nobody cares, nobody changes anything.'

'The reason people were on that search was because they already cared.'

'Come on, Jake, you don't believe that. Some people were there because it was exciting, some were there to walk their dogs, some to get a bit of sun, a bit of gossip. Some – like poor dear Dani – were there to make videos. The missing woman, Claire, was just a pretext, soon to be forgotten.'

'But she hasn't been forgotten, and her death seems to be echoing on.'

'Only in a perverse way. Because we live in a society where men regularly kill women. Look, Jake.' She turns to him, puts a cautious hand on his arm. 'I'm sure you're not a bad guy, but you're a guy. You can't understand this stuff unless you've experienced it.'

He weighs this up for a second. 'You seem to underrate empathy. It strikes me that by listening to people, by – I don't know – reading books, people can understand all sorts of things outside their experience. Otherwise, we're all just trapped.'

'No, Jake, *we're* trapped. *Women* are trapped. You're not, and never have been.'

'That sounds a bit defeatist to me.'

'I don't care what the truth sounds like. You see, even when you found Claire's body, the discovery didn't bring anything along with it, did it? She's dead, the world continues, the river flows past.' She looks wistful, pulls at a weed growing up from the dead wood. Tears at it with the tips of her fingers. 'As a policeman, aren't you struck by how *small* tragedy is, when it all comes down to it? These events that end a life, uproot a family; they cause all that pain and pouf . . .' She lets the tattered stem fall. 'Gone. Huge in the moment, and then tiny thereafter.' She catches herself. 'You didn't come here for a philosophy lesson.'

Jake has had similar thoughts, often in fact. The indifference of the world to individual tragedy is so manifest. 'Life goes on' is a cliché, a soothing thing to say, a palliative remark, but it is also bitterly accurate: death stops one person, all other life persists in its wake. Even the most bereaved relative has to eat and sleep and dress and talk; the clock still ticks, the rhythm of existence never changes.

He stirs himself from the gloomy thought. 'I came because I'm interested in what you've got to say. I don't entirely agree with it, but I understand the point of view. Did you see anything suspicious during the search?'

'You mean apart from my own behaviour?'

'That's a given.'

'As I said, I was somewhat sceptical of my fellow searchers. If you ask me to accept a killer was there, revelling in it all, I could well believe it. It wasn't sombre, it wasn't reflective.'

Jake gives a wintry smile.

'What?'

'It always strikes me that people who want the best for the world are a little bit disappointed in those that actually live in it.'

She bristles, and doesn't acknowledge the point. 'Emma and I didn't speak to our fellow men and women much. We harrumphed a bit over Dani and her showing off. I did notice a man away from the group, who wasn't searching, but kept showing up at various points humping a pack. He had his eyes on the ground, but I remember saying to Emma that I couldn't imagine him seeing anything.'

'I've met him. He lost his daughter to an intruder, and his wife left him.'

'I'm no psychologist, Jake, but that might be a good place to start.'

'Places to start are not my problem. By the way, did you see someone get angry with Dani during the search?'

'As I said, I wasn't thrilled with her behaviour myself. I think there was a man grumbling at her, but it wasn't violent or anything. He was being forthright, but still polite. He was there with an Indian lady, I think. Said his piece, and moved on.'

She stands up, and makes a move to go. The sun is behind her, bright halo encircling the flame of her hair, so she looks for a second like a torch burning bright. Jake stands alongside her. He is only three inches taller.

'I know I'm a member of the hated patriarchy, but you

might try and see that you don't have the monopoly on good intentions.'

'Please try not to patronize me.'

'Maybe you could do the same in return.' He holds out a hand, impulsively. She pauses, then responds. Her touch is cold. She turns on her heels and walks back to the house. Jake lowers himself down on the soft grass by the side of the stump. It has been warmed by the sun, and he sinks back gratefully. There is a pleasant sweet scent of damp and old mud. He mulls over his conversation with Jess. He still needs to ask David, Rajni's husband, about the row he clearly had with Dani, but did it mean anything? It's been a long day already, and soon he is breathing deeply, asleep.

Livia shakes him awake a couple of hours later. The sun is behind a cloud, a chill has descended. It's one sign of summer coming to an end, the way late afternoon no longer clings to the warmth of its preceding hours, as if each day enacts in miniature the annual coming of the cold.

'Lovey, I hate to disturb you, but we need to get Di.'

Jake is a little frustrated with himself. 'I'm sorry. Some help I'd have been if a killer had come.'

She helps him to his feet. 'I've no doubt that you would have leapt out of the reeds to save me. How was Jess? She came back with a strange expression on her face. I just told her that you had a bemusing effect on everybody.'

They walk back up to the car. 'It was interesting. She strikes me as someone who could really help us. Equally, she's clever enough, no question, to hide something crucial just to leave us aimless and confused.'

'Why would she do that?'

'There's more to her than meets the eye. She's involved in all this, but I just can't work out how.'

Chapter Thirty-Three

A week passes. The whole area feels like it is in lockdown, especially in the evenings and at night. People hasten home with the dusk, the long stretches of riverbank are empty of walkers and runners, no chunky-suited toddlers waddling and throwing bread for the ducks, no friends sitting companionably. The weather helps, as autumn reaches forth early, with gusty winds and squally showers. Many more leaves dance down and carpet the ground, become slick and slimy, mulching when you do walk on them.

The media response to Dani's death was fevered and intrusive. Online influencers were keen to make a martyr of Dani, in a way that both commemorated her work and rendered their own more sympathetic and clickable. The hunt for pity shares was more intense than the hunt for information itself. Jake, the Luddite, the martyr against technology, spent too much time with Aletheia, hunched in front of a screen, looking for reactions that might mean something, might point to the presence of a hidden killer. To little avail.

Martha had wholeheartedly embraced the toenail theory

as the most concrete means of establishing the notion of serial murder. The concept now had its own place on the whiteboard. Martha was insistent on drawing the correct inference from it. She has taken to issuing notes to the group, sent via Aletheia's device, which meant they did not need to wait for the nightly library sessions to understand her thinking. Sample:

What does it take for Jade, Isabelle and Dani to end up (mostly) naked and drowned?

1. A killing method that leaves no marks.
2. Unconsciousness in the water.
3. Space and time to prepare the body.
4. Some sort of mental pathology that wants to do this.

Questions:

1. Motive – what message is being sent?
2. Method – how can you kill without showing?
3. Will they strike again and who?
4. What has the death of Claire to do with this?

Meanwhile, Livia has become rather distant, immersing herself in her job as a vet, lingering on her rounds, dashing off to fetch Diana, finding excuses not to be around conversations about the case. When Jake does see her, she seems to be moving as if broken, leaden of heart. She has continued to visit Talboys, Jake always lingering outside in a little mossy niche he has found beneath a tree that keeps off rain and wind. His suggestion that Jess might know more than she admitted was met with general acceptance, but no real suggestions for how to take the suspicion further. Livia became a sort of spy in the camp, in case any grounds for more serious intervention might arise. She also genuinely embraced the concept of pottery as therapy, sitting with Emma, John Coltrane humming in the background, the wheel turning, clay tactile and moist and shifting from formlessness to form in her hands.

Jake called in regularly at the barges, where Maud was always around for coffee and conversation. He finally met the Ukrainian family, Alex and Yulia, who lived there. They were stoical, as you might expect from a family who'd left a war-torn country.

'I'll always walk with Yulia when she goes out,' said Alex dolefully, 'but we are not frightened by a man who skulks in the dark. A beautiful boat in a beautiful land, we can live with the danger.' They had not been involved in the search for Claire at all, and gave the impression that the whole episode was happening a little distantly from them.

That afternoon, Jake is a mile or so upstream of the barges, heading there to speak again to the Ukrainian's neighbour Vaughan, who had not been able to provide police with much of an alibi for any of the relevant dates. Jake found his brand of effortful charm somewhat wearying, and his views on women certainly did not do much to alleviate the suspicions around him. But maybe he was just an old roué, an anachronism, left over from a time when dashing men could pinch bottoms and anatomise ladies with impunity. How sinister, in the end, was that?

The rain has cleared, and the river is running fast beside him, writhing boisterously in full spate. The wind has torn down a few branches, which find their way into the water, coursing past Jake, miniature shipwrecks.

It is perhaps because he is aware of the passing flotsam

that he sees her, a body in the water. And when she sees him, she gives a strangled shout and a desperate wave of her arm. It is Rajni, fully clothed, being borne along by the current, panic painted across her normally sedate features. 'Jake!' Her voice is clearer this time.

The river loops up then bends back just ahead, on Jake's side a swampy mass of reeds, with an old alder trunk that has been partially felled and seems to be growing out horizontally into the waters. Jake grabs a piece of driftwood, long and slender, and runs to the tree, kicking off his flip-flops as he goes. He crawls along the trunk, feeling the small branches probe and bruise. Rajni is only twenty feet away, her body mostly submerged, her head dipping back in the water, black hair billowing out like tentacles.

She seems to have lost the power to shout; there is fear deep set in her eyes. He pulls himself to the end overhanging the water, which gurgles and froths beneath him. He clings on with his right hand, knuckles bulging with the effort, and extends the switchy branch out into the middle of the stream.

'Grab hold of this, and I'll pull you in.'

He keeps his voice calm, though he can see the need is dire. If he misses her, she'll be carried away faster than he can follow.

Her body spins in the water, and this helps, because it faces her towards him, arms outstretched. Then Rajni's head goes under. He is afraid she might not be able to raise it up again. Then she surges, or the current forces her up, and one hand grasps the branch. It bends with her weight, curving like a corset. He pulls as gently as he dares, hoping the strain will not snap the branch. He'd read somewhere that alder wood grows harder when wet, rather than disintegrating into drenched nothing, and hopes that is true.

It holds. And just by being dragged a few feet to the side, Rajni is pulled out of the fastest part of the current. In the sheltering lee of the bank, she rolls to her back, chest heaving as she takes in gulps of vital air.

Jake manoeuvres himself into a straddle, his feet dangling into the cold water, and pulls her towards him. She is gasping and murmuring. She puts an arm on top of the trunk, face pressed against the knobbly bits of bark.

'Jake, thank God.' She spits water from her mouth, retches. 'I'm not sure I've the strength to get out.'

Jake is not sure he can easily pull her out while staying balanced himself. He looks around. A few yards away, the bank slopes gently down into the water, where it lies shallow for as far as he can see.

'Hold on tight for a minute.'

He edges back down the trunk and on to dry land. Then he pulls off his running top and his vest, as he knows they'll need dry clothes later, and splashes down the gradient into the river, now in just his shorts. There is indeed an area of shallow water, which abruptly terminates in a shelf-edge falling away to a depth of several metres. It is cold, much colder than his lake. He feels the familiar tingle on his skin, followed by a silken numbness. He swims around to the tree-trunk, where Rajni is clinging, her body racked with shivers. The force of the river shudders into him, makes him gasp.

He finds his voice with difficulty. 'In a sec, I'll tow you round to the shallows. When I say let go, lean back into me.'

She can barely speak with chill. He can see the tension in her jawbone, looming white beneath her bloodless skin. 'I can't let go. I can't let go.' He moves himself closer, puts his arm gently over her head. The rest of her is rigid. 'I can't move, Jake.'

He is right behind her now, whispers in her ear. 'You

don't need to move, just let go. I've got you. We need to get you out and warm.'

She either nods or shudders, he can't tell. He knows he can wait no longer. 'One, two, three, now!'

Whether she lets go or not, he throws his body back in the water, ripping her clear. Her head is on his chest, her body now just submerged beneath the surface. She feels insubstantial, a fleck of nothing. He swims, keeping his muscles relaxed, both legs kicking down, allowing the edge of the current to move them both towards the bank. Soon he can stand. She cannot, so he drags her up the slope and deposits her onto the grass, where she lies, like something cast up from the bottom of the ocean, saturated and lifeless.

Her clothes hang heavy upon her: dark jeans, a thick brown shirt. Jake helps her to sit up, starts rubbing life into her hands and forearms, which are inert, bluish. All her reactions seem involuntary, her whole body convulsing as if she has lost control over it.

'Undo your jeans, take the shirt off, you can put on my top.'

She clearly knows she needs to start warming up. She tries to pop the button on her jeans, which has been pressed into the flesh of her stomach, but her fingers won't obey. Jake, keeping his body distant from hers, reaches down and unhooks it. She clings to the belt loops around her waist and tugs them down a few inches. He grabs the hems by her ankles and pulls, the fabric snags on her thighs, before she wriggles it downward once more. They stick, then shift, then stick again. An air of farce to it all. When Jake finally throws them to one side, he can feel the dead weight of the material. Rajni shucks off her shirt with more ease. She looks small in her underwear; her skin is goosebumped all over. Jake puts his top over her head, pulls it down.

'We need to get you moving.'

Together they stand, him in just his soaking shorts, her in blue knickers and his outsized jacket. 'Let's run to the hedge and back, get the circulation going.' She nods, half-laughing, and starts before him, waggling her arms as she goes. They run back and forth, back and forth. More farce. He feels the blood pumping around his body, the sudden suffusion in his skin, the feeling of life fighting against the cold. The grass is damp and soft, cushioning his feet. His breath comes in deep, affirming gasps.

Rajni now leans forward, taking in air greedily. Her skin is back to its normal brown sheen. She pushes wet hair from her face.

'Dear fucking God. What a sight we must look. But my arms are feeling like part of my body again. I'm not sure how much longer I had left, you know.'

'You did brilliantly. Are you OK?'

She shivers as the wind blows icily across them. 'Yes, but I've got to get my core temperature up. And so do you.' He is beginning to shiver a little. 'Put your vest on, little that it can do, and we need to get somewhere warm fast.'

'I've got a car just over there.' He points beyond a thick line of shrubbery. 'I can get us to a cottage.' Livia's place is nearest, and she should be home. They stumble through a gap in the hedge to where the borrowed Volvo is waiting. He turns the heating on full, delicious hot blasts, singeing the hair on his legs.

Rajni closes her eyes, pulls the top down as far as it goes over her thighs. As the engine purrs, she looks across to Jake.

'I could've died twice, you know. I only jumped in the water because someone was trying to kill me.'

Chapter Thirty-Four

Luckily, Livia is home, and soon has a fire blazing, a hot bath running. Jake sits in a blanket before the flames, while Rajni goes first in the bathroom, Livia adding her own body heat to his. She has called Aletheia and Martha, and they plan to speak all together with Rajni, before they turn her over more formally to the police.

An hour later, they are both warm, hot-flushed in fact. Livia has given Rajni pyjamas and an old wool sweater; Jake is in his thickest hooded top and cloth trousers. They are drinking hot coffee, spiked with brandy. Aletheia is sitting in the corner, notebook in hand, face mildly creased with concern. Martha is on the screen, smoking from her glass pipe. If the ensemble seems odd to Rajni, she is too polite to comment. In a quiet, tense voice, she tells her story from the beginning.

'I've been taking care, you know, around the river. Which isn't easy when you live on it. I have two teenagers, one a girl, and we've been tyrants about them not ever being on their own, especially as it gets dark.' The grandfather clock chimes, orotund sound. 'I better get home soon, actually. They'll be back in an hour, and then David is off shift tonight.'

Livia is soothing. 'Shouldn't you call him?'

'He keeps his phone off when he's working. Always has.'

'We can drop you back, and then report it all to the police. That way they can come to you.'

Rajni drinks deeply. 'That's kind. And I want to tell you all I know while it's fresh in my mind. Jake's mentioned his team before when we've spoken.'

A suppressed snigger from Martha at the use of the phrase 'his team'. Jake knows he'll pay for that one later.

Rajni grins to show that she has noticed. 'Anyway, I've been walking inland in the day, going to work at the hospital and coming straight home, staying cosy in the boat at night. Autumn aboard is lovely, it's nice to be dry and snug when it's so miserable outside. And I wanted to be careful, even if I still couldn't believe, didn't want to believe, the place had become dangerous.

'Today was my day off, and I'd just had lunch, tidied things up. It was such lovely blustery weather outside, I thought I could go for a walk for once. There was nobody around, hardly any river traffic. David had mentioned seeing sandpipers in one of the banks a mile or so north of us, so I went to take a look at them. They're getting rarer and rarer these days, and I've never actually seen one.'

Jake glares at Martha, who is shifting impatiently. In his experience, it is worth letting important witnesses, or victims, tell a story at their own pace. Rajni seems to spot the silent exchange.

'Sorry, I'll get to the point, I promise. I'm just explaining my foolishness, I suppose. I got to the site, which was a bit further away than I'd expected.' Aletheia stands and pulls a map from her bag, which she brings to the table. 'Say when.' She traces along the river course with her finger.

Rajni follows her intently. 'About there. There's a reed bed they're supposed to like. Sandpipers, I mean.' She pauses, holding back a sob. 'Ridiculous to be talking about river birds, but that's why I was there. So I stood back for a while, then crept a bit closer. Sandpipers have this big, bright white belly, so when they move you can see the flash in the green of the reeds. As I was looking, I felt that I was being watched.'

Aletheia is back in her corner. 'Had you felt you were being followed at any point?'

Rajni cocks her head to one side, dredging for the memory. 'I don't think so. I was – and I know this is stupid – I was trying to put some of my nerves out of my mind as I walked. I was trying to not think too much about what was going on.'

'Did you see anything after you felt someone was there?' Martha is twirling her pipe.

'I turned quick, but nobody *was* there. It's a wild enough spot, big patches of bracken and fern, small copses, you know, full of places to crouch behind. When I turned back, I saw the flash of white, two flashes actually, two birds moving to the edge of the bed, and on a patch of mud next to the water itself. I followed them across, now a bit preoccupied, I guess.'

Jake watches her body tense, as she comes to the key part of the story. Livia has refilled her coffee, and she takes several sips, swift little gulps like a cat's. She puts the mug down. 'I better stop drinking that before I get too twitchy. So I was standing there, staring at these wretched birds, my feet almost dangling over the edge. And then, and then, I felt someone behind me, a breath on the hairs of my neck.' She touches the back of her head reflexively. She has long, slender fingers, two rings of white gold on her left hand.

Livia leans forward. 'What then?'

'I felt frozen, paralysed for a second. I started to turn around, then got this hard cylinder thing pressed into my back.'

'A gun?' Aletheia is taking notes of everything.

'I guess. I don't know. A weapon. Definitely solid. I hear a whisper, 'Look back at the water.' So I do. And all I can think of is those women. What had happened to them. How David and the kids would get told about my bloated body washing up. How they'd cope or not cope. How I didn't want to die. So I jumped.'

'You jumped?' Martha looks impressed.

'Yep, fully dressed. In I went. I couldn't think of another way out.'

Martha is genuine. 'You're a clever woman. You both know he wants you in the water, so you go in yourself first. I bet he didn't see that coming.'

'Was it a man? Martha just said "he", but can you confirm that?' Aletheia is precise as ever.

'I was using the universal "he", Al,' says Martha, unrepentant. 'Bearing in mind that most scumbags are men, and no, Jake, that doesn't mean that most men are scumbags. Though they are. Anyway, enough of me. Rajni, did you sex this attacker or not?'

Rajni offers up a faint chuckle. 'I didn't. The whisper was soft, could've come from a man or woman. I honestly couldn't tell you. It could've been absolutely anyone. I assume it was a man.'

Jake keeps the conversation moving, conscious that

Rajni might crash at some point. 'So what happened after you jumped?'

'I hit the water, went all the way in over my head, accidentally swallowed a mouthful. God it was cold. I thought through all the medicine I knew about cold-water deaths. I closed my mouth, knew I needed to not inhale any more of it. It was a very fast current, like being pulled along rails. When I got my head out I was already twenty feet downstream.'

Aletheia asks the crucial question. 'Did you look back?'

'I did, but it was all a blur. I saw a figure in waterproof clothing, greeny-brown, hood up, no sign of a face at all. He – or she I suppose – had a backpack on. He was just turning away, heading back to the woods. And then I got swept around the bend, lost sight of him. I kicked off my shoes, and tried to strike out for the bank, but it was impossible to get out of the central stream. The water seemed to want to take me on, and down.'

Livia strokes her arm. 'How long before you saw Jake?'

'It felt like an hour, but probably not more than ten minutes. I was so cold, and just overwhelmed. I felt this massive tiredness, this urge to give up. It was like feeling sleepy. And then I saw him, and got my final wind, I guess.'

Livia sits back, pursing her lips. 'Thank God you did. It sounds like you nearly didn't make it.'

Then the tears, the reaction, the surge of sheer relief. Rajni crumples, crying. All pretence at control gone. Aletheia picks up her phone, calls the hospital and asks for Dr David Saunders. She speaks softly to him for a moment, and then hands the device to Rajni. Livia takes her to the bedroom to speak to him.

She comes back immediately, and hugs Jake. His body

is experiencing its own reaction: the somatic pleasure of heat after cold, relief after deep fear; and then the tiredness that follows, as if his central system needs to reboot itself. He hugs Livia back firmly, finding her warm and real and tactile in his arms.

Martha coughs. 'All right, we'll all gather around and sing "Kumbaya" shortly. Let's focus on the new information, while all our brains are working. Well, while mine is. Well, while mine is a bit.' She inhales on her pipe, billowing smoke.

Aletheia sees the need to take charge. 'David'll come and pick Rajni up now, and then I'll have to report it all. The cops can forensic that scene, see if our attacker left anything. But what have we got new?'

Martha is ticking things off. 'A hard cylinder for a weapon. What could that be? Something that leaves no mark on the body. So is it a gun that's used as a threat? Would you drown yourself to get away from being shot, though? Not sure I would, and I've actually been fucking shot. Anyway, it's a big new variable. What else? A backpack. A figure not noticeably very tall or very short. Some sort of ability at stalking.'

Livia positions herself on Jake's knees, keeps an arm protectively on his shoulder. 'You think he followed Rajni?'

'He must have. He's not hitting random people. She was on the search too. That's another thing confirmed.'

Aletheia keeps writing, thinking aloud. 'Here's another. Our guy might be skilful, but he's not infallible. He didn't expect Rajni to jump, didn't have anything in place to stop her. He should've incapacitated her right away, controlled the situation better.'

'He might in future.' Livia voices a troubling thought.

'That's right. This whole episode might make him frustrated, move again, be bolder.'

'Or it could put him off.'

Jake scowls. 'It could, but I don't think so. The timing is interesting. Not at night again. No precautions. It's like he's losing control. I keep thinking that he's come so close to getting away with this. If he'd stopped after Isabelle, the case gets closed, right? He'd left nothing for us to pursue. He wins if he stops. But then he kills Dani, now this. He's losing his ability to be secret, losing his desire to. That's a problem.'

Rajni appears at the bedroom door, wraith-like, walking like she is floating. 'David's on his way.' Aletheia goes to make her call to McAllister. Ten minutes later, the two doctors are in each other's arms, murmuring shared sentiments into each other's necks, the picture of relief and reunion. They depart in a tight, unbreakable clinch, barely squeezing through the front door.

Martha waves laconically, her face animated as ever by irony. 'I'm not precious, but couldn't he have maybe said a little thank you?'

Jake closes the door behind them. 'I guess they're entitled to have other things on their minds.'

Martha is brisk. 'We need to remember we got fucking lucky there. Rajni was a clever, resourceful woman, and she had a lot of luck on her side today. Jake's right: our killer is ramping up and we've been too passive on this case. So *we* need to start drawing some actual conclusions. Or we're all going to have blood on our hands.'

Chapter Thirty-Five

The next day, earlyish, David reappears at Livia's cottage. Jake had been too exhausted to walk back to Little Sky, and Aletheia had happily slept in the tiny spare bedroom. She, Livia and Diana had all been up before him, and headed off to school and work and – in Aletheia's case – to a conference with McAllister.

Rain is falling, whispering at the window. Jake had awoken with a ferocious appetite, and is eating porridge with cream and brown sugar, raisins, bananas and his own apples with their explosions of wild sweetness.

He is sitting in the porch overlooking the lane when David's car pulls up. An old and slightly battered Honda. Jake had always thought doctors earned a ton of money, but these two never seemed to show it. Their lives appeared deliberately, unostentatiously comfortable, and no more.

David is slightly awkward, wary of intrusion, perhaps warier of overstating his gratitude. Saving someone's life is an onerous act, when it comes down to it. Jake has seen it before: how it places a responsibility on the one saved and, perhaps unfairly, an obligation of sorts on the saver. You are united by an overwhelming event, and neither of you are able to forget it.

David walks through the gate, and Jake extends a hand, which is clasped with fervour. With his other, Jake passes over a coffee from the pot, and gestures him to sit down.

David begins to talk. 'Jake, I don't know what we can say to thank you.'

Jake feels the flush of embarrassment. 'Say nothing. It was lucky I was there. And you're lucky your wife's so tough and quick-thinking. There's no need to say more. I'm just glad she's OK.'

'And she is, I think. She slept all night, and is still dozy as all hell. I don't want to leave her for long, but the kids are currently killing her with hot-water bottles and kindness. I said I was going out for supplies, and she wanted me to come thank you. Said we should've been more grateful last night.'

'Don't even consider it. I think when your wife nearly dies, you're entitled to focus on each other.'

'She spent two hours with the police when we got back, and then I almost hurled them overboard to stop them bothering her, and then she collapsed. She did ask me to mention one thing. You guys talked about whether the attacker was a man or a woman. She still doesn't know, but she says she thought she smelled perfume in the air just before she jumped. Sweet and flowery.'

'Any more than that?'

'No. But she wanted to tell you.'

'I wanted to ask you something else, too. About something that happened during the search for Claire, it seems you had an argument with Dani, the YouTube woman?'

'I wouldn't call it an argument. I just told her to take care about who she might upset with her filming. She didn't agree with me, but it never got heated.' David's voice is toneless, curiously distant. He speaks a little like a textbook. So much so that when he expresses concern, it sounds rehearsed. Jake can't imagine him having much of a bedside manner.

'You don't think it had anything to do with her death, do you?'

'No, I don't.' And Jake still doesn't. 'But that search seems to be at the heart of this: all the victims after Claire, including Rajni, were on it.'

David stays to finish his drink. The conversation is awkward, desultory. After five minutes he stands, shakes Jake by the hand once more.

'One last thing. Rajni and I talked about how the attacker was going to do it, you know, knock her out before drowning her. You've said before there's no evidence of obvious trauma. We had two ideas, medically speaking. One would be a rare anaesthetic, something that no coroner would automatically check for. There was a drug we used to talk about at medical school: Suxamethonium. A short half-life, so it disappears pretty quickly from any blood tests, and it just shuts down your systems. There might be a puncture mark, but not big, from a needle; easily missed. The other is some sort of electric shock that makes you pass out. I just don't know if it would be possible without leaving a mark. How's your physics?'

'I am the most arts student of all arts students. But it's a thought.'

'The cylinder at her back could've been a gun, or a pretend gun. But he could've had something else too. An adapted taser, a kind of stun weapon? A syringe? I don't know, I wanted to share it.'

'That's helpful, thank you.'

Jake releases his hand from the shake, and David impulsively hugs him. 'Thank you. You'll never know how grateful I am.' He seems instantly to recoil at the proximity, though, becomes sheepish once more, head bowed, retreats to the car and putters off.

Jake stands in the garden, lets the rain smatter upon his face. Down the lane, he looks at the trees huddled together, abashed beneath the downpour. Each day now they are a little less green, a little more earth-toned, a little barer of life. He sees Livia walking to the house, rustling in her waterproofs, her ringlets smoothed flat by all the moisture.

'Was that the grateful husband?'

'When shall we get married?'

She pinches the skin at his waist. 'That's an interesting non sequitur. The better question is *how* we should get married. I insist upon a whole week in Croatia, a horse-drawn carriage, a parade of bridesmaids in pink chiffon, and a menu based upon the theme of fruits of the land and sea.' She squeezes again. 'Just kidding.'

It's the first real joke she has made since Dani's death, and Jake hopes it signifies a breakthrough. He is less convinced when, a beat later, she sighs mournfully. 'But I can't think of weddings while this is going on, can I? Someone is out there, and the thought of it is consuming, isn't it? And it consumed Dani.' Her voice trails off. She shakes her head as if to clear the sensation of guilt. 'I need to get back to work. I think our wedding should be natural and simple, like getting engaged in the bath.' She pecks his cheek.

'Before you go, if I can't be romantic, can I be practical? Have you heard of something called Suxo-methodi-something? It's a drug David mentioned as a possible means of incapacitating someone.' He wishes he had written it down.

'Sure. You mean Suxamethonium. At uni, we'd have Sux races with the medics. You'd inject it, and see how far you could run before it blocked all your neuro-muscular junctions and shut your body down. It would be a useful thing for a murderer to have in his kitbag, no doubt.'

'There's nothing worse than tales of crazy student doctors, there really isn't. Would a pathologist know to test for it?'

'I'd assume so, but I don't know.'

'Could you dig around your medical memory for any other drugs like that, and we can see?'

'Sure, I've got some textbooks in the study. I'll take a look this afternoon. Aletheia has called a special meeting tonight at Little Sky. She wanted me to tell you. She's invited McAllister too. It's a chance to make a decision on all this, I think.'

After she has gone, he decides to walk to Meryton. The rain has stopped, though the sky remains seal-grey. The idea of a swim in the lake has lost its appeal for the moment. He hasn't seen Martin George in a while. The figure with the backpack glimpsed by Rajni – could it be him? Jake has never seen Martin without his pack, certainly, but it is hardly something that identifies him alone. Aletheia was intending to pick him up today, to speak to him.

Without realizing it, he gravitates towards the bookshop.

Its owner Sam is perched on a stool before a shelf, filling an empty space in the crime section.

'Jake, how are you? I didn't expect to see you. The word is that you're on the track of this mysterious killer.'

'Something like that.'

'There's a big protest stroke vigil in town tonight. A call to keep women safe. Men only welcome if accompanied. Whatever else these deaths have done, they've made everyone a feminist, at least on the surface.'

Jake had thought about that. Since the very first announcement of the disappearance of Claire, one of the central narratives had been around the safety of women, the problem of toxic masculinity. Jess would approve.

He starts to run his finger along a lower shelf, marked 'C – except for Christie' in Sam's teacherly scrawl. Casey, Child, Chesterton, Cole, Conan Doyle, Connelly. Agatha had her own section near the door. Sam's theory is that most people on holiday like to have a Poirot on hand in case the weather turns rainy, and he wants always to be ready to encourage the impulse buyer.

He looks back over his shoulder. 'I've got a Carl Hiaasen here for you.'

They'd spoken a month ago about Jake's slow appreciation of that author, and his stories of more or less wacky, sun-soaked Floridian crime. About as far from Jake's experience as possible. Martha, no slouch herself in the field of comic detective fiction, is a noisy advocate, and she has gradually been converting Jake.

'I'll take it. And do you have anything on electronics for a beginner? Apparently, I need to brush up on my physics.'

Sam drops down lightly, and burrows deep into a box

in the corner of the room. 'We got given a whole bunch of textbooks by a retired teacher the other week. I think they were about science. Do you want it on general physics, electronics or electromagnetics?'

'I better take all three. I've no fucking idea if I'm honest.'

'Spoken like a true Renaissance Man.'

Jake comes over to pay, and Sam holds the books back for a second. 'Jake, I know you'll be interested in our friend Martin as a suspect, because of who he is and how he behaves, but take care. I'd hate to see him railroaded because he's an easy target.'

'You still don't trust the police, do you?'

'I don't trust authority, but you're just scruffy enough to make me want to believe in you. I don't want to be disappointed in that.'

'I understand. We'll look at him, but there's no desire to drag him in unless there's reason. He's an odd one, I know that. We had a fairly unusual chat the other day. But does that strangeness, all the misery he suffered, make him an actual suspect? I honestly don't know. I can't promise we can rule him out.'

'I've no interest in arguing against myself, but once people get destroyed by tragedy, maybe they don't feel it the same way in the future. Maybe they lose the ability to feel at all. Maybe that's what makes a murderer.'

Something to ponder when Jake gets home a few hours later. He prepares the library for the conference, laying a fire, checking the fridge is stocked. He grabs some potatoes from the store, bakes them, removes the flesh and mashes it with cheese and herbs, and hard-fried pieces of sausage, before returning the mix to the skins to brown that evening. He chops half of his remaining summer vegetables as crudités to have with his own bean dip, which is creamy and tart with garlic.

Then he picks up a book on general physics and sits by the window. Outside, the clouds descend further, until they seem to touch the tree-topped ridge in the distance. The soothing sounds and the impenetrable prose eventually get to him, and he sleeps. His face smoothed of care for the first time in what feels like a long time.

Chapter Thirty-Six

There are six for the council of war that night. Livia drops Diana off at Jo's house for a sleepover with her children, to be presided over by Jo's husband, a quiet and faintly shambling man, who is likely to be beneficently lax when it comes to sugar intake and bedtimes. Jo comes back with Livia to Little Sky.

Jo hugs him before Livia does, and immediately talks shop, her mind as ever on the paper. 'We gave the tale of Dr Rajni's rescue a big show today, and your name is once again lighting up the sodding internet. We won't be able to move for vultures for the next couple of days. But well done, old chap.' She lights a meditative cigarette, keen to enjoy her domestic freedom for once, waves it in the air. 'We do need an occasional hero in this godawful mess.'

Livia gives her a playful shove. 'You smoke outside, and leave my fiancé alone.'

'That's why I was hugging him, to congratulate him on punching so successfully above his weight. And I was going outside anyway. I don't smoke with pregnant women, thank you very much.'

She winks, and shuffles out to stand under the eaves, smoke circling above her damp hair, watching the downpour. Jake takes Livia in his arms. 'You told her then?'

'I think it's more or less obvious now, isn't it?' She shifts, and pulls up her jumper. Her stomach is round, hard, the skin taut. There is the faint hint of a dark line wending downwards from navel to beneath the elastic of her trousers.

'I reckon so.'

'Are you saying I look fat?' A wicked grin, and she releases him from the clinch. 'Al told me to get Jo, because we could use some local knowledge beyond mine. Our little team is great on brains, but a bit short on experience of the area when you think about it.'

'We can trust her.' Jake is needlessly solemn.

'You bet your hairy bottom you can.' Jo bursts back in, her final smoky exhalation wreathed above her head, hovering in the doorway. 'And this is more than just a story to me, you know. I find the TikTokers and YouTubers generally insufferable, and pretty disrespectful to the skills of actually trained journalists like me. But the fact is: we lost someone who was digging around, acting like a reporter, and that matters. And that's before we get to the fact that we shouldn't be living in a place where women can't walk by a river without being knocked out by some perv.'

Jake watches Livia's reaction to the reference to Dani, and sees a small deflation, a sag in her bearing, that manifest sense of guilt. Would finding the killer ever remove that?

He has a big pot of coffee broiling and pours a mug for Jo. Livia is drinking fresh mint tea, will have to rely on resilience alone to stay awake if the meeting runs long. He takes a peek outside. Aletheia and McAllister are walking up from the lake, dark shapes in the dusk.

They eat first before going to the library. It is a strange meal, an unstated feel of looming magnitude. They talk and laugh thinly, make extravagant attempts at moving the conversation along. Jake had read about meals like this in diaries from the war, the tension almost tangible but never quite acknowledged.

They head to the library, Martha's screen at one end of the table. Pads and paper to hand, more drinks, atmospheric lamplight, a hearty fire that spits and crackles. Cyprian the cat is in front of it, asleep. She opens a weary, lizard eye at their arrival, and then rolls over.

The whiteboard has been photographed and cleared. It now has four new headings: MOTIVE, METHOD, OPPORTUNITY, PHYSICAL EVIDENCE.

Martha blips on and wastes little time on any preamble. 'I want to move things on this evening, my fellow drones. We might need to make some intuitive leaps to get things going, and that might be clumsy, but we've got to make progress. So challenge only when you need to. Do we agree?'

McAllister is the least accustomed to Martha's manner, and quails slightly. 'Is there a risk that we go down the wrong path too easily?'

She lights her pipe. 'Yes, Chief Inspector, there is. That's why you challenge something if you don't agree. And if you're shy about arguing with a woman with no legs and an authority complex, then I'm afraid you're in the wrong place.'

Chuckles around the table. McAllister tries to rally. 'Are you smoking anything illegal there, Martha?'

'Yes. Any more questions?'

Aletheia gives McAllister a sympathetic glance. 'Best to go along with it, in my experience,' she whispers.

'In which case, Jake, I might trouble you for a beer. This might be a long night and I don't want to poison myself with coffee.' He goes to the fridge and opens a bottle, sits back down.

Martha is drinking from a bottle of unlabelled liquor. 'I want to say something else. I've been examining the data taken from the phones of Isabelle and Dani, and I've got some theories. Dani's phone was damaged at exactly 7.37 in the morning, which is when I can confidently suggest the attack on her actually happened.' Her face softens a fraction. She normally keeps her expressions as part of her general armour, buffed-up and steely, one way she protects herself against the world. 'Livia, listen, we can't afford guilt to slow us down. And if I can't convince you that you shouldn't feel guilty, I can show you that you've got no real grounds to. Dani was probably dead by eight, before you ever saw her sign. You couldn't have saved her.'

Livia sits forward, eyes gleaming. 'But, I still thought—'

Martha is ironclad once more, stern and forbidding. 'But, but, but. This is not a fucking therapy session. I don't care what you thought. I care about reality. Dani's phone went dead in the early morning, way before you could've possibly worked out she was in trouble. So park it. Give yourself that freedom.'

Livia looks around the room, awkward. She weighs up her response. 'I will. Thank you.'

Jake wonders for a moment whether Martha would make that detail up, just to soothe Livia's conscience, and realizes that no good could come from him finding out the answer.

Martha continues. 'Now let's look at what we know, or think we know. Claire's death started this, but it doesn't share many of the physical aspects of the later deaths. Conclusion? Claire was not murdered. She died swimming on a warm day. Her death, though sad, only became exceptional because of the mystery around it and how long it took to find her body.' She pauses, eyes black and dilated. Nobody says anything to deny what she has said.

'But Claire's death has an impact on the community, local and wider. It gets interest. It brings people together. The three women who died, and the fourth who nearly did – our chum Dr Rajni – all went on the search. *Our killer must have done the same, or witnessed them doing it.*'

Aletheia is making notes as normal, soft sound of pen on paper. There's no music on, and Jake goes to remedy that. When he had first come to Little Sky, first tried to understand classical music, he had been seduced by the ready romanticism of Mahler, its brassy and plangent obviousness. He puts on Symphony No. 3, very quiet, so its rise and fall doesn't impinge on the conversation.

He sits back down. 'That gives us a range of suspects, quite a broad one.' Then he asks the question he had been pondering all day. 'Have you spoken to Martin George?'

Aletheia shakes her head. 'Can't find him. He's pretty nomadic, as you know. We'll get to him. There's no real reason to prioritize him as a suspect at this stage, beyond his basic weirdness.'

McAllister is pensive. 'Weirdness, plus opportunity, plus access to the river. I don't hate him for it, to be honest.'

Martha accepts the baton here. 'Which brings us to motive.'

'Actually, I wonder if method comes first, M.' Aletheia looks up from her notes. 'The method is striking, and speaks to some sort of message, some sort of meaning. I think motive follows from that.'

'OK, Aletheia is right, though her alliteration there was a little clumsy. Method. Our women are all strong, basically fit. How do they end up in the water?'

Livia has been thinking about this. 'They need to be incapacitated but not killed. The killer needs time.'

'Isabelle was left with her underwear on,' points out Jake, 'which might mean the killer was hurried, made to finish before he was ready.'

Martha resumes control of the narrative. 'And what does he need time for? Strip clothes, paint toenails, make them go in the water to drown. Five minutes?'

'Is it possible?' This is McAllister, completely engaged in the thought, the flicker of light dancing within his beady eyes. 'Is it possible that they were made to strip and all that with a gun, without being touched? Yer woman Rajni felt a gun at her back, or what could've been a gun.'

'It's possible, but it doesn't explain the drowning. If the killer held down the victims, subdued them, there'd be marks. The absence of marks is a key feature. I just can't believe that people can be made to drown even at gunpoint; they need to be out of it, unconscious I think. Which brings us to two theories, offered by Rajni's husband, Dr David, to Jake, which I'd already been looking at.'

The table turns to him, and he marshals his recollection. 'Right. One was a drug, like Sux-a-something.'

'Suxamethonium.' Livia supplies the name.

'The argument, though, against that was a drug would be visible in the blood. Liv, does that make sense?'

'It does, but pathologists don't test for all drugs, they can't, nor can they know all possible variants of every muscle or neuro inhibitor. Our killer might know more than them.'

McAllister interjects. 'Our killer could be a doctor?'

Martha nods. 'The thought did occur. It'd be one reason why it's been so hard to establish means of death. Plus Claire and Rajni are both connected to the hospital. Jake, remind us of the other method?'

Jake answers a little sheepishly. 'I don't fully understand this, obviously. But an electric shock or charge can leave you incapacitated, can't it?'

'That's right, but there are problems with it. Say a supercharged taser was used, there'd be scorch marks or contact marks. Plus, it wouldn't knock you out, it would just paralyse you.'

'That might be enough, though?' This is Livia, the scientist in the room. 'If you're paralysed, you could be stripped and dropped into the river, held down in the shallows?'

'Perhaps. Nobody's really tested this. And I'm not sure it would be possible without visible damage to the body.' Martha puts down her bottle. 'There's one other factor. The phones of two victims, the only phones we've discovered, were both damaged.'

Jake leans forward. 'Were they both equally damaged?'

'More or less, and both seem to have been interrupted by something, maybe electrical.'

'But could it be water?'

'Yes in the case of Isabelle, but probably not in Dani's case. So there's something that might suggest some form of electrical interference, though.' She frowns. 'So where does this all leave us? Do we accept that our victims were incapacitated with something at least?'

'Something which we have no physical evidence for at all, remember.'

'That's a fair point, Jake, though a little sneery. So let's move on to physical evidence, shall we? Al, you've been thinking about this. I'm going to smoke my illegal drugs and listen.'

Aletheia stands up and stretches her legs. She is, as so often, all in dark tones, purples and blacks, and seems to float around the room. 'I want to focus on two things: the toenails and the drowning. On the first, which was Jake's great spot, what does it mean? It's a message, surely, a finicky thing to do at a kill site, so it must be worth it for some reason, worth the risk.'

Jo has said little, slightly overwhelmed by the process. For all her cynicism and regular reference to worldly journalism, she probably has not been party to many meetings like this. Martha and Aletheia are impressive people, clear-minded and formidable. Jake sees that more than ever. Jo finds her voice. 'It's creepy, obviously, but it's something about femininity, isn't it? Doing your nails is a kind of act of dressing up, looking nice, doing something small to look prettier, I don't know, more fucking feminine. Isn't it?'

Aletheia laughs. 'That must be right. The follow-on to what you're saying is that by doing it to our victims it becomes a sort of political statement. Women are pretty. Or women are commoditised for being pretty. Or the killer wishes he could fit into a world where prettiness prospered, and women knew their place.'

Livia looks out into the dark night. The rain has stopped.

A miserly moon has risen, pared and sterile. She stands and opens the window for air. Jo takes it as an invitation to smoke out of it, and follows the conversation, half-turning and puffing into the coolness outside. Livia sits back down. 'Plus, the women are all involved in trying to find Claire. So the killer could well be saying something about women and their place in the world, or about, you know, the sisterhood.'

'Is the killer a man then?' McAllister is forthright.

Aletheia points her pen at him. 'Excellent question. Yes, probably, but women can have a view on other women's place in the world.'

Livia nods sadly. 'Look at me with Dani.' Jake starts to demur. 'No, listen, I decided that she was a flirt, no better than she ought to be, as my mum would say. I objected to her as a woman, and I'm a woman.'

'That wouldn't be true about, say, Rajni.' Jake offers a rebuttal.

'No, but what did Jess say to you? And say at that impromptu speech she did during the search? Something about the need to dramatize the plight of women, to bring home just how toxic the world is for us. Attacking a doctor would do that – even a doctor is reduced to nothing if she is a woman. Could all of this be a means of raising a feminist point, even in a horrific manner?'

Aletheia writes something down. 'Maybe. One other piece of physical evidence. Chief, did you know that there were bins all along the riverbank, at lengthy intervals?'

'Sure. We checked them for weapons.'

'Quite right. I looked again today at what the cops collected from the bin near where Isabelle went in, which is probably our most accurately located murder site. There was a plastic bag, empty and lacking prints.'

Martha raises her eyebrows. 'Ooh, that sounds exciting.'

'Wait for it, my friend. It'd been previously full of river water, the same make-up as the water nearby, in fact. Here's my theory. Our killer incapacitates the women, and drowns them by immersing their face in a container of river water, before taking his time to do whatever to the body and pushing them in. He drowns them on dry land, paints their toes and strips them when they are already dead. That's why there's no marking.'

Jake looks at the board. 'Which brings us to opportunity. This is bold stuff. Even if it takes ten minutes, it's out in the open, and brutal. It involves manhandling a body without causing marks. It involves nudity in public, flashes of flesh which would attract attention.'

'But what's the conclusion from that?' Martha asks, a faint note of petulance in her voice.

Jake pauses. 'I don't know. He's a local, he's confident in the countryside, he's a planner, he's decisive, maybe sociopathic. He knows where there are no prying eyes to catch him.'

Livia interjects. 'But he's getting wilder, taking more risks. That was Jake's point, too. He could've stopped, preserved himself. Chief, you were ready to pack it in, weren't you?' McAllister nods. 'I wonder if Dani did something that provoked him in some way, came close to uncovering him?'

Martha nods. 'I think that's it, she was a professional provoker. It would be good to know more of what she knew. There was nothing of use in her place, was there?'

Aletheia is looking through the file. 'Nope, we looked at where she lived, and combed through all her social posts. I suppose we could go again at that.' She yawns. It is late.

Jake can feel the drooping of his eyelids, the staleness in his breath, the feeling of exhausted thinking.

Martha senses the entropy of the meeting. For someone who has consumed the most inappropriate intoxicants, she remains in firm command. 'So what do we know, and what shall we do?'

They turn to McAllister, as the official arm of the investigation. 'I think we should re-examine the blood of all the vics, testing for a range of drugs. We should look into the electroshock point. And we need to really examine these people without clear alibis, who we know were involved in the searches: they're our prospect list.' He gestures at Aletheia, who goes to the board and writes down some names. On it, Jake sees, as expected: Martin George, the potters Jess Molloy and Emma Bateman, Dr David Saunders, Antonio and Wayne (two of the boys from the gym; MC is not on the list), Vaughan Mitchell from the barges, Sam Fryer from the bookshop.

'From everything that's been said, one of them is probably our killer.' He frowns. 'The damnedest thing is that we've still got almost nothing to show us which one.'

Chapter Thirty-Seven

Before Martha hangs up – while Livia is seeing Jo and McAllister to the door; thence a long walk in the damp and misty fields, and finally home – she says to Jake, faint mischief in her eyes, 'I want to conduct an experiment on you. Can you come to my place tomorrow at a reasonable hour?'

And that is why he finds himself on the bus the next morning, heading to Martha's house on the other side of the city, faintly perturbed by what she might have in mind. The window is open, letting gusts of fresh air into the stale and stained interior. He has two books with him, one on electromagnetics, the other a novel. He spends half an hour trying to read the first, but sleep keeps overwhelming him, that feeling of being dragged slowly under, pleasantly helpless, the words too hard and weighty for his consciousness to bear.

Martha lives on the outskirts of the suburbs, more or less in the countryside itself. Her house is on an isolated lot, and looks like it has been dropped accidentally from the sky into the natural environment. It is big and square, and utilitarian. No comfortable curves or old-beamed crookedness, no charm. 'A house, not a fucking antique,' as she once put it. She needs wide corridors and doors, flat ground, space and functionality, a home that makes her life easier. And that is what she has created.

Someone still helps her look after her garden, evidently, because it is well-tended, if a little on the wild side. Sprays of flowers in blues and purples and oranges clinging on against the change in season, dense grass mown into alternating lines. Two grey squirrels, the colour of dirty smoke, pour themselves up and down the trunks of copper beeches, so fast as to seem fluid. A bullfinch hops, delicate and regal, on the lawn.

Martha is in her library, and she shouts him in through the open front door. She is sitting in front of a table littered with electronic detritus, a screwdriver rather raffishly skewering her purple-blond hair.

'Thanks for coming, Jake. I hate to drag you away from your important duties of soaking up undeserved praise and being an occasional lifeguard.'

'Hello to you.'

She swivels to face him. 'I won't offer you a drink, because I don't want to ruin the experiment and I need all your wits about you. Are you ready to have your mind blown?'

He sits down on an old overstuffed armchair. 'Why am I scared that you might mean that literally.'

She smiles sweetly. 'Because you have wisdom beyond your years. Now what do you know about electromagnetics?'

Jake reaches into his stained suede bag and pulls out his book, throwing it to the floor. 'About as much as I could read of that without falling asleep.'

'As much as that, eh? OK, I'll do the uber-dummies guide if I can. A bit of background: I get a lot of pain still in my legs, which I generally combat with drugs and alcohol.'

'Am I allowed to say: and great bravery too?'

'No. Don't be wet. I medicate with drugs, including legal drugs, and it gets me through. But – and I hate to admit weakness here – when I'm using whatever I'm using, it means I'm sometimes operating in an impaired fashion. Now, me impaired is still a shitload better than most people unimpaired, I think you'll agree.' There is bravado in her voice. Jake inclines his head in assent.

'But it isn't an entirely brilliant way to be living all the time. So I started investigating something called "transcranial magnetic stimulation", which you will have never heard of. But it's basically a means of using electromagnetic force to help with pain, and also to help with some of the stuff that comes with that chronic pain, which is to say anger and depression and sorrow.' She pulls the screwdriver from her hair and scratches her thigh with it thoughtfully. 'I'm being frank with you here, Jake. There are parts of my life where I feel full to bursting with . . .' – she reaches inwardly for the word – 'with a sort of antipathy towards the world, and myself. When I look around this rattling old house and think, What's the point of it all?'

Jake tries to speak, but she cuts him off. 'I'm not fishing for compliments, or for a worthy explanation of life's meaningfulness and my own contribution to the greater good. I don't want to be told that everything's all right.'

'I wasn't going to. I just wanted to say that I understand. I'm just pleased that I'm here to be told it. Now carry on with your science lesson.'

'You're already confused, aren't you?'

'Yes, I am.'

'You don't need to understand much beyond the fact there's technology that can impact your brain function, using electricity and magnets. What you do is build a big coil, charge it with electricity and then that creates a magnetic field that in turn creates a current in the brain.'

Jake has horror-movie visions of American lunatic asylums in the 1930s, patients strapped to chairs under steel helmets with wires protruding, jolts and screams. 'Is it the same as electroshock therapy?'

Martha has turned back, is fiddling with the apparatus on the table. 'It's like its cooler, gayer cousin. Non-invasive, non-painful, and you can target it at different parts of the brain, depending on what you want to achieve. One way of thinking about it is it's like an induction cooker: there the coil creates a magnetic field that induces a current in the pan and heats it up.'

'I can follow so far, but I'm not quite sure why we're talking about it.'

'Here's the thing about this type of stimulation – as I say, it works using this magnetic field, not direct contact, so it leaves no mark.'

Jake stretches his legs, rotates his ankles, watches the thin bones in his feet push against the surface of his skin, like lines on a fan. The body is essentially a mystery to him, he realizes; he can believe almost anything is possible. 'You said it's non-painful, not dangerous.'

'That's the clever bit. It's not dangerous at the levels used in medicine. But what would happen if instead of connecting it to a small battery, you juiced it up with a big old capacitor and really went for it? I ask the question non-rhetorically.'

'What's a capacitor?'

'It's like a really fucking big battery, Jake. You could've worked that out from context.'

'So your theory is that a big transcranial blast, as it were, could – instead of doing all that lovely therapeutic work – be used to knock someone out, leaving them insensible?'

'Yes.'

'And you think I'm going to let you try that with me?'

'Yes.'

'Not a chance in hell. No. Nope. Nyet. Non. Nein.'

She simpers slightly. 'It's just been so good talking about this technology, bearing in mind how it's helped my mental health.'

'Nope again. Don't play the mental health card with me.'

'Look, it's probably a bit risky, but fine. The bottom line is we need to prove the point, and you're the only person here for me to experiment on. So enough of your blathering and look at this.' She shows him the device she has been working on: a short stubby pole with what looks like a half-eaten doughnut at the end connected to a much bigger square pack. 'The power itself is the main problem, you'd need to carry it with you if you want a big enough jolt.'

'Hence the killer with the pack who Rajni saw.'

'Exactly. You need a load of extra power to turn this from a little tingly thing to a knockout machine. You could store that in your backpack. And then I think the whole thing becomes like a portable solar flare for the brain. Do you understand that?'

'No.'

'Of course you don't. Rendering you unconscious is going to be no loss to science. A solar flare sends out a signal that basically can knock out electric systems, cause a massive reset. This thing should be able to do that to your brain, and leave no mark. Should, Jake. In theory.' She smiles, flutters her eyelashes. 'We do need to try it in practice.'

'Could it kill me?'

'I doubt it.'

'Yep, I'm going to need more certainty than that.'

'I'm joking, wet pants. We won't go full blast, just a little taster to prove what's possible.'

'No. It's not that I don't trust you. But I absolutely don't trust you.'

'Just come over here and at least take a look to see if this could all be carried by one person. I'll show you the working parts.' He stands at her shoulder. The capacitor is large and bulky, and could just about fit into a heavy pack. She points out some of the connective lines, and the details of the coil itself, which sits at the head of a thick, stubby stick about the size of a truncheon.

Martha picks it up in her hand. 'See, this is something that Rajni could have felt in her back, before she jumped in the water to escape. And look over there at how the wire could be reduced to the right length to go down your sleeve and come out into the coil that you hold in your hand.'

He leans forward to see, his head close to Martha's. He can smell the coffee on her breath, the lavender in her soap. When she grins, her teeth are white, with faint yellow stains just above and beneath her gums.

'Sorry about this, Jake.'

And then nothing.

Chapter Thirty-Eight

Martha's face, concerned, peering down upon him. Purple hair dangling just above his nose. He cannot remember falling to the ground. He is there, though, prone, the back of his head throbbing, his limbs numbed, feel of hard wood on his back. Experimentally, delicately, he wriggles fingers and toes, then arms and legs. Everything seems to be functioning approximately as it should.

'Jake, how are you feeling?'

He rubs his head wistfully. 'Angry and betrayed. How do you feel?'

She offers her hand and half drags him into a kneeling position, before he makes his way to the armchair, falls gratefully into its soft recesses. It is an odd sensation, hard to describe. He feels like he has been in some sort of high-impact crash, but also that he has no impact injuries to account for. He touches himself gingerly, expecting soft spots or bruised flesh, gets nothing. It is like he has been in a videogame that was switched off and on again.

Martha wheels herself across to him. 'No, seriously, what do you feel? It might be useful for the investigation.'

He reaches for a glass of water. He has a faint headache around his eyes, the colours of the room – the scarlet of a cushion, the turmeric yellow of the walls – seem brighter than before.

'I seriously can't believe you did that. You could've killed me.'

'Jake, come on. Do you think I'd have risked it if I'd been at all concerned?'

He rubs his neck, again expecting stiffness but encountering none. 'I do, yes.'

'Well it doesn't matter, because you've not, in fact, died. You dropped to the ground like a shot, though. Boom. You were out for four minutes, which – I'm not going to lie – was a terrifying time for me.'

'Oh no, you poor thing. Now I'm *really* worried about your mental health.' Jake is more or less muttering to himself.

Martha is ignoring him. 'I'll be fine. And I've been vindicated. This definitely feels like a plausible way of knocking someone out, doesn't it? And I held back some of the charge; I could've put you down for longer. What can you remember?'

'Nothing. One moment I was talking to you, trusting you as a friend. The next one, flat on the floor. All trust lost forever.'

'Really, as much of a blank as that? So I could have done stuff to you without you knowing? Not that I would, of course.' She waggles her eyebrows, before putting her serious voice on again. 'And how do you feel now?'

'A bit odd, a bit weak, but basically fine.' In fact, he

begins to get a surge of adrenaline, as the proof of Martha's theory settles in. 'The question is, just because you could do this, could and would anyone else?'

'I've been thinking about that. The science isn't complicated. It's actually been around a couple of hundred years, since a chap called Faraday, if you're interested.'

'I'm not.'

'And the use of transcranial magnetic stimulation in therapy is relatively well established.' Martha rolls the technical terms around her tongue; there is clear delight in the prospering of her theory. 'You need someone with a degree of expertise in physics or medicine, but nothing outrageous.'

'We do keep coming back to doctors again, don't we?'

'Yes, but with what motive? Rajni and David don't strike me as killers from what I've read. Plus he was at work when she was attacked.'

'We only have her word that she was attacked. Is it possible she jumped in to alibi him? That there was no attacker at all? We have him there at the search, and arguing with the last victim. That's not nothing. Is it possible they're thrill seekers knocking off people for their own pleasure?' Jake poses the question rhetorically, a nagging sense there might be something there.

'It's possible, I suppose. We should check scientific backgrounds of everybody else on the list. I'll do that this afternoon. Then you and the guys can talk to whoever we think is a likely candidate.'

'You're making me lunch first; it's the least you can do.'

She has a meal already prepared in another room. Great, generous platters of food: cold meats and cheeses, bowls of crisps, a Greek salad, bread flavoured with rosemary and garlic. A cool-box of beers, necks protruding from ice. As they clink bottles, she looks rueful for a second. 'I'm sorry Jake, for magnetizing your brain without consent.'

He wonders whether he should be angry, but cannot quite find it within him. It was a useful experiment all in all. 'Forget about it. Unless I'm feeling euphoric as a side-effect and the rage will build later.'

'Don't joke. I've been taking lesser hits from it, and my rage has come down. To a barely simmering level, but still.'

They talk over the case more, testing each other's thoughts.

Martha sums things up. 'We're looking for someone with a bit of a science background, without an alibi, who wants to pretty-up women before killing them, either for personal or political reasons. Shouldn't be too hard to find, even in the depths of your unchartered countryside.'

Jake agrees with the assessment, apart from the final statement. He realizes, with a stab of regret, that even after all of this he still has no clear idea of who the killer might be.

Chapter Thirty-Nine

Back in the library at Little Sky, a cold evening, mist hanging from the eaves in an icy drape. Livia is at her cottage with Diana, ahead of an early school-trip in the morning. Jake and Aletheia with steaming drinks (fresh cream with dark chocolate melted in it) at the kitchen table, a list of names in front of them. Martha has spent the afternoon conducting background checks, and they are prioritizing whom they should target. Thus far it reads as follows:

> *David and Rajni Saunders – medical backgrounds.*
> *Jess Molloy – science degree, pharma background.*
> *Antonio Cruce – works for electrician.*
> *Martin George – science degree, masters in physics.*

'What do you think, Al?' Jake scratches his nose sceptically.

'I think it's a solid theory. Some sort of shock that knocks out phones at the same time, and leaves no mark. We have evidence for that. Right? So who could do that? Someone with the right background knowledge.'

'Yes, but you don't need to be a scientist to know about science. Take Sam, for example: he's got a bookshop in Meryton, he could be a huge science autodidact, reading all the right books that come in. The man Vaughan, who lives on the barges next to Rajni, he could be an electromagnetic hobbyist for all we know. And literally anybody in the world can become an internet expert in anything.'

'Of course. But we need to focus somewhere, don't we? Let's look at these people first, if only to rule them out.'

Jake sips his drink, which is pale, a faint ribbon of dissolving chocolate on the surface. 'I meant to ask. How come that lad MC is not on the main list? How did he get an alibi when his mates didn't?'

'I checked that. He's a carer a lot of the time. His mum has severe MS, and he was looking after her at the key moments.'

He sighs. 'We're still pretty thin on motive, whoever you pick as a possible. What's the next step?'

'I think we need to speak to the folk on this list, see if they give up anything.'

They agree to split the task over the next day. Jake gets himself up early, ahead of the light, the sky empurpled and threatening, the air cold as he runs. The lake takes the magenta hint from above, looks dark and imperial, its surface inky and flat, liquid smooth as stone. When he dives into it, it swallows him in a languid mouthful, before he pops up, splashing and frenetic.

Dry and warm, swaddled in thick top and jeans, he

walks all the way round to the barges. He waves at Maud, who seems to want to speak to him. He realizes that, if he agrees to stop and chat, the morning will be lost. With an apologetic wave, he jumps across her deck to the next one, and makes a further move beyond. He has to take care; there are all sorts of exposed surfaces and cruel-looking obstacles aboard, hooks and entangled lines, looped wires and jerry-cans.

Rajni is cleaning the outside windows and waves him down into the galley for coffee. They talk of how she is feeling, her sense of lucky escape. She seems a normal, conscientious, grateful woman.

'It's hard looking out of the window sometimes. The river there, coiled and menacing. I used to love staring at the water. It's never the same from instant to instant, never the same twice. Now I sometimes have to shut the curtains. David says I'll get over it, but I don't know.' She clasps both hands around her hot mug, as if to remove the sensation of cold from her memory. She hands Jake a ginger biscuit fresh from the oven. The smell of spice is warming in itself.

'It reminds me a bit of when Jill died, actually.' This was the teacher she had mentioned before.

'Tell me about her.'

'She lived in the barge one over. Vaughan's place now: she called it *Pequod*, after that novel *Moby Dick*. She'd have laughed at it being renamed *The Playboy*. She was a very jolly, warm woman. They both were, she and her husband, Frank. They both worked at the school: she taught English, he taught technology, you know. But they did more than that. They looked after children, "my waifs and strays" she called them. If she came across difficult kids, neglected or struggling at home, she'd give them special attention, have them over. Teach them about the river, fishing or rowing and so on.' Rajni looks wistful.

'How did she die?'

'Disappeared off the boat one evening eight years ago, found three days later, bloated and unrecognizable.' She puts her hand on her neck. Jake can see the vein throbbing there. 'She either slipped or jumped. No sign of foul play. No reason to think she wanted to end it all, but who really knows what's going on inside someone's mind. Even someone you love.' She lets the idea linger unspoken. 'You don't think, do you?'

Jake has not considered a connection up until now. 'It seems like a long time ago. Was there an autopsy?'

Rajni nods distantly. 'There was, and a coroner's verdict: death by drowning, you know, misadventure. No suicidal tendencies, no note, no sign of trauma.'

'What happened to Frank?'

'He stayed for a while. We tried to look out for him. But he withered, if I'm honest, just pottered around the place, struggled with the upkeep. He had family somewhere and they eventually took him off the boat, and sold it to Vaughan a few years back. I think Frank died two years ago.'

Jake lets the silence build in the room. The barge creaks and shifts, there is the subtle murmur of water, no louder than a liquid whisper. Rajni stares out of the window once more.

'David mentioned to me some theories about how the attacker might be doing this.' His voice, as ever, is gentle, hardly louder than the coursing current outside.

'We've spoken about it. I thought drugs; he thought some form of electric shock.'

'Have you heard of transcranial magnetic simulation?'

Her eyes widen, faintly impressed. 'I have, but it's more David's area than mine. He's a neurologist, he might even have used it sometimes. What's the idea, that someone cranks it up and uses it as a sort of blackout device?'

'Something like that.'

She purses her lips. 'You'd need a big power source, I think. But it could work. I mean, David would know better.'

Jake doesn't really know how to phrase the next question delicately. 'We're checking on people who had a connection to the search for Claire, who don't have an alibi.' Rajni nods politely. 'That does include David, who was on the search and had a row with one of the victims, Dani.'

The temperature in the room drops ten degrees. Rajni's body stiffens. 'You can't be serious, Jake. I'm his wife. He's a doctor. Why on earth would you think that?'

'I don't think anything. I'm simply pointing out that he doesn't have an alibi, and – as you've just said – he's maybe got some expertise in the right discipline.'

Rajni takes Jake's mug from his hands, her face now distorted. 'You've been talking to me, leading me on. You're not a policeman, but you're probing away like one, and you're doing it against my David.' Her eyes are alive with anger, glistening with uncried tears. 'I think you should go. I'll always be grateful, Jake, for what you did. But I won't hear anything said against my husband.'

'I have to ask these things, look at every possibility. Or how else can we get an answer?'

'I'm not going to help you think of an answer that involves David.'

Jake raises his hands in mute apology, though does not feel he can actually apologize. He lets himself be ushered back up the steps into the blustery morning. He sees Vaughan disappearing into his own barge, a few feet away. Had he been listening? He turns to ask Rajni if she thought it possible, but the door has already been slammed behind him.

Jake's next move is to find Antonio, the leader of the gym lads. Aletheia has an address for him, an old labourer's cottage a mile or so away, not on the river, but not far from it either. Jake shrugs up his collar, stuffs his hands in his pockets and decides he might as well walk. There is a bit of rain in the air, but not enough to make him uncomfortable. His thoughts wander as his body moves automatically, his eyes for once not seeing much of the landscape that surrounds him.

When he gets there, Antonio is on his way out, back to work. He's wearing jeans and a jumper, stained with paint, holding a Tupperware container of pasta and a thermos flask.

'Jake, nice to see you, man. You just caught me. I always get my food from home, so I know what I'm eating, right. Protein shake and pasta. It's how I maintain the bulk. You should try it, bruv.'

Jake shakes his hand. 'I prefer being the pull-up king of the gym.'

Antonio laughs exuberantly, his teeth big and white. 'You are that, man. Hey, have you come up with MC's tattoo yet? I thought something like "woman repeller" on his stomach. Crack myself up.'

Antonio lets him into the main sitting room, which is barely furnished apart from an old sofa and a beanbag. There is a TV connected to an X-box and nothing else. The place smells of deodorant, a pungent, flowery scent. A gym bag sits in the corner, half-open.

Antonio sits down on the beanbag, knees near his face. He looks bigger than ever in this small space, a bear in his den. 'I'd offer you a drink, man, but I just run out of milk. You don't drink water on its own, do you? I could probably manage that.'

Jake shakes his head. 'Antonio, do you do much work with electrical stuff, circuits or coils or magnets?'

'Nah, not my area. I'm just an apprentice at the moment. And my boss mainly has me stripping out old houses, grunt work, you know. Which is fine, because I can sometimes turn it into a bit of cardio, you know what I mean?' Big laugh again.

'You know about building an electromagnetic coil?'

Jake tries to read the response for signs of concealment.

'Nah, I wouldn't know where to start with that. What's it do?'

'Knocks people out, or at least I think it can.'

'That sounds like a dangerous thing in the wrong sort of hands, don't it, Jake? More dangerous to those girls, no doubt.'

They talk some more about the phenomenon of the drowned women, but Jake cannot help but feel that it matters little to Antonio. The deaths don't seem to touch him, to ruffle his blithe self-confidence. At most it had been something to fill up conversation, something exciting in a local area too often filled with sameness.

Jake gets up to leave. 'Say hi to the boys for me.'

Antonio shakes his hand. 'I will. I'll tell my boy MC you've got plans for him.'

Jake makes the walk back home in the gloaming. Aletheia is pacing the walkway by the lake, hands half-buried in her trench coat. Her face is alive with urgency.

'Jake, I've just been with Jo. The killer's written to the local paper.'

'What?'

'He says he's doing all this to protest against the feminisation of the country, on behalf of all the rejected men everywhere. It's like an incel manifesto. You can imagine the reaction. And one other thing.' She places a warning hand on his thigh. 'He says he's getting ready to kill again.'

Book Five: Delta

All the rivers run into the sea; yet the sea is not full.

Ecclesiastes, 1:7

Chapter Forty

Aletheia hands him a piece of paper and they go inside the house so he can read it.

> More than twelve men commit suicide every day in this country. No protests, no prayers, no calls for men's rights! One woman goes missing and the whole world stops!
>
> Men are second-class citizens. We are losing our jobs to women not because they are better but because they are women.
>
> We need to fight back! We need to stop feminism! We need to stop pretending women have things tougher. They don't. We are the unlucky ones. We do the dirty jobs, clean the streets, we fight the wars. We used to be thanked for it. Not any more.
>
> Women get everything. Including sex whenever they

want it. They cry rape when they don't. Sex is their superpower. Men get no respect now.

I've killed these women to show they don't matter. Their deaths are no more important than any man's.

I'm not going to stop now. More deaths are coming.

They are back at the kitchen table. Jake looks up at the clock. Livia is due home soon with Diana. He bites his lip.

'What do you make of it, Al?'

'It was emailed in from an address which looks made up for the purpose, a kind of a sick joke about the location of the murders: wildswimmer@menmatter.org. Martha is seeing if she can look behind it, but normally people use software to hide their IP addresses. We might get lucky and our chap might be a moron, but probably not.'

'When did it come in?'

'It sat in an unread email box for two days. Jo just happened to check and found it. Apparently these days they don't respond to readers as quickly as they used to.'

'I wonder how that affected the killer. Would be frustrating for him, this not getting attention straight away.'

'I guess. It's out now anyway.'

Jake pours two glasses of cider from a big bottle. It is cloudy and half-sour. 'It doesn't mention the attempt on Rajni, interestingly. I wonder why not?'

'I noticed that, but it probably doesn't fit into the point of the letter, showing off how dangerous and lethal he is. Anything else you spot?'

'Lots of exclamation marks, which are either a sign of someone not quite in control, or someone trying to look out of control.' Jake had a thing about exclamation marks generally; he used to hate getting texts with them, thought they were miniature distress flares of self-importance.

'Or someone who uses exclamation marks a lot. People do, however much you moan about it.' Aletheia takes a birdlike sip of her drink.

'Yes, but look at this phrase: *Their deaths are no more important than any man's*. It's quite refined when you think about basic standards of literacy. The apostrophe is right, which must put the author somewhere in the – what? – top 20 per cent of people in the country. The person who wrote this was not stupid, in a literary sense.'

The clock chimes, a round and echoing note. Jake moves to the window, but can make out little in the evening haze. Night is descending, adorned with wispy veil. He puts his head out of the door, sees a light in the far distance, hears the noise of mother and daughter talking and laughing. They are home safe.

They wait until Diana is in bed to talk. Martha blips in, to announce her lack of progress in tracing the email address. 'I'm not thwarted yet, but it's not going to be easy. So tell me about your luck with our science geek suspects.'

Jake is first, arguing that neither Rajni nor Antonio look especially good for this. He remains more open-minded about David, but there would have to be something concealed in his background somewhere to explain such aberrant behaviour. Aletheia then reports back herself. Her account is necessarily brief. 'Jess wouldn't speak to me, because she said I was an arm of the male-dominated state, and I was likely to have internalized the misogyny, not to mention racism, with which I was surrounded.' There is an amused grunt from Martha at this. Aletheia's smile is icy. 'I do like it when white people tell me how I should feel about racism. Anyway, she told me she'd just heard about Rajni, and said that it showed how useless we all are. I got a bit more of a lecture and then the door slammed on me.'

Livia murmurs her lack of surprise. 'She's a prickly one. Not sure that makes her a killer.'

Aletheia goes on. 'And I did track down Martin George. He was friendly enough, but it was like talking to a husk of a man. He was happy to sit with me by the river, to talk to me as a copper, but everything he said was low on meaning when you sought to tie him down. Yes, he'd done a science degree and then a masters. Yes, he even knew about the power of electromagnetic stimulation. He half-told an anecdote about being at the Royal Society in the nineties when someone walked round zapping people with a prototype to make their arms fly up.'

'A low dose could do that.' Martha, the acknowledged expert after her own successful experiment. 'That might mean something: he's actually witnessed the technology before. That can't be irrelevant.'

'By the sound of it, anyone with a medical connection could say the same, though. But when I tried to get to the present, he became more vacant, more protective, more cryptic. He said that he watched over women when he could, that he would love to keep them from the river's grasp. That the world was evil. It all made sense to a point, but not quite the whole point.'

Martha leans back. 'So he has ability and opportunity, but what about motive? That what happened to his family somehow made him hate women? I think he's definitely a maybe – he's not exactly normal when it comes to relationships. He doesn't have that incel, sex-deprived angry vibe of our letter writer, though.'

'I agree, but none of the folk on that list do. Maybe that letter is a blind, trying to point us in the wrong direction.' Aletheia is drinking fresh mint tea. 'Martin also showed me his backpack, which was full of clothes, a few toiletries and well-thumbed crime books. He could've had another pack, I suppose, but no way this one had a big battery or a capacitor in it.'

Martha expels a cloud of smoke in frustration. 'What you're both saying is that I come up with a brilliant explanation that should blow the fucking case wide open, and we get nothing from it.'

'Yes, that's more or less it.' Jake can't really sugar-coat it.

'I'll go back to checking that email then.'

They go to bed, a sense of overweening depression in the house. Jake lies wakeful for an age on his side, watching Livia sleep in the half-light, thinking. She now lies on her back because of the bump, and it makes her snore gently, a pleasant enough rasp and rattle, soothing in the dark. Her face is smoothed of tension, her skin cross-hatched by the shadow so it looks like she is from an old, faded painting. As the light leaches in, grey and unpromising, Jake finally falls asleep himself.

The next day, Aletheia goes to meet with McAllister, and Livia goes to her office, a pottery lesson scheduled afterwards. Jake promises to meet her there, as normal. After a morning of self-punishing exercise, he is lying in the library, his mind still restless as before. Finally, though, some ideas seem to be beginning to coalesce. He feels there is one person who is being overlooked, counted out. He needs to do some more work to make the connection.

He is planning to get up, then nearly falls off the sofa when Martha suddenly comes online accompanied by a loud bleep. Aletheia has left her device at Little Sky for exactly this purpose.

'Jake.' Unusually, Martha takes no time for the mild, companionable abuse that exists as the foundation point for their communication. 'I've found out who sent the email. I couldn't get to the IP address, but I looked around the place to see if anything like it had ever been used before. Check this out. A message board from five years ago, a debate about how to defeat the patriarchy. What fucking else? Anyway, here it is, someone ironically using the "menmatter" address.' She flashes the reference on the screen. 'And if we scroll down further, they're talking about going on a freedom walk, a sort of protest. Look here at the picture that gets posted a day later.'

Jake is up and at the table, peering at the image, which is out of focus, over-pixilated. Five women arm-in-arm, wearing bright pink T-shirts with slogans scrawled across them. At the end, arm extended, long and lean and muscular, as if she is holding her colleagues at squeamish distance, a familiar-looking woman, tall and angular and slightly severe, hair pulled up taut atop her head.

'Jess.'

'Yup, I'd bet your balls to a bag of sweets she sent the letter. And I wasn't expecting that.'

He thinks for half a second. 'Livia's gone to her house today. I've got to go.' He runs out of the room without saying goodbye. All he can think is that the woman he loves is, even now, sitting metres away from someone who has declared to all the world that she is a serial killer.

Chapter Forty-One

He runs hard towards the river, his breaths snatched and short. He decides to go through Caelum Parvum in case he can pick up a lift there. As he comes up to the Jolly Nook, he spots with relief Rose's car.

He bursts in, sees Rose drinking coffee with Sarah.

'Rose, I need your help and car. Livia might be in trouble.'

Rose shifts quickly from his normal state of languor. 'Of course. Let's go.'

They are soon speeding confidently through narrow roads, around tight bends fringed with overhanging hedges, still damp and dense with dripping leaf. Rose's brand of hypnotic dance music plays softly in the background, low enough that Jake can explain everything that has happened so far.

'D'you think the cops will be there already?'

'I hope so, but we're probably closer, and I don't know how quickly Martha could've raised the alarm.'

'What's the plan? Do we kick the door down, bust in?'

'Let's see what it looks like. They know I'm coming to pick up Livia later, because I always do, so there's no reason to think anything different needs to happen today. They don't know that we've got an evil genius like Martha on our side. They don't know we know anything.'

Rose manoeuvres around a tractor skilfully, if a little dangerously. A deep honk of rebuke follows them. Rose sticks his hand out of the window in half-apology.

'He's not to know he's blocking an intrepid crime-fighting team.' He looks across at Jake, whose hands are fussing and fretting the seat belt. His teeth flash off-white. The look that comes from him is one of sympathy.

'Jake, she'll be OK. And so will the little one.'

'I was going to tell you myself, you know.'

'There's no hurry for that sort of thing. Plus, you've met my little sister, and she's as nosy as all hell. She seemed to guess, I don't know, because of some tiny change she said she'd spotted. Thickened waist or something like, that I'd never of dared to say. So I've known for ages. I'm really pleased for you both, you're a nice little family.'

Jake's mind is racing, and he is not quite paying full attention. Yet is there something wistful in Rose's voice? They had been joking for the last few months about his relationship with Aletheia – maybe he was searching for something meaningful himself?

He puts it out of his mind for the time being, catching glimpses of the river now, between gaps in the hedges, khaki-coloured in the dour light of the day. They are coming close to Talboys.

Rose knows the whole area intimately, every dip and dell, every ridge and treeline. He pulls up a few hundred yards from the path to the house, slowing so the engine noise will not reach them. 'I've got my shotgun in the boot.'

'Expecting trouble, were you?'

'Let's just say I was going to relieve one of the big boys of some of his grouse at some point.' Rose is an unrepentant poacher, even though he no longer needs – as he had done as a very young man – to ply the trade for economic reasons. He likes the challenge, the thrill of the trespass, the redistribution of natural plenty.

He opens the boot silently, grabs the gun, checking its load and tucking it under his arm.

'And the plan is, Jake?'

'You hang back, Rambo. I'll go up as normal, no drama. You linger and listen out for signs of trouble.'

'That's a roger from me. I'll find a dry patch by that yonder gate.'

Jake leaves him there, pads down the garden path towards the house. The rain has given everything a glossy sheen, has brought out the colours of the plants, a hectic collage of brightness. There is a sweet smell of smoke in the air, and Jake sees a thin curl spiralling from the chimney.

Nobody answers to his nonchalant knock, so he tries a little more firmly. Nothing. He pushes at the door, but it is locked and steadfast. He moves along the edge of the house, keeping his feet on the soft grass, away from the flower borders that might take his footprints. He works around to the studio window, which is wide open. Inside, it is quiet. Two of the wheels have been in use, and they've been half-heartedly tidied. Scents of coffee mingle with the smoke from the fire and that earthy reek of wet clay. A record player hisses somewhere, having reached the end of the side.

Jake can feel panic rise, acrid in his throat. When he shouts for Rose, it is in a voice that sounds unlike his own. Rose hurtles around the corner, gun under his arm.

'Gone?' He takes in the situation quickly. 'River?' It is both question and fearful conclusion. They turn together and head towards the riverbank path, which curves off in both directions, soon swallowed by the surrounding woodland. With a gesture, Jake sends him upstream, and he moves off himself at a run downstream, the thought bouncing around his brain that the killer would not want Livia's body to be caught in the reeds outside her own house. Like one of the previous bodies had been.

Jake keeps his eyes scanning both the reedy bank on one side of the path, and the line of trees that borders the other side. The river meanders today, slower than running pace for once, rain-gorged and replete.

Movement and colour ahead. Jake increases his speed, gasps out her name. 'Livia.' He rounds a small bend, sees Jess leaning forward, her long legs on the bank itself, staring into the water, dressed in black, the rose-red of her hair the most visible thing about her. 'Hey!' His voice is louder, and she turns, face pale and insouciant, lip already curling. Behind her is Emma, in blue dungarees, wearing a big backpack.

It is only when he gets close up, uncertain of what he is going to do, that Emma moves back on to the path, and he sees Livia is crouched behind her. She is pulling up pink flowers on long stems. Her face is fixed in concentration.

She beams when she sees him. 'Jake, I'm glad you're here. We've just been doing a bit of plant-picking for artistic inspiration, and Emma's seeing if she can use some of this river clay for her sculptures. Look at these. Snakeroot, apparently. Looks nothing like a snake to me.' The flowers are made up of a series of tiny, bell-shaped petals that cluster, each one upon the last.

'You look a bit flustered, Jake.' Jess's voice is pointed.

'I'm wondering why you're walking by a river when you know women have been attacked here. Liv, what are you doing, my love?'

Jess's voice is mocking. 'I'm afraid I rather insisted, Jake. I thought three of us would be able to withstand any dastardly man, whatever his evil intent. And the big serious policeman did warn us poor little women only not to venture out alone when it was dark.'

'This is hardly a thing to laugh about.'

'I'm not laughing. I've told you. I think it's disgusting that men can make us afraid of our own landscape. That's one of our points of this walk. Wasn't it, Livia?'

Livia is looking intensely at Jake. She seems ill at ease, but not in any deep state of fear. Jake reaches out a hand, and guides her off the bank and onto the path. 'Maybe we can all take a walk back now.'

Jess looks impassively out across the water. 'Yes, I think our little expedition has served its purpose.'

They make the return journey in a group, strolling, Jake clutching Livia's hand tight. As they turn towards the house, he spots the revolving blue flash of light pulsing through the foliage. He slows down and pushes Livia slightly behind him. Ahead, on the path to the far side of the property, he can see Rose standing, gun cradled in his arms, watching them intently.

Jess and Emma are late to see the police car. Jake speaks gently from behind them. 'We know you wrote the email to the paper, Jess. As you'd expect, the police want to speak to you about it.'

He senses Livia stiffen, but Jess turns back, her expression untroubled. 'You know, I rather thought they might.' She spins and strides towards Talboys, full of purpose, leaving the three of them behind. Emma looks distressed, says nothing. Jake watches as two police officers emerge from the garden, put their hands on Jess's shoulders and march her to the car. When he looks back at the path, he sees that Rose and his gun have melted away.

Chapter Forty-Two

On the road behind the house, McAllister is waiting by his own car, rocking forward and back upon his heels, a picture of patience. Jess has already been whisked away in a police car, never once looking back at them, her home or her partner.

'Shall we see Livia home safe, and then maybe you'd like to hear what Ms Molloy has to say for herself at the station?'

Jake nods. 'I think I would like that. Can you follow us home?'

Five minutes later, Jake and Livia are in her car. Jake is driving with one hand, the other resting in her lap.

'Thank God you're OK. Why on earth did you go outside with her?'

'She really didn't give me much choice. I was more or less frogmarched out. Short of doing a runner down the path, I'm not sure what I could've tried. Plus, I thought – after that letter, which looked like it was from a man – the chances of her being the killer were pretty small.'

'What was she up to?'

'Oh, I think she wanted you to show up like normal and find us missing. She wants to unsettle you. Wants to do that to any man in fact, I think. She's like a performance protester. She terrorizes poor Emma, who seems to just want a quiet life as a potter. I'll miss her. I enjoyed doing art with her.' She pauses, puts her elbow on the bottom of the window. 'I still can't believe Jess is the killer. Can you?'

'Let's see what she has to say for herself, shall we?'

An hour later, Jake is sipping unappetising coffee in a small room adjoining the interrogation cell at the Meryton police station. He's been here before and it hasn't changed. The same stale smell, of cleaning fluid and sweat, the same sense of scruffiness, of being a shabby home for stray furniture. He is sitting on a plastic chair, his arms on a sticky table with wonky legs. He looks through the two-way mirror at Jess, who is trying to look indefatigable. Her long neck is stiff, her head held high, face sculpted to show nothing but scorn. Only her hands, knotted in front of her, bone-white, betray any form of anxiety.

She has refused a lawyer, refused so far to say anything much to anyone. McAllister now enters the room to begin the process more formally. With him is a constable Jake has met before: John Stevens, heavy-set, balding and terribly keen. He sits to one side, as a note-taker.

At first it doesn't appear that there'll be much for him to write down. McAllister and Jess stare in silence, weighing each other up.

He is first eventually to speak. 'What d'you have to say for yourself, Miss Molloy?'

'It's "Ms", as I'm sure you know.'

'"Ms" or "Miss", not really any difference in the real world, is there?'

'You're trying to provoke me, but I won't be provoked.'

He lets the pause linger. 'Why did you send an email saying you were the killer of innocent women?'

'Who said I did?'

'I'm saying you did. It came from an email address that links back to this message board conversation a few years ago.' McAllister pushes a piece of paper across the table. Jess looks at it, inscrutable. 'You'll recognize the face of the woman on the right of the picture.'

Her voice remains brisk. 'This doesn't prove anything.'

'So you're denying writing an email claiming to be a killer?'

'I'm neither confirming nor denying anything, apart from this.' Jake leans forward imperceptibly. Jess remains broom-stiff. 'I'm saying that women live in a society that glories in endangering them, treating them as cheap and disposable receptacles for pornographic male lust. I'm saying that these recent deaths are not shocking, because they're part of the world that women have faced for millennia. I'm saying that the next generation of young men are following their forebears, but are even worse, in fact: mired in toxicity and frustrated, degrading sexual desires. I'm saying that any letter that reflects the debasement of the male mind is accurate and should be widely seen. I'm saying that the circus around these women's deaths was unseemly, sensationalist and symptomatic of the problems we all face.'

'How do you know that the letter does "reflect the debasement of the male mind", if you didn't write it?'

'I was talking conditionally, Chief Inspector. I confirm nothing, deny nothing further.'

'Did you kill Jade Fortescue, Isabelle Abbas and Dani Jones?'

A pregnant silence. Jess is unflinching. 'I mourn their deaths, but if by dying in these circumstances they inspire a revolution, a revolution against misogyny, then they'll not have died in vain.'

'Did you kill them to inspire a revolution? Did you send that email to inspire a revolution?'

'I've nothing further to say, in my own defence or otherwise. I know I'm in the grip of a patriarchal institution, within a system that has historically failed to respect or support abused women. I'm prepared for that.'

McAllister seems to sense she is daring him to lose his temper. Instead, his voice becomes softer, his eyes milder. 'Ms Molloy, you do see that, if you didn't kill them, you're now taking up vital resources, you're becoming a distraction and all you're doing is putting other women in danger. And that makes you no better than a killer yourself, or the uncaring system you object to so strenuously.'

'If you've got evidence against me, Inspector, you must proceed. If not, I'll go and tell my story to whoever listens.'

'You have no story, you've told us nothing. We've got your computer, your phone; we'll find some evidence, don't worry about that.'

Jess bows her head in response, does not speak further. McAllister stands up and stalks out. He bursts into Jake's room, visibly fuming. Behind him is Aletheia, her heavy black boots clicking on the cheap linoleum.

McAllister is pacing. 'You're a woman, Aletheia, do you have any idea what she's up to?'

Aletheia is calm as ever. 'It seems to me she either killed the women to make a point about how little women are valued by society, and wants to put the blame on a man. Or she's using the fact someone else is doing the killing to make her own political points after the event. Have you got the warrant for her place?'

'Aye, they're turning it over as we speak. Her companion or partner or whatever she is, she's sitting in our waiting room, placid as anything. She's saying nothing too. What d'you make of it, Jake?'

'If she killed the women, she did it for a man to be blamed. So either way she's not going to admit it now, because it'd defeat the whole point of the exercise. She'd just be seen as a maniac and mad feminist to the outside world. And our only evidence is an email that she probably did send, but doesn't actually prove anything.'

McAllister leans back, hands on his head. 'Let's see if we get anything from her house. I'd love to find a giant magnet or whatever fucking thing you brainiacs have been talking about. We won't know for a few hours. I can hold her overnight, no problem. See if a night in a cold cell wobbles that middle-class resolve of hers.'

'If I judge her right,' says Aletheia, standing, 'she'll be only too pleased to play the martyr that way.'

She heads off to bring the car around. Jake lingers at the front of the station, glimpses Emma inside, sitting motionless. He goes in to find a seat next to her. She offers him a faint smile of acknowledgement, but no words.

He is brisk. 'What a mess. Why is she getting herself caught up in all this? Why get you caught up in all this?'

Emma seems to be wrestling with something. After a minute, she grasps his hand. Her fingers are damp and strong. 'I keep out of Jess's politics. It's always enraged her:

my passivity, she calls it. But you've got to know, she acts this way because she cares. She cares too much. I want to shut the world out, have done since I was a girl. Get lost in music and art. She wants to change the world, and failing to do it makes her mad.'

'Mad enough to kill people?'

Throaty laugh. 'She's mad enough to fight anyone, she's mad enough to sacrifice herself, she's mad enough to go to prison. Not mad enough to harm a woman.' The laugh becomes a rackety sob. 'We wanted a quiet life together – it's so typical of her to find a way of . . . fucking it up.' She lets go of Jake with a push, is silent once more.

Aletheia is outside in the car, and she shows him the online headlines about the letter, which Jo's paper was the first to publish and has been picked up widely ever since. 'Incel killer's anti-woman manifesto', 'Mad meninist manifesto', 'Killer blames no sex for women-hating murder', 'Toxic incel culture of the inadequate male has real world consequences'. The reaction is loud and fulminating, the comment pieces pious. The general sense is that the online environment has spilled across into real life, that an inadequate man, representing hordes of inadequate men, has finally gone too far.

'If Jess isn't the killer,' Jake muses quietly, 'then I wonder what the real one will make of this.'

'And if Jess is the letter writer, she'd be pretty pleased with this response.' Aletheia lets her phone fall to her lap. 'Do we have any other leads?'

He looks at his watch, there is still much of the afternoon to go, the sun poised high above them.

'Drop me off on the high street. I want to mosey about.'

'Do you want to share your thinking first?'

'I'll go through it with you and Liv and Martha tonight. There's something I want to check first.'

She leaves him five minutes later, drives off with a soft purr, splashing through the puddled street. A thin drizzle is falling. He heads off towards the school on the corner of the high street, an old redbrick Victorian building, its motto above the doorway, etched in everlasting brick: 'Ex Umbris in Veritatem'; 'From the Shadows to the Truth.'

An hour later, time spent in the school library going through records, talking to an old teacher who had been working there for the last decade, making a call to an elderly and confused woman, Jake emerges, worry etched manifest on his face. The rain is coming down harder now, thin rods from the blackening sky. He needs to speak urgently to McAllister or Aletheia.

The road outside is potholed, and he has to take care to avoid soaking his feet. He walks close to the hedge bordering a playing field. The weather has turned the afternoon to half-night, a grey pall that makes every shape a shadow.

To his left is a thin-trunked tree, limbs like manic arms exhorting upwards. Next to that is another. And another. They shift as the wind blusters across the field, rustling and quavering. The fourth tree sways like the rest, but as he comes close to it, it seems to jerk forward.

It was not the wind. It is not a tree. Jake glimpses a hooded figure, then crumples down into oblivion.

Chapter Forty-Three

He wakes up in a sort of nightmare, immobile. He is tied to a wooden chair, ankles to each of its front legs, his wrists affixed behind the slats at the back. His shoulders ache, his fingers feel thick with blood, so he imagines he has been in the position for at least a little while.

The room is exactly the sort you'd expect to find if you were to wake up imprisoned by a serial killer. Little natural light, a single high window, mostly shuttered, hinting at a thin line of encroaching gloom. There is almost no furniture: a chair similar to the one to which Jake is bound, a rucksack in the corner with the top flap half-open, an old wardrobe with the door falling off its hinge. The place smells musty, seldom-used, faint tang of dried sweat.

Jake flexes his arms, tries to break his bindings, but the ropes have been drawn tight and expertly knotted. He cannot move his legs either, no matter how hard he strains his muscles. Sweat trickles from his forehead, speckling the dusty floor; more runs down his back, turning cold and sticky. His breath quickens, panic rises, and he fights it down, swallowing it like the acid in his throat.

It is very quiet. Jake can hear nobody moving nearby, no sounds of traffic or conversation. There is the faint rattle of rain against the window, a hushed whisper of wind. Otherwise, nothing. He has not been gagged, so he presumes he is in a place where his shouts will not be heard: some deserted farmstead, or a labourer's cottage huddled into the broad sweep of empty fields. In the countryside, nobody can hear you scream. He tries a shout, loud in his own ears, an obscene noise that is swiftly swallowed by the void. He is alone. Not dead, but forcibly removed from the equation.

Jake fights fear by marshalling his thoughts. He works through the logic of his assumptions, the fragments of evidence he has been putting together. First, that Claire's death was indeed a catalyst for someone, tipped them over the edge, awoke within them some hitherto suppressed desire for violence. Second, that sex is key in this. The stripping of the bodies, the painting of the nails, was a telling sign: a travestying of the idea of a relationship, of the need to be intimate. Third, that Jess was correct. Her letter was a hoax, but her theory is still sound: that a frustrated male – in her view, an example of this era's *typically* frustrated and toxic male – has been operating with apparent impunity.

Jake hears the noise of a door being opened and shut, footsteps in the hall outside, something sung quietly under the breath, tuneless. The door into the room is kicked open. Jake knows who it is already. He shuts his eyes, speaks before the man enters.

'Michael, we can sort this out. It's gone far, but we can pull it back.'

When he looks again he sees the figure standing in the doorway: pale, drawn, hostile. Tight black jeans, his top shrugged off onto the floor. An unhealthy expression, filled with disgust. The voice is slender and vaguely effeminate, contrasting with all those thick, taut muscles glowing pale in the half-light.

'Call me MC, and I'll tell you exactly how far I'm willing to go. You're as good as dead, and the bitch you live with is next.'

Chapter Forty-Four

MC lingers, his outline silhouetted by the light behind him. Jake can sense he wants to sound in control; he can sense too that it is hard for him: there is a writhing mass of doubt and pain there beneath the solid surface. He smirks, effortlessly. 'Stay where you are. I'll be with you in a second. Oh, I'm sorry. You've got no choice in the matter, being tied as you are to that chair.'

The door closes again. Jake curses himself softly. The hints – only hints, mind, only tiny suggestions that did not coalesce easily into a workable theory – were there all along. Jade's shy boyfriend, never identified. More could have been done to find him. They must have met by chance, maybe at the gym. Maybe she pitied him, thought he was sweet, lacking in the swagger of his friends. Did something go wrong, a misjudged word, a laugh in the wrong place?

For behind this all, Jake has realized, was the mysterious death of the teacher a decade earlier, Jill Hayes. A woman, a strong woman, who tried to nurture problem children, help them feel at home in the landscape, in the bounteous places by the river. Her death – maybe it was suicide, maybe it wasn't – would have been unbalancing to any of those who had come to rely upon her. A boy like Michael, vulnerable perhaps, bullied, one of her waifs and strays. Jake tries to guess at what the death could have meant to him. Made him scared and angry, certainly. And maybe turned the river into a potent symbol, something that could wash away a dominant, female figure with no trace at all.

Jill had also been married to a technology teacher, Frank, someone who probably knew about electromagnetic theories, enough to spark the imagination of a determined student, alone in the world, wanting to have power, dominion over the people who scorned him. The internet could provide the rest, as could contact with anyone experiencing a long-term and serious condition that required new methods of pain management. Like MC's mum, his caring responsibility. It all adds up: an inventive and evidence-free method of murder was there to be discovered.

It was all of those things that led Jake to the school earlier, to find out who had been close to Jill and her husband. Was it anyone whose name was also on the list of those without an alibi? Actually, no. But what if someone's alibi was too easily accepted? The field could have been narrowed wrongly and too soon. They have been drawing broad conclusions, as Martha said; they could have missed someone. They had.

MC's alibi had been his relationship to his sick mother. But how much could a lonely woman, suffering from a severe illness, have really known about the movements of her carer, who came and went, who controlled her medicine, helped her in and out of sleep? Jake has spoken to her, intruded upon the confused and sad life of someone who has no idea what her son has been doing, has no idea really where he is from one day to the next.

Jake now knows that this carer had, as a young teenager, regularly fled his domestic responsibilities to spend time with the Hayes family. He was someone who was shy, who struggled with female relationships, who probably then spent a lot of time alone, on the internet. Did he spend those hours reading theories about the exploitation of men by an over-feminized society? Could he have been all the while working on his killing device? It was plausible. A sad, but ultimately strong and physically formidable figure, triggered by the hoopla surrounding Claire's disappearance – what might he not be able to do?

Jake hears MC's returning footsteps come down the corridor. The young man stalks into the room, and stands a foot away from Jake's chair. His body seems to be swelling, engorged with blood. He cannot stand still, feet shifting, hands twitching. A mass of nerves, of roiling, irrepressible energy. Danger emanates from him in waves, like a stench. Jake recoils despite himself.

MC leans closer. He has a sweet-smelling cologne on, dense and sickly and unsophisticated. That flowery smell Rajni had mentioned. His eyes are dilated, and Jake wonders if he has been using some sort of steroid. He has seldom seen such an obviously over-worked torso in the flesh, humped and veined, throbbing.

Jake holds MC's stare, desperately thinking of a way to take control of the situation. But MC is in no mood to stay still. He paces in a circle, arms flexing up and down as if attached to invisible weights. Back close again, his mouth dry, toothmarks visible on the surface of his encrusted lips.

'How d'you get on to me anyway?'

Jake keeps his voice measured, almost passive. 'How did you know I did?'

'Oh I've been watching you, on and off. You've got a good rep, man. You're a super cop according to the internet. You don't look that super to me now. No, I've been following you, ever since we first met. Not all the time, just keeping an eye. I was going to stop the stalk today, after that confession got published, someone pretending to be a killer, to be this horrific sex-starved loser. I thought I was home free, someone else admitting to what I did. But when I saw you in my old school, I got suspicious, called my ma and found out she'd just been speaking to you. I figured I had to step in. I had the kit in the van already. By the way, did you believe the confession?'

'I believed it to a point. You know it was written by a woman who'd been on the searches. She was exactly right about the killer, what sort of man he was, sad, desperate, hated himself and women in equal measure; she just wasn't the killer herself.'

MC's expression darkens, and he steps forward, swinging a huge swooping backhand across Jake's face. Pain shoots into him. His chair falls sideways to the ground, jarring his shoulder. MC pushes him back up again. 'That fucking bitch knows nothing about me. The letter said I was doing it because nobody wanted to have sex with me.'

Jake's left eye is half-closed. He can feel a thin line of blood trickle into his beard. He tries to think of a response that wouldn't provoke MC further. 'So why have you been doing it?'

MC walks over to his rucksack, pulls out an iron rod just over a foot long. Slaps it experimentally against his palm.

Comes back close again. Jake wonders what it is used for, why it was in his pack. 'People have underestimated me my whole life. Maybe I got sick of it. You underestimated me, Jake, admit it. Now look at you. You're not thinking that now.'

He turns away, and then spins back suddenly, smashing the rod into Jake's ankle, trapping it against the wood. The pain burns white in Jake's eyes, stops his breath. Vomit wells in his mouth. He swallows it.

'Look at me, Jake. Women see pictures of me on the internet and say I'm perfect, the dream body, the dream man. They say they can't wait to get close, touch me, squeeze my big muscles. It's not my fault if it doesn't then work when we meet in real life, when I touch them back. Women are told, taught the whole time, to hate men, to not have sex to punish us, to make up for all the years we ran the world. Aren't they told that, isn't that what girls learn now? You do agree, Jake, don't you?'

Jake speaks between gasps, spittle flecking his mouth. 'I think things are changing all the time. It's sometimes easier to get on with people when they're just a picture on the screen.'

MC is pacing once more, tigerish. 'Things went wrong with Jade. She always thought she was too good for me. She liked me quiet, and sweet. But sometimes I wanted something rougher. She wasn't up for that, as if what I wanted didn't matter. Then I got this idea. That I could punish them more than they could ever punish me. Women who stared and didn't put out. They were everywhere. Whores in their minds and on the screen, and then prissy little virgins when it mattered. It started with Jade; she was the first I silenced. Then that woman Isabelle, she was sort of an accident. I'd been swimming, she was there, looking at my body on the side of the river, then got all shocked when I showed her more than she bargained for. She didn't know I had a way of keeping her quiet, just sitting there in my bag.'

He grabs his crotch suggestively as he speaks. There is spittle at the corner of his mouth. Words continue to pour out. He is unstoppable as the river itself.

'All of a sudden, I'm this genius killer, and nobody knew. Like a superpower, I reckon. I could of stopped then, or at least waited a bit. But that Dani, the sneaky whore that she was, looked at everything I'd ever done online. The things I was – you know – into. Sex stuff. Places where I'd posted. She would've made everyone laugh at me. I know she would've. She thought you were fucking great, though, Jake. Why do women do that, like you? You don't look after yourself like I do.'

He comes close again. 'You're in pain, Jake, I can see that. Your body hurts. You think you can't feel worse, but you can. That's why I'm going to leave you here while I go after your woman. She lives with you, doesn't she? One big fucking happy family. And you've even got a lake, haven't you? Your perfect life. Imagine her face down in it, Jake. That body you've touched, completely bare to the cold water. Imagine that.'

Jake tries to surge forward, rocks the legs of the chair, shifts his entire weight to make a grab for MC's face with his mouth, desperate to tear flesh, do anything that might stop him. MC takes an agile step backwards. 'Uh-uh, Jake. That's going to cost you. Look at this.' He holds the rod up. 'I'm an electrical genius, aren't I? This is my other little toy: a cattle prod, gets cows moving when they're stubborn.

I've had a play with it, given it a bit of zing. I never used it on the women, because believe me when I tell you it leaves a mark, and I was too clever for that. It'll hurt like all hell, I reckon, Jake.' He crouches, keeping a foot away from the chair. His face is calm, smoothed. 'You'll let me know, won't you?'

A crackle, and a terrible surge of heat and shuddering, speech-destroying agony. The chair topples. Jake screams, a wild animal cry that seems to echo in his head. Then darkness overwhelms him.

When he awakens, he is back upright again. He can smelled singed hair. His top has been torn off, and he can see the ugly mark where the prod touched him, a smear of blistered skin, bubbled and raw. MC is sitting on the floor in front of him, legs crossed. He smiles faintly when he sees Jake is conscious once more.

'I thought that would be a bit painful. You appreciate, Jake, that I could've hurt those women, but I didn't. No, I came up with a way of easing them to death, easing them into the silence of the water. My brilliant machine. Doesn't hurt at all, does it? I had to use it on you a few times to get you back here, and you were quiet as a baby. I used it to turn them to mannequins, posed them as I wanted, even painted their little toes. Pretty, quiet girls, the way I like. And then I watched the river claim them.'

Jake can think of no strategy beyond keeping him talking.

'Why did you paint the nails? I couldn't work that out.'

He smirks. 'I think women should be pretty, like they used to be. Delicate, you know. They should look the right way to please a man. You can't say that any more, but it's true. I did it first to Jade as she slept.' He strokes his fingers down his bare arm, sketching the line of his tricep in dreamy fashion. Jake feels a spasm of revulsion. 'And maybe I wanted to link them all up, all the pretty girls I was giving to the river.'

'How did you come up with the magnet? Was that Jill's husband who taught you?'

MC smiles reflectively. 'You *are* a super-cop, Jake, you have worked some things out. Yep, he was a great man. Gentle. Good husband. He saw that I was skilful with my hands, could make machines work. Said I had a talent. He taught me some of the theory, but after Mrs Hayes died and he left . . .' His voice breaks for a second. 'Well, I took it on and did things with it. Jake?' He becomes earnest, looks almost young, face glimmering white in the twilit gloom. 'Jake, have you ever heard of anyone else doing this? I reckon I'm the first. I hope people'll say that. A couple more bodies, and then I'll move away, and they can wonder about it and talk about it. I'll leave a note, and the magnet, maybe my little pot of pink nail varnish; they can look it over, admire it, stick it in a museum. The work of not a fucking desperate and toxic man, but a sort of artist, a sort of genius.'

Jake thinks his only chance is to get him close if he can, and throw every ounce of his strength into knocking his body into him. First, he needs to provoke him, get him back to that condition of heightened, frantic, uncontrolled tension, make him slip up.

'Michael, you're no genius. You're someone who creeps out women. You can only get them close to you by knocking them out. Nobody's going to be wondering about you. They know your type. You're just a normal, sad, sexless man who works out too much, wishes he could get laid more easily and blames the world instead of himself.'

A heavy pause. MC giggles, makes no effort to rise. 'Jake, I know what you're doing, and I don't blame you. You want me mad and in your face. I'm cleverer than that. Shall I tell you how clever?' He stays cross-legged, raises his body on both hands, lets it swing in the air. His triceps bulge huge. 'The Black policewoman who helps you is currently driving off to follow up a clue. It came from an email I sent to the police. It's an eyewitness that says they saw a man with a big backpack coming out of a tiny cottage about ten miles away. Looks an awful lot like that weirdo who wanders the riverbank night and day. She'll be gone for hours. It does leave Livia on her own, I'm afraid. That's her name, isn't it? Livia?' His expression becomes dreamy, his words a delicate whisper. 'I never heard of that name before. She's at home, and shortly she'll see a bit of cloth in that tree of yours.'

Jake chokes back his dismay.

'Yes, Dani told me about that sweet little romantic thing when she was gushing about you, Jake. I'll get Livia coming up to the house, and wait for her near the lake. Then zap. Bye, bye, wifey.'

'She's pregnant, you know.' Jake can't believe this is the first person he has actively told, wishes beyond anything he didn't have to, scarcely hopes it will have any impact. And it doesn't.

'Two deaths for the price of one. Probably for the best, Jake. This is no world for a little one to come into. Sad, but there you go. I wouldn't want it to be a boy, growing up second-class among the feminazis. I better get going, Jake. I'd hate to miss my appointment. And, in case you're worrying, if Livia doesn't come to me, I'll make sure I come to her. I know where she lives and you're not going anywhere, are you?'

He gets to his feet, picks up the bag from the corner. Jake has never felt such hollow desperation. 'You doing this, it doesn't make you less of a loser, Michael. Women can always spot the creep, you know. And they talk about it to each other. They name names. That's why they've always stayed clear of you. You reek of desperation. Probably why you wear that aftershave, you're trying to hide the stink.'

MC comes to the middle of the room, well out of Jake's reach. 'You're doing a good job of trying, Jake. But I won't react. Though if you want another tickle, I certainly don't mind doing that.' He raises the cattle prod. Jake bites down so as not to give him the satisfaction of hearing the scream.

Chapter Forty-Five

Jake wakes up on the floor. He is still tied to the chair and there is a puddle of vomit by his face. His legs have gone to sleep. He strains every muscle for a desperate period, eyes bulging with effort. Nothing.

He feels pain everywhere, his very bones seem to have absorbed it, and the ache seeps back into him from his ankle upwards. There is also a stabbing sensation in his side. He looks down, his face and beard sticky with blood and sick and sweat. A rank, sour-scented top-note in his nostrils. The arm of the chair has broken off, and one of the shards has pushed into the flesh just beneath his ribcage.

It hurts, but he doesn't think it is dangerous. What it does mean is that the chair's structure has been weakened: the arm connects up to one of the slats at the back, and so a gap is there, perhaps to pass his arms through. It is awkward work, his hands still bound. With trembling fingers he can reach the giant splinter. He grits his teeth and pulls it from his side, grimacing through the sting.

He takes a deep breath, steels himself, then raises his whole body up and slams it down on the ground, letting the broken wood take the impact. It hurts. It adds bruise upon bruise upon wounded skin. Does very little else. Desperation fills him like a drug, a sort of inverse euphoria that makes him feel strong. He lifts himself up again, higher, and falls more savagely down. A cracking sound like a gun shot, a shattering.

He grits his teeth, tensed to check if he has damaged himself at all. No extra pain. The chair is a shambles now, wood poking at all angles, like broken bones. He finds he can manoeuvre his hands, still behind him, more easily, actually push one of the sharpest spokes of wood into the knot. A feverish five minutes follow, wrists moving left and right, sawing blindly against the rope, the fibres slowly loosening, tearing. Each second of delay a stab of panic within.

One wrist finally comes free. He raises his hand, purpled and obscene, like a liquid glove. He shakes it, jump-starts the circulation, letting blood flow again, which returns along with pain, a sort of cumulative shriek inside him. He holds his other hand up, repeats the process. When his fingers are functioning again he unties his legs, and stands, his body gripped by tremors. He puts weight on his ankle. Immediate agony. A cry of anguish bubbles from his lips. He tries again: the pain surges, but the ankle does not buckle. It will hold up, he thinks. It has to.

It takes him a moment to break the lock on the door, using a leg of the smashed-up chair. Outside it is dusk, the sky smoky, the hour beginning to turn late. The rain clouds have cleared and the sun is low, swathed in pale haziness, a scarlet hint at the base of the horizon. Dark is an hour away. He is shirtless and cold, swings his arms to warm himself, uses the ragged remains of his top to clean his torso and face. He must look like a terrible mess. There is nobody to see it, though. The landscape all around is still, a silhouetted bank of trees to one side, branches spindly and crooked, unmoved by the chill breeze that is shivering him. To the other, the ground falls away, wide fields of grass, studded with muddied pools. Beyond them something glimmers in the last rays of light. It must be the river.

Jake has no real idea of where he is. MC said he had used the electromagnetic device on him a few times, which meant he could have been repeatedly knocked out for several minutes. He could've been driven miles in that time. There are no obvious landmarks to help him: the gloom has swallowed the hill line.

He makes for the river at a slow run, his ankle killing him, a wretched stab with every step. But it doesn't stop him; he pushes the pain into the back of his mind, an ignorable constant, a sustained hum that he can bear for a while. He hears the water before he sees it. Rushing in spate, rain-swollen. There is a path stretching in both directions. Which way to go? A wrong decision could mean everything. The end of Livia, of their child, of what his life had so joyfully become. The thought of her, face smoothed in death, claimed by the water, enrages him.

He makes himself think. A river flows in one direction, and if you're using it to dispose of bodies you'd want as much scope for removal as possible. You'd want to have your base upstream, as high up the river as you can go, letting the cleansing water carry things away from you. MC has been cunning, patient, rational, but Jake has also glimpsed how unhinged he is: he sees the river as mystical, he attributes some warped meaning to it.

It isn't much, but it is enough to set Jake following the river downstream, letting its swift current pace him, lead him along into the deepening dusk. The next twenty minutes are the worst of his life. He runs as fast as he can, hard and determined but ungainly, lopsided, unsure whether each pounding and pain-racked step is taking him further from home. The river itself bends infuriatingly, never showing him much of an expanse beyond.

And then: something. A knot of familiar trees just visible. A stile and a track that runs off the bridle path. Then a bench he had sat on once with Livia, in an idle afternoon, hot and drowsy and joyful. Jake realizes that from here he can strike a line cross-country that will take him to Agatha Wood on the other side of Little Sky, get him close to home and the lake. If Livia is not there, it will mean she hasn't seen the sign yet, and he has a chance to get to her before MC does.

The realization, the fleeting hope, gives him energy. His strides lengthen, the pain diminishes further, as he moves over and down the undulating hummocks of land. There is enough light to spot the gap in each hedge, and soon he thinks he can see the broad smudge of black that denotes his own trees.

He crashes through some flimsy undergrowth, finds the pathway that began as a game trail when the wood was young. He makes his way to the south side, softening his step as the change of shade – a shift from dense green-black to a lighter charcoal hue – tells him the edge is near. He comes out a few yards from his lake. He shifts his body silently now, each motion swallowed by the inky night-time all around.

The water ripples gently, a heaving carpet. Beyond the

lake on the other side, he sees the lamps that dot the path all the way up to his house, which must be there, but it looms as an absence, unlit and unseen.

Then he is not looking towards the house. His breath is stilled. Underneath one of the lamps stand two people. One wide and bulky, carrying a backpack. Ahead of him is someone Jake would know at any distance, her body slender but not bent or cowed, her feet on a scrap of ground that overhangs the water.

Chapter Forty-Six

Jake needs to get close, unobserved. He kicks off his shoes and shorts, and eases into the lake, naked. It is even colder than he expected, his own core temperature lowered by his journey over the last hour. It numbs his ankle at least, making it feel normal for the moment. He pushes into the deeper part, submerges himself. The water swallows him. Darkness is everywhere, he can see nothing, hear nothing beyond the ripple of liquid. He is enrobed in it. He makes for a dark silhouette in the middle of the lake: Reacher Island. The name feels ridiculous in the circumstances, but the scrap of land serves a purpose. It hides his approach, and takes him within a hundred metres of the opposing shore, within touching distance of his target.

He realizes he is pale, a lucent white in the darkness, moon-bait. He shifts behind a bush that borders the water. Quiet descends. He peers around the foliage. MC and Livia are spotlit, haloed, he can see every detail of their expressions. They can see little, he thinks, beyond a few feet in front of them. He listens, his own heartbeat almost too loud in his ears.

'It won't hurt a bit.' This is MC, high-pitched again, almost a whine. He is behind Livia, must be pushing his device against her back. Jake wonders why she doesn't risk diving in, doing what Rajni did.

Her voice is steady, but he can tell it is saturated with fear and distaste. 'You'll leave my daughter alone. You promise.'

'I've no interest in one so young. You are all I want.'

Livia sobs. 'And Jake?'

'It's too late for him, I'm afraid. I couldn't leave him alive. He knew too much, as you now do. So either you go alone, or you and your daughter go together. It won't take much to pick her up tonight.'

Diana must be somewhere close, Jake thinks. Maybe at Jo's house.

MC continues to speak, his voice oily. 'Soon it will be peaceful. You'll be beautiful. It's almost like a union. Like sex.'

Livia makes a disgusted noise. MC's tone hardens. 'It is what I say it is.'

'What about my baby?' Livia is choking the words. Jake can see tears rolling down her cheeks, miniature pearls in the light.

'There will be no baby. There will just be darkness. And that is better. Are you ready?'

Jake realizes it is now or never. He pushes himself headfirst into the water, his stomach scraping against the rough ground. He has swum all parts of the lake over the last couple of years, knows the depths and shallows, the silty slopes where the weeds cling to your legs, and where the water runs clear up to the sides. Livia is standing near a deep part, but there is the hint of a ledge in front of her that rises up to within a foot of the surface.

Jake is swimming straight at them, a fast breaststroke, no splashes. He is trusting that they are blinded by the light around them, like actors in a theatre. He keeps his head down, counting in his mind the distance covered by each stroke. He risks looking up. He sees Livia's legs buckle. She collapses to the ground, dead faint, one arm trailing down into the water. MC stands over her, his whole attention given to the sprawling body beneath him. His face is ecstatic.

Jake pulls close, every fibre within him singing now with rage, and plants both feet on the ledge. He surges out of the water, like a monster from the depths. With both hands he seizes MC, and then falls back into the lake, dragging him away from Livia into the blackness beyond.

The water is Jake's element. He has gone through the feelings of cold and fear and uncertainty. MC might be strong but Jake is wild and strong. He is now the predator, mobile and unforgiving, relying on his victim's shock. He drags him away from the shore, spluttering and gasping, then pivots on top of him, pushing him down beneath the surface. He can hear a keening noise, a sort of angry wail, and he realizes it is his own.

MC thrashes, but Jake gets a grip on his throat, squeezes tight. He closes his eyes, takes a huge breath in, lets himself roll in the water, heading downwards like he is falling. MC is trying to grab hold of Jake's body, but it is smooth and slick. He tries a bear hug, but Jake leans into it, kicking his legs hard and forcing MC downward. They are locked together beneath the surface; the world is pitch-black, closing in on them.

Jake can feel his own lungs beginning to scream, knows that MC must be running out of air. He doesn't seem to be weakening, though, and Jake doesn't know how long he can hold out himself. He bites down on his lips, determined. After a while, he begins to feel faint, bright lights explode in his vision. He can feel MC sag. He stops pushing, kicks up to the surface, one hand on MC's shirt, bringing him up behind him. He has become a dead weight, heavy as carrion, now floating on the surface, rolling to his side, as the wind-ruffled waves shift and sway him.

The air is like a joyful benison. He sucks it in. He takes his hands from MC's body and strikes out for the side of the lake. Livia hasn't moved, sprawled, limbs a deathly tangle. Jake pulls himself out, crawls over to her. She is inert, embalmed in the light. He strokes her hair, calls her name. No response. The breeze touches every part of him with chill. He says her name again.

It takes long moments for her eyes to open, green as the ground beyond. Confusion written upon her face. He tries to be calm, screaming inside his hope for her to be fine. Her voice is a whisper. 'The last thing I remember, I was about to be pushed into the lake. The thing is, even after he said you were dead, even when I almost lost hope, I knew you would come. You always do.'

He laughs, covers her in a soaking hug. She is warm, an embodiment of life, something to cling to. She is crying, speaking his name. Then she stiffens, her arms go to her stomach. 'Oh God, Jake, what if he's harmed the baby?'

Chapter Forty-Seven

He helps her rise to her feet. She totters. He holds her more tightly.

He tries to sound reassuring. 'I don't think the baby'd be affected. It's like a switch-off thing for your brain; your body keeps working all the time.' That sounds right. Nothing had happened to him after being knocked out after all. But he is a man; she is a pregnant woman. Livia doesn't straighten. He keeps talking. 'But we'll get to a doctor straightaway.' He feels a lurch in his stomach. They'll have to deal with the body in the lake too. She peers behind them, but the water is dark, placid, concealing what it must have killed.

Arms locked, they walk the soft-lit path towards the house, she half-holding him up on his bum ankle. Reaction and cold is setting in for Jake. He is shivering, his skin coarse and pimpled with raised goosebumps, his wet hair lank against his shoulders. Livia forces a smile that dies before it reaches her eyes. 'I'd suggest getting you out of your wet things, but you don't seem to be wearing any.'

Jake smiles, despite the pain. Getting him out of his wet things. Their joke, since the beginning.

'I was in a bit of a hurry to get into the lake. It seemed important at the time. Plus, you know, weaponised nudity.'

She traces her fingers on his scorched and damaged skin. The cold water has helped soothe them, but the burns are deep and angry. She clucks. 'What on earth did this?'

'Our friend had a modified cattle prod, seemed to lose his temper.'

'Jesus, you poor thing. We'll fix this up with something inside.' They are a hundred yards from the house, which has never looked more inviting, even in its unlit and looming state.

Livia suddenly stops, makes a noise between a giggle and a wail. Controlled hysteria. She's trying to hold things together, he can tell. 'I was just thinking of the shock he must've felt. Standing over me in the full glory of his realized plans, and then this giant nude hairy man pops up from the dark water. Serves the fucker right, of course. But what a sight. Were you like a male Aphrodite coming out of the waves?'

'I think it was a bit more butch than that.' He can't help but laugh too, relief making him almost hysterical too. She pauses, turns into him, and gives him a hug, stilling his shudders for a second. It is a good thing she does – Jake will think later – because it means she looks behind them at exactly the right moment.

He's still alive.

Running across from the lakeside, just now caught by the lamplight of the path, his face a mask of purest hatred, is MC. Staggering more than running, actually, his clothes clinging tight to his thick muscles. He is wielding the cattle prod, which he must have grabbed from his pack. It crackles in the still of the night, as he thrusts it at them. He is close, too close. In mid-swing, he has aimed the weapon at Jake's head when Livia pushes Jake roughly, and he stumbles to the ground. The prod swoops through the air, its momentum unchecked. Jake is scrabbling in the muck, desperate to climb back to his feet as Livia lurches for MC's wrist and pushes it down, away from them. Her move forward startles him, he looks momentarily confused. The tip of the prod touches his chest with a loud cracking noise. She leaps back just in time, away from the spark and the burn and the shriek of agony that rises and is immediately choked off. MC collapses to the floor, still.

Livia doesn't move, then staggers. Jake finally manages to stand; he reaches out and checks her movement. Holds her close to him, feels the adrenaline coursing through her. 'Thank you,' he whispers in her ear. 'Thank God you saw him.'

They cling, frozen in time, their chests heaving in unison. Minutes pass. Livia looks at the bedraggled body, smoking in the evening air. 'Is he dead?'

Jake approaches him carefully. The stink of burnt flesh rising like a sacrifice. He checks the pulse. Nothing. A slab of past life. 'I think he was half-dead anyway. In no condition to survive that sort of shock, especially soaking wet. Come on. Leave him there.'

They hurry to the kitchen, locking the door behind them. Jake crouches in front of the stove, blowing on its embers, watching the flame flicker and surge, willing the waves of heat to enter his body. Livia gets the device from the library, calls Martha.

She's there, thankfully, and blips on right away. She can sense something has happened. Livia blurts out as much of the story as she knows: her abduction, the lake rescue, the final surprise.

Martha listens, but is busy throughout, tapping at her unseen keyboard. 'Slow down, slow down. And get your feller lurking in the background there to put some clothes on. I don't want to see his junk at the best of times, and certainly not when it's been shrunk by the cold.' She grins. 'Liv, it's important you don't get stressed now. It's not good for your little one.' Her voice is tender, and Jake realizes just how much Martha has invested in their collective companionship. He reaches for his robe, in the basket above the stove, and comes to the table where Livia is sitting.

'Can you get Al, and call the cavalry?'

'Already on it. She's not far, actually; she was already on her way home. He sent her off on a wild goose chase, didn't he?'

Jake nods. 'He wanted her out of the way to get to Livia. He was going to kill her, finish me off, and then probably disappear.'

'It was a hell of a catch, finding him. Less impressive was you being jumped in a playing field, of course.'

Jake lets that one pass. 'You were right about the electromagnetic thing, M. I don't think there's many folk in the country who'd have come up with that.'

The pause lingers, as they assess all that happened. Livia has heated some sweet tea. Jake wraps his frozen fingers around the mug. Her expression is troubled. 'I killed him. I killed someone. What will happen about that?'

Martha is brisk. 'Liv, you know you did the right thing. On a practical note, I don't know what Jake saw, but I reckon it was a desperate man, soaking wet, falling and being done over by his own device. We'll all celebrate what a badass you are, but you'll get no other credit than that. Now hold tight, it's going to get frantic there.'

As ever, she is right. Ten minutes later, Aletheia bursts through the door, McAllister not far behind her. Through the window, they see the emergency lights of two big Land Rovers, which must have barrelled over the fields, an ambulance in its wake. Jake can make out a paramedic and a police officer crouched over MC's corpse.

Aletheia is in official mode, directing efforts, getting a full search away on properties linked to MC. She spends five minutes with Livia, murmuring, hand clasping hers. Jake catches a little. 'Leave everything to us now. It'll be fine, just you see.'

Chapter Forty-Eight

It is not quite that simple, but Aletheia is as good as her word, helped by Martha and McAllister, all determined to bring matters to as clean a conclusion as possible.

Martha somehow manages to get a doctor out to Little Sky while their statements are still being taken, before MC's body has been fully examined and removed. She is a middle-aged woman, who seems to have been plucked from a dinner party, an incongruous figure in a canary-yellow frock and borrowed green wellies. She arrives, unheralded, over pitch-black fields, on a motorbike driven by a silent figure who refuses to take his helmet off, and sits aloof on the bench by the lake, waiting to take her home.

She strides confidently into the kitchen, where Jake and Livia are sitting, hands still clasped. 'I'm Dr Sampson, and I desperately want to get back for pudding so let me take a look at you.' There is something kindly in her eyes, though, despite her bluff tone.

She takes Livia to her bedroom, examines her, listens to the baby's heart. Jake stands in the corner, fists clenched throughout. The amplified pitter-patter that emerges, haunting and foreign as whale song, is music to his ears.

Dr Sampson has her eyes closed as she listens. She opens them. 'I have to say, my dears, I've never been asked to do a house call in the middle of a murder investigation with an electrocuted corpse on the lawn outside. Nor to worry about the impact of a home-made magnetic device on an unborn foetus. So I'm not relying on precedent here. All I can tell you is that the vital signs are remarkably normal, Mum is disgustingly healthy – really sickeningly good-looking – and my rusty anatomy tells me that your brain is nearly two feet away from your uterus. That makes me confident things are OK. Or as confident as I can be. How's that?'

She is addressing Livia, who is lying on the bed, shirt pulled up, bump glistening. Her eyes are closed, but Jake can sense the welling up of relief. A tear trickles down her cheek as she sits up. 'I'm happy-crying, I promise. Thank you, Doctor, and thank you so much for coming out. It looks like we disturbed your evening.'

'I was sitting next to a man who wanted to tell me about every jot and tittle in some contract he was overseeing. I could actually feel *my* uterus shrinking. No, I've enjoyed myself rather more doing this. And now I get to straddle a big silent hunk on a motorbike for the journey home. I should be thanking you.' She pats Livia's hand, pulls her top down.

She stands by the door, an incongruous figure in her bare feet and piled-up blond hair. 'You look after yourselves, especially if you're going to insist on having such an exciting time while being pregnant. I'd tell you to live a bit more quietly, but I can't abide wrapping strong and healthy women in cotton wool. Pregnancy's not a sickness, as I always say.' Her voice, so rich and brassy, softens. 'Just don't push your luck too far if you can help it.'

The next day, Little Sky is quiet, gloriously and defiantly so. A cold wind blows, making the trees shuffle and whisper. Jake and Livia are walking past the lake, its surface ruffled with waves like scrawled lines on a page. The heron stands a few yards from where Jake had emerged from the water, poised on its pinky-grey legs, judicious and untroubled, re-establishing – without knowing it – the place as nothing more than landscape, habitat.

Livia is going to pick Diana up from Jo's, and give her the full story. They stop at Livia's cottage to watch McAllister's press conference. The identification of Michael Cork as the killer, the itemisation of all the evidence accrued at his home, where trophies of the three victims, including intimate garments, has been discovered. McAllister spends some time – in a room packed with journalists, joined by a less soberly dressed crowd of social media folk, contemporaries of Dani – explaining the murder method, without quite revealing enough detail to make it easy to copy.

Michael's device has been examined and revealed to be something of an engineering feat. He had taken the basic principles of a pain management system used by his mother, who had severe multiple sclerosis, and constructed something that was turbocharged and deadly. The police have discovered piles of notes taken first from his lessons with Frank Hayes, Jill's husband, whom he idolized. It is clear that her death and his departure left Michael increasingly solitary, devoted to muscle-building and haunting the dark recesses of the internet.

Under alternative names, Michael took part in various Reddit threads on the subject of building an electromagnetic machine that could knock people out, and clearly made the crucial breakthrough about a year ago. The furore around Claire's disappearance was a trigger, unbalancing his mind further on the subject of male–female relationships, compounded by some sort of fracture in his unsuccessful relationship with Jade. He'd told Jake that she had wanted him to be shy and kind, and had been repelled by his desire for something more violent. That had only increased his desires to that end.

At that point, the device went in his mind from a plaything to an actual weapon, which could be used repeatedly without leaving evidence. He had managed to stun women – Jade, first – into unconsciousness, before stripping them, painting their nails – McAllister winces at this detail – and drowning them, probably by placing their heads in a bag filled with river water. Once dead, they could be placed in the river, unmarked and inexplicable. McAllister speculates that he had been hurried in some way when he was killing Isabelle, which is why she had been found still in her knickers. She had been unlucky enough to attract his attention by simply looking at him, and then being repelled by his advances. A victim of appalling chance, and no more. Dani's brave investigation – McAllister gives her this due – meant that she was a threat, and she was killed partly to protect the killer's identity.

Claire Davidson, the woman whose tragic disappearance began all this, he intones, died of natural causes, of drowning on a hot day. He pays tribute to Claire's husband, Steve, who has never wavered in his desire first to find his wife, then to learn what had happened to her. The camera cuts to him, seated in the front row, head bowed, muscles taut in his neck. McAllister goes on to praise, and commiserate with, the families of the other victims, who – he hopes – will find the beginnings of peace, now that the killer has been discovered.

Jake's name is mentioned briefly, the implication being that he had been involved in the final stages of the hunt. Michael's death was termed 'self-inflicted in the act of trying to commit violence on another victim'. His cattle prod had been modified to contain enough potential power to kill a human – he was brought down by his own lethal weapon. Case closed.

Livia turns to Jake. 'Aletheia knows how to tie things up.'

'She's a good person to have on our side, all right. She could even make Rose go straight.'

'That I would like to see.' She strokes her thigh, thoughtfully. 'What will happen to Jess now? I thought I'd go and check on Emma, if you don't think that's too weird.'

'Not weird by your standards of generosity. I think they'll have to decide whether or not to prosecute Jess for obstruction. Sending a fake confession is a pretty awful thing to do, and it could've cost someone.'

'Even if a matter of principle was at stake in her mind?'

'She wasn't exactly tolerant of other people's principles, though, was she?'

Livia is silent for a moment. 'Will you put in a word for her?'

Jake lets that notion settle for a second. 'I will, but I'm not sure a member of the patriarchy asking for a favour will make her very happy. That's a reason to do it on its own, of course.' They both smile. He thinks that, in the end, the authorities won't take the trouble of prosecuting someone who might actually welcome the platform to criticize the judicial system. Jess and Emma could go back to their cottage, their pottery, their attempt to escape from the world. Whether or not they will be happy together, Jake couldn't say.

Livia heads off in her car, leaves Jake to stroll through Parvum. It is empty as normal, the cottages set back from the road, mostly out of sight, a long history of concealing their secrets, good and bad. He goes to the church to sit and glory in the peace. The pleasure of tedium. He closes his eyes.

When he opens them, a heavy-set man is standing in front of him, bald head gleaming in the morning light. He looks nervous, is shifting his feet, plucking at himself. It is Paul Sansom, the man who – a lifetime ago – had threatened Jake.

He stutters a little. 'I just wanted to say that we're quits, mate. I don't want trouble. I've had two visits from folk who put the scares on me and I want out of it all. I heard your name on the news this morning. Listen: I've got a job and I don't want people saying I'm some sort of crim. So call it off, call it quits.'

He holds out a hand. Jake does not take it. He wonders who Aletheia had sent to scare Paul, a man previously so confident in his ability to dominate the men and women around him. A bully's confidence, of course, always liable to be undermined.

'Are we quits?'

Jake leans forward, keeps his voice quiet. 'I can't control the cops. I do know that they hate wife-beaters. If your missus appears anywhere in public looking bruised or scared or even a bit upset, I don't know what they'll fit you up for. But they'll come for you. You understand that?'

He nods.

Jake sinks back, stares at the ground once more. Paul doesn't move. Jake waits a minute. 'I'm not your mate, either. You can go.' He watches through half-lidded eyes as Paul shuffles away.

Can you ever interfere to make a toxic relationship better, he wonders? Jake had got involved with Paul and Louise, but had he actually helped? He remembers the sight of the defiant woman, bludgeoned and bruised, and thinks it may well happen again. Her stubborn refusal to leave, her boyfriend's appetite for violence – maybe they will never change.

He shakes his head. All around him is soothing. He closes his eyes. There is always tragedy and pain. And there are always moments of peace, healthful repose. You have to cling to those whenever you can.

Epilogue

The day of the wedding dawns icy cold, but clear, the sky limitless and blue as the sun shrugs up from the horizon, bright and willing. By mid-morning it is warm enough for T-shirts and flip-flops, for pleasure boating on the river, for picnics in the woods. Autumn clutching at summer's memory, a feeling of holiday, especially after the fearful events of the last month.

Jake has walked to the church at Bluntisham, one of his favourite old buildings in the area, a beautiful melding – or collision, depending on your perspective – of Anglo-Saxon and Norman architecture. At its front is the porch, a miniature anteroom; above it, carved high in the wall, is an ornate rose window, somehow still delicate despite its stony heft. The porch itself has tall, time-blackened beams curving up to form a roof, an addition at some point in the thirteenth century, wearing its age – like the rest of the building – with hardy grace.

Rose and Lily had suggested getting married in the porch, Lily pointing out first that it was a tradition going back to the medieval period, and then that it would look splendid on Instagram. Jake relished the first point: he wasn't religious, but loved the history of this place, the endless weathering, the constant tread of footsteps that connect ever backward to the past.

He is wearing his best clothes, which is not saying much: clean, sea-blue cloth trousers; a new white vest; a short-sleeved white shirt he had 'ironed' by putting it between two boards and leaning a heavy tractor tire on top; scrubbed, brown boots. His hair is pulled back, his beard trimmed and scented with some oil Rose had lent him. The churchyard is empty, just him and the gravestones, stubbornly upright in a sea of grass and late wildflowers shimmying in the breeze: milky-white yarrow and clover, imperial purple mallows.

They are not having many guests. Aletheia has driven up in a big SUV, bringing Martha with her. Jake has spent a week laying down wooden pathways – 'don't call them fucking "walkways", Jake, for God's sake,' in Martha's own words – across Little Sky. The house itself, the modern bit at least, is predominantly on the ground floor, with wide doors. It has taken little to make it work for Martha, and Jake is glad she is here, staying for a week.

The two women, his closest friends really, push through the lychgate and come up the path together. Behind them are Rose and Lily, and Sarah from the Jolly Nook, face bright and carefully made-up, in her best frock and an entirely unnecessary hat. McAllister arrives alone, in a dark suit, looking sheepish, until he is pulled almost literally into the conversation by Lily. They are soon joined by a harassed Jo and husband, their children in tow, an argument begun in the car between them imperfectly suppressed.

A small crowd for a momentous occasion, Jake thinks, but a reflection of who has come to matter to him. He is nervous, though not at all sure why. He loves Livia; she loves him. When they aren't rescuing each other from homicidal maniacs, they have a shared devotion to the place they have made home, to natural beauty, to a quiet, peaceful existence. They have a spot to retreat to, somewhere that is remote and just theirs. A haven. Maybe that is the worry, maybe all that isolation means pressure, maybe it will mean more strain in the months to come: they will have to cope, amid the bountiful silences, with just each other, and a jealous child, and a mewling, uncooperative baby.

Livia then makes her entrance and all concern is washed away. Diana comes first, aglow in pink, her face clenched with pleasure and concentration, relishing being at the centre of attention. She holds the rings on a pillow in front of her, a picture of studied balance. Behind her is Livia. She is magnificent in a cream dress, cut just above her knees, tight around her bump. Her skin gleams coppery in the mild sunlight, her hair spilling across her bare shoulders in dense metallic coils. Jake's breath comes short at the sight.

The ceremony is brief and simple, the party – an open house for the local farmers and villagers, plenty of broached cider barrels, a huge hog roast – runs long across the rest of the day at Little Sky. Rajni and David, the doctors, make an appearance, approaching with caution, carrying a cake made by Maud, their neighbour from the barges. 'This doesn't mean I totally forgive you for suspecting David,' says Rajni, her voice still a little austere, eyes gleaming with a hint of frost. David, by contrast, is far more relaxed: 'I told her you had to suspect everyone, Jake. It's part of the gig. And I was suspiciously right about the murder weapon too.' Rajni smiles, and the tension slowly dissipates, helped by the interventions of Martha and Aletheia. Jake and Rajni will be forever united by the one saving the other, he knows that; there is a connection that cannot really be broken. No need to spoil a happy event.

As dusk comes, Jake finds himself standing alone by the lake, the sun a pink smear low on a dark canvas, the rosy light shimmering back on the water's surface. It will be his third winter here when it arrives, and his life has been transformed utterly in that short time. He came fleeing responsibility, he has made himself a place in a community. He came tired of crime and violence, he has continued to find occasion to confront them. He came seeking solitude, he has found family.

A gentle cough behind him. His wife, flush with the life inside her, takes him by the hand and draws him home.

Playlist

This is the fourth Jake Jackson book, and the third with some music recommendations. I listen to the same music that Jake does while I'm writing, so this is a chance to join us while you are reading. I've made a playlist on Spotify that you can find. In this book, Jake tries his hardest to get into jazz, like every hard-boiled detective should. He mostly succeeds, as does his author. You can see what you think.

'Come, sweet death, come blessed rest', by Johann Sebastian Bach, arr. for cello by Sheku Kanneh-Mason

9 Preludes, Op.1: No. 2, Andante con moto, by Karol Szymanowski

Spiegel im Spiegel, by Arvo Pärt

'Let There Be Light', *The Songs of Distant Earth*, by Mike Oldfield

Nocturne No.1 in B-Flat Minor, by Frédéric Chopin

'Getaway Car', *Reputation*, by Taylor Swift and Jack Antonoff

'Betty', *Folklore*, by Taylor Swift and William Bowery

'So What', *Kind of Blue* by Miles Davis

Concierto de Aranjuez: Adagio, *Sketches of Spain*, by Miles Davis

'Blue Train', *Blue Train*, by John Coltrane

'I Put a Spell on You', *I Put a Spell on You*, by Nina Simone

Symphony in D minor, CFF 130: III. Allegro non troppo, by Cesar Franck

'I'm Just a Lucky So-and-So', *Ella Fitzgerald sings the Duke Ellington Songbook*, by Ella Fitzgerald

Concerto No. 21 In C Major, K. 467: I. Allegro maestoso, by Wolfgang Amadeus Mozart

Symphony No. 7 in E Minor: V. Rondo-Finale, by Gustav Mahler

The Hebrides Overture, Op. 26, MWV P7 'Fingal's Cave', by Felix Mendelssohn

Canon in D Major, by Johann Pachelbel

'In a Sentimental Mood', by John Coltrane and Duke Ellington

Köln, January 24, 1975, Pt 1, *The Köln Concert*, by Keith Jarrett

Symphony No. 3, 1a. *Kräftig. Entschieden*, by Gustav Mahler

'Requiem For a Dream', by Leama, Paul Oakenfold remix

Acknowledgements

People who listen to me on the radio, or know me from elsewhere, will be familiar with my non-complaining refrain that I have no friends. If I did have a friend, it might be Dr Xand van Tulleken, who provided the murder method in this book. I was looking for a means of incapacitating someone without leaving a mark, and the ingenious answer came from him. Needless to say, if the science is somehow off, the fault is entirely his.

I was lucky to have two editors for the novel: Kathryn Cheshire who got it going before she pardonably left to have a baby; and Jo Thompson, who came in and made it all infinitely better. Anne O'Brien is the copyediting guru who thankfully exposes my many irritating mannerisms. If the prose is somehow off, the fault is sadly mine.

My other friend-types at HarperCollins have been there from the start: the wonderful Liz Dawson and Maud Davies. I apologise to the latter for stealing her name to use on an elderly character with fat fingers. My agent, Cathryn

Summerhayes, is also long-standing and long-suffering, so I better thank her as well.

Away from books, there is my Times Radio family, who manage to help me keep going despite 3 a.m. starts. And my actual family, of course. My parents, despite recent ill health, are endlessly supportive, and tend to pop up at literary events however far away from their house I schedule them.

My two eldest children won't read this book, because they can't be bothered. I love them anyway. My little one is too young, and I love her because she still seems to like me.

As ever, my wife is my inspiration, consolation, and reason for continuation. This book, like all my others, is dedicated to her.